CW00547428

Cover Design by: Aubrey Joy Rosales of Jai Design (Instagram username: designjai)

Edited by: Ashley Olivier, Cara Flannery and Tracey McKinney

Proofreading by: Ken Snyder and Kelly Sweeney

Dedicated to the ones who helped me make this possible.

Words cannot say how grateful I am to all of you

The Community

Chapter 1

THE COMMUNITY BY-LAWS FOR THOSE TURNED IN

I.   The youngest a person can be turned in is the age of twelve.

II.   All persons must be turned in with a full medical evaluation from a Community registered doctor.

III. All persons over the age of eighteen turning themselves into the Community must specify where funds will be sent. Upon completion of the transfer of funds, the person then must turn themselves in to the Distribution Center.

IV.   Those in debt have the right to request a transfer to a new household or unit. However, this will result in a fine added to their debt.

V.   If a person in debt is returned to the Distribution Center due to poor performance, a fine will be added to their debt.

VI.   Upon being assigned to a household/unit, a trial period will take place for ninety days. If the household/unit returns the person in debt to the Distribution Center before ninety days, the household/unit is subject to a fine.

VII. All persons in debt who can no longer work in a classified skill set will be classified as Medical Waste.

VIII. All persons with the classification of delinquent will immediately be classified as Medical Waste.

Evie sat on the hard chair and glared at the large glass plaque across from her. She could read the words easily, though each line only made her angrier. The words stretched far across the wall, ready for anyone who entered the building. Along with the words etched into the glass, she could clearly see her reflection. Her long brown hair was fashioned in a simple braid that fell down her back. Her full lips were a pale pink with only basic chap-stick to keep them from getting chapped. The only real color on her face were the bright blue eyes she inherited from her father.

If it were at all possible, Evie would break the plaque into pieces. Or better yet, she'd watch this entire building burn to the ground with a huge smile on her face. She'd hated this building from the moment she'd stepped into it.

Evie could remember walking into the Distribution Center with her mother and older brother Ryder. Their father had left them behind for another woman, leaving her mother alone to care for two children. Unfortunately, he took all their money with him, leaving them nothing to live on. Her mother, Emily, filled Ryder's face with kisses while tears ran down her face. She made so many promises to the young boy. Promises of paying off the debt soon so he could be free and they could be a family again. Promises to get a job and reunite all of them again. Evie watched with tears in her eyes as her brother was escorted away into the building.

But as soon as the Community had handed Emily that fateful check, her eyes seemed to change. Evie never did find out how much money her mother received for Ryder, but whatever amount that had been given her was enough to turn her mother into the greedy woman she was today. As soon as Emily's eyes landed on the check, her eyes went wide and a sickening smile spread across her face.

Evie knew then that, soon enough, she would be turned in as well.

And she was right. On her twelfth birthday, her mother took Evie to the doctor for the medical evaluation. As soon as she received the paperwork, she forced Evie to go to the Distribution Center.

Her mother did not look back once. Not even while Evie was screaming and crying for her while case workers dragged her deeper inside. At the time, her mother was pregnant with Evie's twin brother and sister, thanks to her current lover. Emily had left her screaming child behind while patting her large pregnant belly. Evie had no doubt that she was counting down the days until they could be turned in as well.

With the memory fading, Evie hadn't even realized she had walked over to the plaque and was raising her fist up, ready to punch a hole right through it. She didn't care about the glass shards that would dig into her fist, but rather about getting revenge for herself and her siblings. A loud voice over the intercom brought her back to reality.

"Number six-seven-seven-five, report to office twelve for your assignment."

Huffing, she grabbed the large black backpack she had left on the chair beside her. That was another way the Community degraded those turned in. By taking away their birth names and turning them into numbers. Upon completion of their training, they are assigned numbers and are only referred to as such. Evie wondered if they hoped that those in debt would forget their real identities and simply dissolve into numbers. But she wouldn't allow herself to be completely degraded like that.

Evie flipped the strap of her bag over her shoulder and made her way down the hall. She had been waiting for about three hours for her case worker to finally call her into his office. It was difficult for her to keep a scowl off her face as she walked down the hall. Her head was pounding, her eyes felt heavy from exhaustion, and her stomach churned in hungry discomfort. Eating was not allowed while waiting to be summoned into her case worker's office.

It had been years since Evie had been in Marcos's office, but she knew where to go. He had been her case worker ever since she was turned in. The middle-aged, obese man had always treated her the same way she assumed he treated everyone else in debt: like the dirt beneath his feet. Evie knocked on his office door and entered before he even had the chance to acknowledge the sound.

Marcos glared up at Evie from his desk. "I did not give you permission to enter."

Evie closed the door, refusing to shrink away from his glare. "You paged me. I figured that was permission enough."

He huffed when Evie took the seat across from him. She couldn't deny that it felt good to stand up to someone in the Community who looked down on her, especially knowing there was nothing he could do about it. As soon as she was turned in, Evie's life was owned by the Community. Any physical harm to her would result in him paying the price they had attached to her. After all, Evie was now Community property, and if you broke Community property, you had to pay for it.

She sat and watched Marcos's large fingers work over the keyboard. The man had a hard time typing at his desk with his large stomach in the way. His chair seemed way too small for him and looked as if it could break at any moment. Evie knew he already had her new household assignment. He was forcing her to wait, wanting to watch her squirm. Unfortunately for him, that wasn't working. Evie had long ago learned to be patient. This man, however, was arrogant and thought all his cases were beneath him, although Marcos was hardly a high-standing member of the Community.

She calmly waited until Marcos finally opened a folder on his desk.

"I see you asked for your contract to be transferred to the Laborer's Unit."

"Yes, sir."

While the Community wouldn't have allowed her to become a laborer, Evie could have gotten a spot in Sanitation and Paperwork for the unit. She hoped for the opportunity to work in the unit so she could see her older brother more often than once a week. Ryder had been lucky to get a position in the Laborer's Unit. The food was better, and they received their own special housing. Anyone in the Domestic's Unit, however, was not so lucky. All of their meals and housing were determined by the ones who owned their contract.

Marcos smirked at her. "There are no positions open. And even if there were, you're much too low on the waiting list for a transfer."

Evie didn't give him the satisfaction of showing her disappointment. She knew she would not get a position near her brother, but Evie couldn't deny that she hoped to have some good luck for once. Like her, many other women in debt had family in the different units across the Community. Of course, they would all try to get a position in the same unit as their loved ones. Evie couldn't help but wonder if the waiting list was real or if the Community just randomly chose women to fill those spots. A sick way of giving them false hope.

"You are being assigned to one of the highest members of the Community. You will be in the service of Elias Huntley and his wife, Sara. Have you ever heard of them?"

"I have not," she said back, glaring at him from across the desk.

Marcos released a loud and obnoxious grunt while sitting back in his seat, the chair groaning under his weight.

"Elias Huntley is one of the most powerful members of the Community. Hell, I wouldn't be surprised if he finally gets a place on the council within the next couple of years. But seeing as you've only been in the service of one person after your training, I shouldn't have been surprised you haven't heard of him."

Evie gritted her teeth, her eyes threatening to spill tears. She had been in the service of Oscar Hillard for seven years. He had treated her more like a daughter than someone in his service due to debt. When he lost his battle to cancer, she was heartbroken.

Marcos leaned forward and resumed typing at his keyboard, the seat groaning again as he moved forward. His obesity disgusted Evie, as it easily gave away the fact that the man wasted so much money on food. Miscellaneous candy wrappers scattered the desk and filled the trash can next to him on the floor. Candy, like many other small luxuries, was expensive. It was all money she believed that could go to better things. To help others in need, even. But Marcos didn't care for other people. No, Evie bet that he enjoyed spending his money on himself. Perhaps if he had a wife, he would learn to care for someone other than himself, but no woman in the Community would be attracted to him with his oily hair, greasy skin, and arrogant attitude.

"As usual, you will have every Sunday off. They already have a cook, so you will be doing whatever other chores and tasks they assign to you."

Evie listened and tried to ignore the annoying clicking of the keyboard. She knew he wasn't actually doing anything behind his computer screen. He simply wanted to look busy and important. Evie longed to tell him how stupid he looked to her. This man was a Community worker, not a high member of society. But Marcos believed in his delusion that he was just as important and well-known as they were.

After a few more minutes, Marcos finally raised his head to look at her. "Do you have your identification card?"

"Yes."

He nodded and stood, grabbing two black bracelets off his desk. "Hold out your arms." Evie did as she was told, and Marcos secured a black band around each of her wrists. The cold metal inside of the bracelet made her shiver. "They've been programmed to new remotes. Mr. and Mrs. Huntley will each have one."

Evie didn't miss the loss of her previous electric shock bracelets. The short time she had them removed had felt like a blessing. Mr. Hillard had never used his remote, either. Not once did he force her to feel the pain that many others in debt had suffered from. She doubted that her new household would be as merciful.

She never understood why a new assignment meant new bracelets. Her previous ones were much smaller than the new ones on her wrists. These were much larger. The thick black bands covered most of her wrists, hiding the silver lining inside. They pressed tightly against her skin, only giving enough slack for her to bend her wrists to work.

Marcos slouched back against his chair, and Evie was amazed that it hadn't collapsed under his weight. "You have thirty minutes to make your purchases. I'll meet you in the lobby and take you to your new assignment."

Evie was silent for a moment before gaining the courage to ask her desired question. "Sir, may I please know how much debt I have yet to pay off?"

Marcos snorted. He simply leaned forward in his chair and returned to typing away on his keyboard. His eyes did not leave the screen.

"You have a long way to go. The Community will let you know when your debt is paid."

Evie gritted her teeth in frustration while grabbing her bag before leaving to go do her shopping. On the rare visits to the Distribution Center, she had always tried to find out how much debt was left under her name. But not once had anyone who worked in the building answered that question.

The Distribution Center had a large store for those in debt to get their necessities. She grabbed a small basket and walked inside. Immediately, she went to the aisles holding what she needed. She already had two pairs of slacks and two basic black shirts inside her backpack. There was no need for her to get more personal clothing. Her assignment would probably provide a professional uniform for her to wear. She proceeded to seek out other needed supplies, flying through the aisles at record speed while she strolled along. A toothbrush, toothpaste, alarm clock, socks, tampons, and so on. It was always her goal to get enough supplies to last her for a while. She had been there many times over the years, nearly holding a map of the store inside her head from memory.

As Evie made her way to check out, she couldn't help but cast a longing look at the food section. Of course, the Community would tempt them to add to their debt by placing expensive treats in front of them. Lines of several different candy bars seemed to be presenting themselves to her. Without thinking, her feet led her to the candy, and her hand slowly reached for the largest chocolate bar. Her mouth watered as she imagined how the smooth chocolate would taste on her tongue. As soon as her fingers touched the bar, she could almost feel a jolt inside her chest. She withdrew her hand and took a step back.

'It's not worth it. Don't add onto your debt. It's not worth it,' she told herself before forcing her feet towards the register.

Evie's favorite meal as a child was a cheeseburger with a large strawberry milkshake. She could almost remember the taste of the juicy ground beef with cheddar cheese along with the sweetness of the strawberry shake. The cherry on top was always saved for last. Evie longed to have such a meal again, but she felt obligated to save every penny and work to save her older brother and younger siblings. Indulging would only prolong all of their suffering.

Evie's items were charged to her identification card and bagged up. As her card was swiped through the machine, she winced. The disappearing dollars felt heavy on her heart, a ghostly reminder of her servitude. After another thirty-minute wait in the lobby, Marcos came shuttling out of the hallway, gesturing for her to follow him. Evie walked behind him while he breathed heavily and stomped outside to the car.

As soon as she took a step out of the Distribution Center, Evie took a deep breath. This was the first time she had been outside since leaving Mr. Hillard's house. There was a slight chill in the air from the wind, and the sky was a depressing gray. Evie couldn't remember a single day in her life where the sun was beautiful and shining all day. She believed the Community was cursed with dull weather, an invisible darkness seeping out from every crevice of its windowpanes and doorframes that sucked out all the life around its towering structure.

A sudden movement out of the corner of her eye caught her attention.

She turned to see a large white van open and several men climbing outside. Within seconds of the van door opening, Evie heard the screams and wailing of a young woman. Evie watched in dismay as two men dragged a crying teenager out of the Distribution Center and threw her into the vehicle. As soon as the door closed, Evie could read the words on the side of the van.

HARMONY GROUP

Evie shuddered as the vehicle pulled away from the curb. To the Community, they were the Harmony Group. Those in charge of keeping the peace. To everyone in debt, they were the Harvesters. Those who would easily harvest anyone in debt to send to Medical Waste. Although they were established to keep the peace, everyone in debt knew that they would easily snatch up unwitting figures to toss into their snares. With or without a reason.

"Six-seven-seven-five, let's go!"

Evie jumped at the sound of Marcos's voice and quickly went over to the impossibly black Community car. Evie sat in the back while Marcos heaved himself into the driver's seat. She could have sworn the car shifted as he sat down.

She silently looked through the foggy window at the houses they drove past. The Distribution Center was seated at the very center of the Community, surrounded by several tall businesses and skyscrapers. Evie had not once entered any of those buildings, though. She never had a reason to. The next area they drove through was the Marketplace Unit. The towering structures held several stores for designer clothes and gourmet restaurants. Mr. Hillard, during her time working for him, had never wasted his time or money on such expensive food and clothing.

When they exited the area, Evie saw the many grocery stores she used to shop at for Mr. Hillard. She wondered if she would continue to shop there for her new assignment. Harmony Group vans and men on motorbikes could be seen randomly patrolling the streets. Motorbikes were a rare vehicle in the Community. It was known that only those in the Harmony Group used them for their patrols.

Soon enough, they passed through the large gates of the Community Board Unit. Evie remembered how Oscar Hillard would complain about this horrible place. He and Evie were under the same belief that such large and expensive houses were nothing but a waste of money. She smiled at the memory. The houses were massive, surrounded by private fences and beautiful flower beds. Many individuals could be seen working outside.

The house Marcos parked in front of was by far the largest in the unit. The front yard had a tall black fence all around it with beautiful flowers along the walk path. Evie thought it was a waste of blossoms, as they couldn't make the house look any less intimidating. Tall brick walls loomed over her when she stepped out of the car. The large structure oozed luxury and superiority. The black roof atop it contrasted deeply against the light gray clouds in the sky.

Just looking at it sent a chill down her spine.

Marcos trudged down the path as Evie wordlessly followed behind, staring at the concrete beneath her feet. Out of the corner of her eye, Evie could have sworn she saw movement from one of the large windows. Was someone watching her? It was possible. Perhaps one of the Huntleys. She shrugged the feeling off while Marcos rang the doorbell to the house.

When the door opened, Evie lowered her eyes to the ground.

"This way," a sharp feminine voice snapped.

Throughout her training, Evie was taught to never look up to anyone while in service. They were to keep their eyes to the ground until given permission to raise them. Evie had to be on her guard. Oscar Hillard was far more lenient with such standards. She immediately knew that this household would be starkly different.

Evie obediently followed Marcos into what she assumed was a sitting room. She was not allowed to raise her head, but the carpet she walked on was a dark red color, and she could scarcely see the lining of the ivory walls. The faint smell of cigarette smoke gave away that someone smoked in the house. She stood in the middle of the room, holding her bags tightly in her hands, refusing to let them fall to the floor.

The feminine voice was the first to speak out of the three of them. "This is it? This is the only one you have available?"

Evie clenched her fists in anger, pressing her lips tightly together.

"Y-yes, Mrs. Huntley," Marcos sputtered, clearly trying to be respectful. "This is number six-seven-seven-five. She has had extensive training. She is trained in domestics, cooking, financing, gardening, and musical entertainment for you and any guests you may have. More specifically, the piano."

The woman scoffed, and Evie felt shame color her cheeks.

"I don't want any of these mutts touching our grand piano. My husband handles our finances. And how is a girl this skinny supposed to be fit for manual labor?"

Evie bit her tongue and fought the urge to snap at the woman. *"Maybe if everyone in debt was given a decent meal, we wouldn't look so damn thin!"* she thought bitterly.

"Yes, madam. She is fit for domestic labor. She served her former assignment very well."

"Then why is she here and not with them?"

"Her former charge was Oscar Hillard. He passed away from cancer."

"Oh," Mrs. Huntley paused. "Well, I don't want her. Send her back."

Evie felt like she was going to be sick. Being sent back meant a large fine being added onto her debt.

"I'm sorry, madam, but your husband has already signed her contract. She must stay for at least ninety days, or you and your husband will face a fine. It's Community policy." There was a puff of air and Evie could smell cigarette smoke.

"That will not be an issue. Charge us. I don't care. Send her back and send us someone not as scrawny." She did not bother to try and hide the disgust in her voice.

"Your husband is the one who signed the contract. He is the only one that can send her back. Just give her a chance, Mrs. Huntley. If you aren't satisfied after ninety days, your husband can send her back. Then there would be no penalty against you."

Evie knew that if Mrs. Huntley pushed the issue, she could very well have her sent back. She was quite surprised Marcos was even pushing for Mrs. Huntley to give her a chance. Perhaps he wasn't as cold-hearted as she thought.

An aggravated sigh escaped the woman's lips. "Whatever. Expect a call soon. I'll be speaking to my husband."

"Thank you, madam. Here are the remotes for you and your husband. Six-seven-seven-five is very obedient, so I doubt you'll ever need to use them."

"I'll be the judge of that," Mrs. Huntley retorted flatly.

Evie still didn't look up, but she could hear the shuffling and heavy breathing of Marcos walking away. He had been dismissed. She flinched when the front door opened and closed. The transaction had been completed. She was now under the charge of this household.

Her eyes were on the floor, but Evie watched the expensive black heels as they circled her atop the plush carpet. Evie knew the woman was looking for flaws. Anything that could be used to convince her husband to send Evie back to the Distribution Center.

The woman finally stopped her assessment of Evie and stood in front of her.

"Look at me."

Evie raised her eyes and looked at the woman she would now serve. Sara Huntley was a beautiful woman. Her brown eyes and eyebrows stood in contrast to her expertly dyed blonde hair, but she wore it very well. Her tailored black skirt and blouse fit her slim body perfectly. Evie had no doubt this was a woman who would settle for nothing less than the best quality clothing.

Evie also took the quick opportunity to get a good look at the room. It was filled with beautiful paintings and a large red velvet couch. The accent tables neatly organized around the space looked to be made of mahogany with glass tops. The lamps appeared to be crystal, and they gave off a comfortable light. There was no doubt that everything else in the house would be just as nice and, most likely, expensive.

Mrs. Huntley gave Evie another head to toe look over before speaking. "So, I'm stuck with you for ninety days. Or until I speak to my husband and ask him to get you out of this house."

Evie swallowed and tried to find the correct way to address the arrogant woman. "Yes, madam. I'm sorry."

Mrs. Huntley rolled her eyes and dropped down on the velvet couch. "Well, you know your manners. While you're here, you will address me as madam. I'll give you one week. If you don't do things to my satisfaction, I'll be speaking to my husband and you will be gone."

Evie nodded and released the breath she was holding in. She was relieved the woman would at least give her time to prove herself.

Mrs. Huntley continued, "Mary is another in debt who works in my house. You will report to her and she will give you directions for your everyday tasks. You will also follow any directions my husband and I give you. Do you understand?"

"Yes, madam."

Mrs. Huntley stubbed out her cigarette in the cut glass ashtray on the small side table beside her before shaking out another from a slim case. The chain-smoking didn't surprise Evie; most higher members of the Community had the habit. It was an easy way to broadcast their wealth as cigarettes were expensive and often rare to find.

"Mary is in the kitchen down the hall. You'll begin tomorrow morning. Now, get going."

Evie didn't hesitate. Her hands ached from holding her bags for so long. She turned to leave, but Mrs. Huntley's voice stopped her.

"I almost forgot. What should I call you?"

Evie turned and looked back into Mrs. Huntley's arrogant face.

"Madam, my number is—"

"I'm not going to remember your fucking number," Mrs. Huntley snapped, waving a dismissive hand. "We need a name for you."

Evie swallowed. "Madam, my birth name is—"

The woman interrupted, offering a cruel smile, "Dog."

Evie blinked as Mrs. Huntley stood and puffed smoke into her face. She felt that the woman was enjoying the feeling of being able to degrade her. She tried not to cringe from the look of pleasure spreading over the woman's expression.

"I'm going to call you Dog." Evie's hands began to shake, her blood boiling as Mrs. Huntley laughed. "That's all you are here. My little errand Dog."

Without warning, Evie felt a sudden sting of electricity in her wrists. She cried out in pain and dropped to her knees, clenching her jaw. It lasted only seconds, but to Evie, it felt like an eternity.

Mrs. Huntley smirked down at her as she pocketed the remotes.

"A reminder of the pain you will receive if I am not satisfied with your work. Now, get to the kitchen."

Evie's eyes burned with tears as she grabbed her bags and rushed out of the room. The last time she felt this low was when her mother had turned her in.

She shook the anger away, making her way to a hallway door. The mouth-watering smell of roasted chicken told Evie that this was the kitchen's entrance. She dropped one of her bags to knock on the door.

"Come on in!" a voice called from inside.

Evie picked up her bag and entered. The room was large with several top-of-the-line pots and pans hanging from hooks in the ceiling. The countertops were made of marble and held a large gas stove. Next to the stove were double stacked ovens that emanated the smell of roasted chicken.

Then, she saw the figure of an older woman bent over the stove. The woman looked up and gave Evie a smile.

"Welcome. Please, take a seat."

The older woman had kind eyes, a full figure and almond skin. Her dark hair, that held streaks of gray, was tied in a tight bun atop her head. On her wrists were the same black bracelets Evie wore. She finished stirring a large pot before bringing a glass of water over and placed in on a small wooden dining table.

Evie returned the smile and walked over to the table. She placed her bags on the floor and took a seat, flexing her aching hands to ease the pain from carrying her things for so long.

"I'm Mary." The woman extended her hand and Evie shook it.

"Pleasure to meet you. I'm Evie, but Mrs. Huntley wants me to be called Dog."

Mary rolled her eyes, curling her lips in disgust. "Why am I not surprised? That woman will do anything to make herself feel better than everyone else."

Evie sipped her water while Mary returned to the stove. *At least I'm not alone here. She seems nice enough,"* she thought. She hoped they would get along during her servitude at the house.

"I'm going to call you Evie in this room. Outside of it, I'll have to call you Dog, as Mrs. Huntley wishes. Once I'm finished with this, I'll take you to your room. We begin work at six in the morning every day, except your day off. Which day do you get?"

"Sundays," Evie replied.

Mary nodded and continued. "As I was saying, we begin at six. We both have breakfast, and by seven, it's all hands-on deck. Mr. Huntley takes his breakfast in his study; he practically lives there. Mrs. Huntley, however, won't be up until about nine. I have a schedule lined up for cleaning tasks for the week. You will need to tend to the flowers up front and the garden in the back every day unless the weather is bad. Mrs. Huntley has gatherings just about every other weekend, so be prepared for plenty of guests. You have four uniforms in your room. One of them is a little nicer for those events."

The entire time Mary spoke, she was either stirring pots or chopping vegetables and looking into her oven. Evie's stomach rumbled at the smell of Mary's cooking, but the older woman didn't seem to notice. Or perhaps she didn't care.

"We eat lunch at eleven, and dinner is at seven. Mealtimes can change if Mrs. Huntley is having company over, which happens a lot. That woman likes to show off her husband's money."

Evie finished her water and looked back to Mary. "When is your day off?"

"I don't have one. Don't need one. Sunday is my easy day. I just cook and clean up the kitchen," Mary said simply, sitting down at the table across from Evie.

"You don't have anyone you want to go see? No family to visit?" Evie knew it wasn't her business, but if she could help another person in debt see their family, she would do it.

Mary smiled and shook her head. "No. I have my son, but I won't be able to see him. He's working for the Community as an engineer."

"Your son was able to become an engineer? How was that possible?" Evie was flabbergasted.

Mary's smile didn't falter at her question. "I turned myself in. All the money went to his education. He still has to work for the Community for a while as an engineer to finish paying off his education. Thankfully, they provide housing for Community engineers. But once the tuition is paid off, he'll be free to work for himself and have a good life."

It was a sudden rush of emotions for her. Evie felt her eyes shimmer and couldn't stop tears from filling her eyes. It felt like a miracle to see a mother who would make such a sacrifice for her child. After she was turned in, Evie was told by many others in debt about how their parents turned them in for the money they'd get in return. Hardly anyone she had spoken to had parents who truly loved them.

Mary looked quite shocked at the sudden look on Evie's face. "Are you alright?"

Evie quickly brushed away her tears with her fingers, sniffling. "I'm alright. Sorry, I just don't see mothers like you often."

Mary raised a brow. "And what kind of mother am I?"

"One that actually loves her child."

It was silent for a long moment, and Evie felt her chest tighten and her heart pound faster. She felt an instant respect for the woman before her. To Evie, Mary was the mother she longed to have. A strong, selfless woman who would do anything to see to her child's future.

Mary cleared her throat, and Evie could almost swear she saw small tears in the older woman's eyes, which had grown glossy and red. Mary rose to her feet. "Come on. I'll show you your room. You can have dinner at seven. We begin working together tomorrow."

The woman did a final quick check on the dinner that was still cooking before leaving the room with Evie trailing behind, bags in hand. As she followed Mary, Evie couldn't help but admire the house. It still felt cold to her, but the furnishings were beautiful. Everything was elegant and placed perfectly in whatever spot it occupied. Never before had Evie seen such expensive decorations and furnishings.

"Just a warning, Mrs. Huntley is a perfectionist. Every painting, vase, and furnishing is in its place for a reason, in her eyes. She will know if it's out of place, so be careful when cleaning. Otherwise, she's going to have you squirming on the floor thanks to those damn bracelets. And God help you if something gets broken."

Evie shuddered. She guessed that Mrs. Huntley would enjoy watching her scream in pain while she called the Distribution Center to send her back into the system. The value of the broken item would probably be added onto her debt as well.

Mary led Evie up an elegant set of stairs. The cream walls were decorated with many beautiful paintings, and the second floor of the house was no exception. However, upon reaching the third set of stairs, the decor of the house changed. The final set was a simple wooden staircase. Upon climbing to the third floor, the walls were bare, with the ivory paint slowly fading away. Evie assumed that no guests entered this floor of the house.

"That room is mine," Mary said, gesturing to a door along the left side of the hall. "That other one is our bathroom that we'll share" She made another gesture to a door on the opposite side of the hall.

She led Evie to the end of the hall and opened the last door to reveal another set of wooden stairs. This set looked old and worn. The nails were rusted over and the wood was slightly warped. The white paint even looked to be peeling away from the walls.

"Our rooms are the same size, but unfortunately, yours is up in the attic. I'm sorry, but it's going to get hot up there in the summer. It gets pretty cold at night too."

Evie gave her a small smile. "It's okay. I can deal with it."

Mary grinned in return and began to make her way down the hall. "Get yourself settled and come down for dinner a little later."

Before Mary completely disappeared around the corner, Evie couldn't stop the words from blurting out her mouth, "Thank you for being so kind."

Mary stopped and turned to look back at Evie with a brow raised. "You seem surprised. Were you expecting me to act like a total bitch to you?"

"I didn't know what to expect. I've never shared a household with someone else in debt before. You could have been a bitch to me if you wanted to. But thank you for being so nice. It feels good knowing I'm not alone here," Evie said, her expression full of sincere gratitude.

Mary paused and slowly walked back to stand in front of Evie. "The way I see it, we're both in debt. We both have a long way to go before we even get a taste of freedom. Now, I'm not saying that if you mess up, I won't report you. Because I will. I won't risk my neck for you. But hopefully, you aren't that dumb. So, if you work with me, I'll work with you. We can at least try to make our time together not miserable. Deal?"

Evie nodded, and Mary's eyes flashed with appreciation.

"Good. Now, go get situated. I'll see you later for dinner."

Mary vanished around the corner and Evie sighed. She made her way up the stairs, closing the door behind her. The steps were quite steep, and Evie had already begun to dread going up and down them every day. As soon as she reached the top and looked around, she let loose a loud groan.

The room was old with a musty smell, like mildew and dusty newspapers.

There was a small window against the wall, but Evie doubted it would give her much relief from the summer heat. She had hope that it would at least give her some fresh air when needed. The bed provided by the Huntleys was small with simple white sheets, a thin gray blanket, and a flat pillow. Her new assignment was courteous enough to provide a small table for her alarm clock. She would have to keep her personal clothes in her bag on the floor, though, as there was no dresser or closet in the small room.

Her uniforms hung on a small hook against the wall. Black pants with a white blouse. The uniform that was designated for the Huntleys' social gatherings was a knee-length black dress with long sleeves and a white apron.

Evie dropped her bag on the bed and went over to open the window. A small rush of air entered. She hoped the room's smell would clear out within a couple of hours, though it would most likely take much longer than that. Everything appeared old and unused.

With another sigh, Evie dropped onto the small bed and groaned in frustration. The bed was hard and worn, with a lumpy mattress that was less than comfortable. Evie felt like she should have known better. In what world would anyone in the Community care about the comfort of those in debt? Especially Mrs. Huntley. Evie was sure the woman was probably as terrible of a person as her mother was. She would find out soon enough.

Her eyes scanned the room and finally rested on a small crucifix above the door. Evie rolled her eyes. She had no idea how anyone was to believe in God in a place like this. Or at least, if there *was* one, then he was certainly turning a blind eye to this world and its suffering.

No. As far as Evie was concerned, there was no God.

Chapter 2

Six in the morning came quickly. Evie went into the kitchen in her new uniform, determined to begin working and impress the Huntleys. Evie refused to be sent back. If that were to happen, all her years of hard work up until this point would have been pointless.

Her back ached from the hard mattress and her eyes felt heavy from lack of sleep. The attic had grown cold in the middle of the night, and the thin blanket did nothing to help. Her pajamas were too thin for such weather. She would have to wear her regular clothes to bed in order to stay warm at night, it seemed. By the time she had finally gotten comfortable enough to fall asleep, it was time to wake up and begin work.

After she got ready and sat down in the kitchen, she and Mary quickly began eating their oatmeal. While they ate, Mary gave Evie instructions of all the daily tasks she would be responsible for.

"Like I said yesterday, you're in charge of the garden and lawn. It's a rotation of deep cleaning. First floor one day, second floor the next day, and vice versa. We both must work together in order to make sure the decorations go back up *exactly* how Mrs. Huntley wants," Mary said.

The entire time Mary spoke, Evie felt her stomach churn with unease and she fought against making a sour expression. She forced herself to keep eating as to not waste the food. From her memory, she found that Mr. Hillard was nowhere near that strict with her. She had to get with the program and fast if she had any hope of appeasing Mrs. Huntley.

"I wonder if Mr. Huntley is just as bad. Maybe he's worse." She cringed at her own thoughts, taking a sip of milk.

Both women finished their breakfast, moving to stand. Mary began to cook breakfast for Mr. Huntley while Evie began washing the dishes.

"Does Mr. Huntley eat his breakfast this early every day?" Evie asked while scrubbing a plate, bubbles coating her fingers.

Mary nodded while flipping eggs and frying bacon on the kitchen's griddle. "Yup. Every morning at seven-thirty on the dot. He's a man who likes a schedule. Lunch is at twelve-thirty, and dinner is at seven. He takes his in his study."

"He doesn't want to eat with his wife?"

Mary seemed to stifle a laugh. "Nope. You're going to see soon enough that they aren't some romantic couple. They get together for social occasions and whenever they need to talk about money and household needs. That's it."

Evie stopped drying the bowl in her hand and gave Mary a look of disbelief. "Seriously? What's the point of being married then?"

Mary shrugged as she slid the over easy eggs onto a large plate. "From what I heard, Mrs. Huntley's father cashed in a favor. He wanted his daughter set up with a good life and a strong name. And this was just after Mr. Huntley's divorce."

"He's divorced? What happened with his first marriage?"

Mary placed the bacon on the plate with the eggs and turned to look at Evie. "This is Mr. Huntley's *third* marriage. No, I have no idea why. I came to work for him while he was still married to the first. Next thing I knew, the first was packing her bags and left crying out the door after six years of marriage. The second was here for four years. The current Mrs. Huntley has been here for three."

Mary poured coffee into a mug while Evie silently put the dishes away in the kitchen cabinets. She couldn't understand why he would marry any woman he didn't love. Or at least, didn't care about. The Community was indeed a heartless place.

Evie took a breath. "So, what happened to the women? Do you know?"

Mary finished his tray and prepared herself to walk out with it. "I think they went back to their parents. Haven't heard anything since. But divorce is sort of a mark of shame in the Community, and I imagine he isn't interested in sharing his personal business like that."

Mary swiftly left with the tray, leaving Evie alone, her mind swarming with questions. Why in the world would divorce be a mark of shame? The higher-ups in the Community could do whatever they wanted. At least, that's what Evie thought.

Mary returned about ten minutes later with a tray full of dirty dishes.

"Last night's dinner dishes," Mary said before Evie could ask.

Evie took them from her to begin washing them while Mary put away the carton of eggs and unneeded bacon that sat on the counter.

"Mary, why is divorce a mark of shame in the Community? Why would they even care?"

Mary was silent for a few moments, her lips pursed in thought.

"Well, I can only tell you things I overhear. You should know, marriage for these old bastards is all about what they can get out of it. There's no love here. They marry a pretty face for sex and connections. It's only ever a black stain on the women. If they get divorced, it's because they're being replaced with a new woman. It looks bad, and the higher-ups gossip more than they wipe their own asses. Once you serve at one of Mrs. Huntley's parties, you'll understand."

Evie washed the dishes, her brows furrowing while her thoughts remained far away. She didn't think her respect for the Community could sink any lower, but she was wrong.

"What is marriage without love? Sex may give a short time of pleasure, but what about having someone to care about you? Someone to stand beside you during dark times or to remind you that they love and care about you?"

Evie knew true love existed. On occasion, she would see the married couples in debt spend any time they had together. She even once witnessed the tears in a woman's eyes because she had to leave her husband and not see him for a week. But such a love was rare. Naturally, Evie felt love for her siblings, but a romantic relationship was out of the question for her, despite her thoughts and feeling for one man in particular.

Evie forced those thoughts away and finished the dishes. She knew she had a long day ahead of her. It was time to focus.

After the kitchen had been cleaned up, Mary led Evie to the back door of the house. "You're not gonna like this next task," she said with a deep sigh.

Evie was confused until she opened the door. The garden was overrun with weeds while the flowers were dead and the grass was overgrown; bushes were unkempt with limbs growing in several different directions. The black fence around the backyard had thick brush and vines growing all around the bars.

"Mrs. Huntley likes the idea of having a garden, but she sure as hell doesn't want to take care of one. I'm sorry, but I just couldn't keep up with it. Mrs. Huntley told me to wait till we got someone new assigned to the house."

Evie gaped at the sight and Mary gave her a small pat on her shoulder.

"How…how long has it been this bad?" Evie exclaimed in shock.

"Well," Mary paused. "The last person who was here was sent back over two months ago. I'm sure you can imagine what came after." She gestured to the wilting scene before them.

Evie took a breath and mentally prepared herself for the task. "Do they have any garden tools?" she asked, her voice small.

Mary stepped out the door and gestured to the corner of the backyard. Evie peeked her head out to see a small, vine-covered structure that she assumed was a shed. The simple wooden door looked worn with spots of mold growing on the corners of it. The hinges were clearly rusted over, leaving Evie to wonder if she would even be able to get the door open.

Her companion stepped back inside, now speaking from the doorway while Evie walked out onto the grass, "Just focus on this for today. I can do most of the housework myself. I'll come grab you for lunch in a bit."

Mary disappeared through the door, closing it behind her.

Evie stomped through the weeds and thorns to get to the shed, leaves and twigs scratching against her ankles. She hissed in pain at their pricks when she tried to pull more thorn covered greenery from the shed. After she cleared a path to get inside, Evie looked down to see tiny, bloody holes randomly dotting her hands. Luckily, she was able to pull out most of the thorns that clung to her palms. Once her hands were dealt with, she carefully grabbed the rusted handle of the door and pulled the door open. Inside the shed, Evie found the tools she needed. It took several hours, but Evie was able to remove all the vines, mow the grass, and pull all the dead flowers from the garden beds.

About halfway through trimming the bushes, A loud slam from behind caused Evie to jump. She turned and saw Mrs. Huntley leaning against the door, taking a drag from a cigarette. Evie's pulse quickened as she watched Mrs. Huntley's thumb run over the button to her remote. One small push and Evie would feel the shock from the bracelets.

Mrs. Huntley looked around the yard and seemed impressed. "Not bad, little Dog. Not bad. Perhaps you will be useful."

Evie averted her gaze to the ground. "Thank you, madam."

She didn't look up until the door slammed shut again. Mrs. Huntley was gone. Evie let out a breath and turned once more to the bushes. She went back to snapping off the oddball limbs when a chill went down her spine. She spun around, but no one was in the doorway. Evie was overwhelmed with the feeling of being watched as the hairs on her arms stood up and goosebumps covered her skin.

Her eyes scanned the back of the house, darting from window to window. Finally, they settled on a large glass pane on the second floor. Evie couldn't see clearly with the sun glaring down on her, but she could have sworn there was a large figure staring into the garden. Perhaps it was Mary? No, the figure was too large. Was it Mr. Huntley?

The sound of the back door opening made her jump. It was Mary.

"Hey, it's almost lunch time! Get cleaned up and come eat."

Evie quickly looked back up to the window, but the figure was gone. Mary's voice brought her back to reality, and she wiped sweat off her forehead before hurrying into the house.

"I'm probably just seeing things," she told herself.

The cool air of the indoors was refreshing to her worn-out figure.

"You alright?" Mary asked, pushing her brows together in concern.

"I'm good," Evie replied quickly, following Mary into the kitchen.

"Mary...which rooms are on the second floor?"

Mary gave Evie a curious look. "The master bedrooms, the guest rooms and the study. Why?"

"Nothing. No reason."

Mary shrugged, and they went into the kitchen. Evie washed her hands and splashed her face with cold water, giving herself some mild relief from the heat. She sat at the small dining table while Mary brought two plates over. Each plate had an egg salad sandwich and carrot sticks.

Evie greedily ate the sandwich while Mary laughed.

"Is it good?"

Evie nodded, her mouth full of the delicious food. Mary chuckled while Evie finished the sandwich and dove immediately into the carrot sticks.

"So, Mrs. Huntley spoke to me this morning. She's having a party this weekend," Mary said between bites of her own sandwich.

Evie swallowed the last of her carrots and looked up. "So, what do we need to do for it?"

"Just clean the house and decorate the entertainment room. I have some shopping to do for the food. It's going to be a rough day for us, but we'll get it done."

"What kind of party is it? Like, a dinner party? How many people?"

"It's just a fancy get together. Usually about a dozen attend but sometimes more than that. It's not even a full dinner. Just some appetizers. They're more about the drinking than the eating. But we get the leftovers," Mary told her with a wink.

Evie smiled. She felt excited for the first time to have the chance at eating some upper-class food. There was no doubt in Evie's mind that the Huntleys wouldn't notice the extra food being gone. Though she just finished lunch, her stomach grumbled at the thought.

"We can talk more about that later. The backyard is looking good," Mary said, sipping from her glass of water. "I'm sure Mrs. Huntley will show it off after you get some flowers growing in it."

Evie couldn't stop herself from rolling her eyes. "Let me guess. She's going to take credit for all the work?"

Mary laughed outright. "Oh, no. Once you please Mrs. Huntley, she's going to rub it in everyone's face that she has you assigned to her house. We are nothing but good labor, and if we have a decent skill at something, we're like trophies for them."

Evie shook her head. It was unsurprising to her that the high-standing members of the Community would take credit for their hard-earned skills.

She went to clear the plates, but Mary shook her head. "Don't worry about this. That backyard is looking great. Keep it up and get it finished. If you don't, you'll be getting an earful from Mrs. Huntley."

Evie nodded and quickly went back to her work outside.

The worst was taken care of. It was now a matter of finishing the bushes and trying to clean up the flower beds enough to make room for new flowers. It would be up to Mr. and Mrs. Huntley to either buy new flowers or get some seeds and grow them from scratch. For one final touch to the backyard, Evie swept the path to remove the grass clippings and dead branches.

She stood by the back door and admired her work.

Yes, the backyard looked much better. All it needed were some replacement flowers in the beds and for the yard to be tended to on a regular basis. Evie walked back into the house and went to the kitchen to look for Mary.

The older woman was preparing dinner when Evie entered. Mary stopped chopping vegetables to look up into Evie's sweaty face.

"Is it alright if I go clean myself up before I do the next task?" Evie asked.

"Hun, just go take a shower. I think you've earned it. And try not to track too much dirt up the stairs. You're going to have to be the one that cleans it up." Mary gave her a pointed look.

Evie thanked her and made her way up the stairs. Upon passing a hallway to reach the next set of stairs, she could hear voices. The female voice was no doubt Mrs. Huntley. Her words were biting, "What's the big deal? We can get another one! And money has never been an issue for you!" Mrs. Huntley's voice was normally commanding and arrogant. Now, she sounded compliant and almost frightened. "Please, Elias. That girl needs to go! She's a scrawny little thing and is hardly working!"

Evie's blood boiled at the woman's words. She shouldn't have been surprised. Of course Mrs. Huntley wouldn't keep her word and give her the full week to prove herself. She should have known not to get her hopes up. It wasn't Evie's intention to stand there and listen, but she wanted to hear the rest of the conversation. Anger was replaced with terror. If she went back, she could still very well face a penalty on her debt.

"No."

As soon as the masculine voice spoke, Evie's body seemed to completely freeze in place. Her muscles tightened and her heart pounded loudly in her ears. All it took was one spoken word to know that this man commanded respect.

Mrs. Huntley's voice began to sound even weaker. "But, darling," the endearment sounded forced, "the girl is just not meant for this house! You have the connections! You can request—"

"I said no."

Evie tried to force her feet to move, but she couldn't. There was a deep, aggravated breath. There was no way to be sure who it was from, but it was clear that Mrs. Huntley was losing her argument. Hope blossomed in Evie's chest.

"Well…what about a week? If she doesn't do well within a week, would you at least consider it? Please?" Mrs. Huntley's voice sounded like a high-pitched whine.

There was silence for a few moments, then she finally received an answer.

"If she does not work to my satisfaction, I will contact the department myself."

"Thank you! I promise I will give her a fair chance! I'll let you know—"

"*My* satisfaction, Sara. Not yours. I will determine if the girl goes or not. You do not need to notify me of anything."

Mrs. Huntley had lost the fight. A feeling of relief washed over Evie. She wasn't being sent back. At least, not yet.

She crept up the next flight of stairs just as Mrs. Huntley came out of the hallway. Evie got a glimpse of her, but the woman didn't see Evie. As Mrs. Huntley stumbled out of the hallway, her face was pale and her full lips were trembling. She had her hands clasped tightly together against her bosom, shaking from the aftermath of the conversation with her husband.

She appeared to be absolutely terrified of him.

"Maybe she isn't afraid at all. Maybe she's just pitching a fit because she lost." Evie shook her thoughts away and climbed up the stairs.

Now she had a new goal. It wasn't Mrs. Huntley she had to impress but her husband. After hearing his voice, Evie hoped she wouldn't have to see him that often. Mary already said he practically lived in his study. His deep and commanding voice echoed through her head.

Evie straightened her back, heading towards the shower. Brooding over the matter would do nothing to change it. She washed herself quickly, as she knew there was much more work to do. After her shower, she met with Mary again in the kitchen.

"Feel better?" Mary asked as soon as she entered the room.

"I do, thank you. Ready for the next task!" Her voice rang out, eager and shrill. She felt energized and ready to move on with her work.

Mary chuckled and gestured for Evie to follow her to the supply closet in the hallway.

"Time to vacuum. Usually, we would do one floor one day and the next another, but both really must be done. You didn't track in much dirt from the garden, but it's better to be safe than sorry. God forbid Mrs. Huntley spot a single speck of dirt on the carpet."

Evie nodded. If a little extra work meant not getting an electric shock, she was more than willing to break the cleaning schedule a bit to appease Mrs. Huntley.

As she began vacuuming, Evie glanced at the clock and realized how fast the day had gone by. Within twenty minutes, she finished the first floor and the first flight of stairs. When she was about to begin on the second floor, her eyes unintentionally went back to the hall that led to Mr. Huntley's study.

The vacuum was loud. Too loud. The first floor was one thing, but any noise outside the study might aggravate Mr. Huntley. She shuddered at the thought of him standing over her while she writhed in pain from her bracelets. Mrs. Huntley already enjoyed it. Hopefully, her husband wasn't as sadistic.

Evie decided to vacuum all the areas besides the hallway that led to the study. Perhaps she could speak to Mary and ask her when the best time to clean that hallway was. It would also be good to ask when the study needed to be cleaned. She hoped that Mary was the one who would do that task. The thought of accidentally breaking something in his office made her stomach churn and heart pound. If she did that, then she had no doubt that he would send her back to the Distribution Center.

As soon as the floors were finished, she went into the kitchen and was immediately greeted with the smell of Mary's delicious cooking. A large roast beef rested on the counter in a roasting pan full of potatoes, carrots, and onions. The idea of having a bite of such a delicious smelling meal made her mouth water.

"Great job today, hun. Dinner is almost ready," she told Evie without even turning from the stove. "I need to finish up plates for Mr. and Mrs. Huntley."
Evie washed her hands and waited patiently while Mary assembled the dinner trays.

"Mary…will I be responsible for cleaning the study?"

The woman stopped and slowly turned to look at Evie. She seemed surprised by the look of worry on Evie's face.

"Is there something wrong with that?"

Evie didn't realize her hands were shaking. Mary noticed and took a breath.

"Let me deliver these and we can talk."

She then rushed out with both dinner trays in hand. After she came back into the kitchen, they sat across from each other at the small wooden dining table.

"Evie, what is it?"

Evie's hands continued to shake, and she didn't know why. Her voice was shaking as well when she spoke, "I was going up to take a shower when I overheard the Huntleys talking. Mrs. Huntley wanted to send me back. Mr. Huntley said no."

Mary raised a brow. "So, what's the problem? Sounds like you won't have to worry about being sent back."

Evie continued to fidget with her hands.

"I…I wish I had a better reason, but when I heard Mr. Huntley's voice, he just scared the hell out of me. I don't know why, but…" Her voice trailed off. "I feel scared to even see him." To Evie's surprise, Mary laughed. It wasn't a cruel laugh, but a light-hearted one.

"Hun, I felt the same way when I first started. Trust me, I get it. To be blunt, Mr. Huntley is not the kind of man you want to mess around with. I'm not sure what business he's into, but I hear a lot of sick gossip from others during their parties here. But don't worry. I swear that as long as you do your job and keep to your own business, you have nothing to worry about." A small weight lifted from Evie's chest.

"To answer your question," the woman continued. "I'm usually the one who cleans the study. But I'll need your help from time to time. And it's always when he's away on business, which is at least once a week."

Mary assembled their dinner plates and brought them to the table. Evie couldn't hold back a smile at the sight of such an amazing meal, even if it was the leftovers from Mr. and Mrs. Huntley's dinner. As they ate, Evie carefully tried to ask the right questions about Mr. Huntley.

"So, what's the gossip you've heard? What does he do exactly? Is he on the council?" Her questions flew out one after the other before she could stop them. Evie's cheeks flooded with embarrassment at her own boldness.

Mary stopped eating, and her face grew cold.

"I don't know the details and I know better than to ask. No, he isn't on the council, but he may as well be. All I know is that if the council needs something, they turn to him. Just do what you're told in this house and don't even think about it anymore."

Mary went back to her dinner, her brows pushing together in disappointment. Evie bit her lip, returning to her own food.

Everyone in debt knew that in the shadows of the Community, there were plenty of people who did dirty work for the council. Most of those individuals dealt with the Medical Waste Facility. The place where all the delinquents and cripples went. Human guinea pigs to be used for what the Community called 'medical research.' No one in debt knew the truth about the facility because those who ended up being taken there were never seen again.

"Is Mr. Huntley one of those men in the shadows?" Evie wondered.

Neither Evie nor Mary spoke further on the subject. As soon as they finished their dinner, Evie started on the dishes and Mary focused on cleaning the rest of the kitchen.

Eventually, Evie spoke. "Do you have a game plan for us tomorrow? What do we need to do to get ready for the party?" She was desperate to have a happier discussion, and Mary seemed thankful for the change of subject.

"We start with the entertainment room and go from there. Don't worry; we'll get it done. We can talk more about it tomorrow."

Evie nodded and finished the dishes while Mary finished sweeping the floor.

"Go ahead and get to bed. I just need to mop and I'm done for the day."

Evie bid Mary goodnight with a wave and began heading to her room.

Once she reached the second floor, a light switched off out of the corner of her eye. The light underneath the door to the study had disappeared. Evie had no idea why, but a sudden rush of panic set in. She rushed to the second set of stairs and made her way up, careful not to trip. Evie paused halfway up and peeked her head over the banister, enough for her to see slightly down the hall.

Heavy footsteps could be heard coming out of the hallway from the study and walked down the opposite direction of the staircase. From this angle, she couldn't quite see Mr. Huntley, but she heard his footsteps retreat to what she assumed was the direction of his room.

Upon reaching her own bedroom, Evie closed the door and took a breath. There was no explanation for her feelings. She had no idea how a man she had never even met nor seen inspired so much fear in her. Evie would see him tomorrow evening, and there was no choice in the matter. Perhaps seeing him would calm her fears. Maybe Mr. Huntley wouldn't look nearly as intimidating as he sounded.

Evie could only hope for the best and forced herself up the stairs and into bed.

Chapter 3

Sleep did not come to Evie quickly, nor did it last long thanks to the hard bed and cold room. Nevertheless, she was able to force herself up and dress for the day ahead.

"Maybe I can ask Mary for another blanket so I can actually sleep at night," she thought as she climbed down the never-ending steps of the staircase.

Evie entered the kitchen to see a plate of scrambled eggs and bacon already on the table.

"We have to get an early start," Mary said as soon as Evie entered the room. "Mr. Huntley will be leaving soon for a meeting, so he doesn't want breakfast. We need to eat and get things ready."

Evie nodded and both women quickly and quietly ate breakfast. Before Evie could start cleaning their dishes, Mary began explaining their schedule for the day.

"So, we need to work on the entertainment room first. The piano needs to be polished for the entertainer Mrs. Huntley hired. She likes to hire a professional. She thinks it makes her look better."

Evie rolled her eyes at the ridiculous waste of money for such a thing, but she stayed silent, waiting for Mary to continue.

"There are some decorations in the closet that we can use for the room. Crystal pieces, special pictures, and all that fancy crap. When Mrs. Huntley wakes up, I'll get her charge card and go get the food. I need to pick you up some black tights to go with your uniform. What's your shoe size?"

"Seven. My regular shoes won't work?" Evie asked, looking down at her plain black sneakers, frowning.

Mary shook her head. "No, we need to completely match each other tonight. I'll get you some black flats. It's part of your uniform for the house, so don't worry about paying for it."

Evie went to do the dishes while Mary grabbed the cleaning supplies from the kitchen. Once the dishes were done, both women went into the entertainment room and got to work.

The room was large and was certainly big enough to host many people. Comfortable chairs and couches made with blue velvet were skillfully placed around the room. Small mahogany tables were at the sides of each chair and couch, clearly for guests to place their drinks. The carpet was a deep blue with the same ivory walls that colored the rest of the inside of the house. A large grand piano sat in the corner of the room, along with the black bench for any piano player to sit in. A large fireplace completed the room with its large mantle holding several beautiful crystal pieces and large brass candlesticks.

Mary pulled the special decorations for the room out of the hall closet. While Mary cleaned the piano in the corner, Evie set to dusting and wiping down the large windows. After about twenty minutes of work, heavy footsteps could be heard coming down the hall. Mary stood at attention and glanced at Evie.

"I'll be right back. I'm just going to see him out."

Evie tried to continue working, but she couldn't stop herself from listening to the small conversation.

"Sir, will you be wanting lunch today?"

Unlike his wife, Mary spoke to Mr. Huntley with confidence. Perhaps because she had worked for him for so long. She must have known him better than anyone in this house.

"There's no need. I'll be back before the party tonight" he said gruffly. "Sara has my card. She'll give it to you before her appointments. Get whatever you need for tonight. I'll be back in a bit."

His voice was a lot less intimidating when he addressed Mary. When the front door closed, Mary came back into the lounge.

"I'll be taking care of his study a little later today. He'll probably be back right before the party starts. Or after. That man doesn't give a damn about any party in the Community. Not even the ones his wife hosts."

Evie was taken aback. "Why? What's wrong with having a party? Especially if you do business with them?" she asked while polishing the brass candlesticks.

Mary snorted. "Hun, Mrs. Huntley is the one throwing these stupid parties. It's all to impress her friends and show off her husband's money. Mr. Huntley doesn't have to do a damn thing to make a name for himself or show off to anyone. As soon as Mr. Huntley makes his appearance tonight, you'll see."

"Okay...so what appointments does Mrs. Huntley have today?"

"Hair and nails. More artificial crap to throw on herself."

Both women laughed and went back to work.

Time was going by way too fast for them. Mary went to cook breakfast for Mrs. Huntley and Evie was tasked with cleaning the first-floor bathroom. It looked almost brand-new by the time she was done with it. As she exited the small room, Mary walked over to Evie. Her brows were scrunched together and the corner of her mouth twitched in aggravation.

"Looks like I have other stops to make," Mary said with an angry scowl. "Now I need to get flowers for the damn garden too. Mrs. Huntley wants to show it off tonight."

Evie sighed, knowing she was going to be the one to plant them when Mary brought them back.

"Hun, you're not going to like this, but I need you to jump on cleaning the study while I'm gone." Mary gave her an apologetic look.

Evie's body tensed. Before she could speak, Mary held up her hand.

"He's not here. Stop worrying. And even if he was, you need to stop being afraid of a man you haven't even seen. He's given you no reason for it, alright? It'll be fine. He won't even be back until later this evening. When I return, we can finish the work together."

Evie nodded. Mary was right. There was no reason to be afraid of a man she hadn't even seen. He hadn't done anything to her.

At least, not yet.

Mary's face was hard and stern as she gave Evie her instructions for the study.

"Do not touch anything on his desk. I mean it. He takes care of it himself. Don't poke into his business. Clean the windows, vacuum the carpet, dust the bookshelves, and clean the chairs and table in his sitting area. It doesn't take long. He also has a paper shredder. Make sure that's empty. Take your time getting it done, and we will work together on everything else when I get back."

Mary walked away without another word, and Evie grabbed the vacuum cleaner and cleaning basket from the hall closet. Her feet were heavy as she trudged up to the second floor and down the hall that led to his study. She took a deep breath and gently opened the door.

It was larger than Evie had expected. Bookcases lined the walls with several different types of literature. On the left side of the room, there were a few large chairs, a small coffee table and what looked to be a wardrobe. On the opposite side, his desk sat in front of the large window. Evie's feet seemed to move on their own as she was suddenly standing in front of the glass panes looking down to see the garden she had worked so hard on.

Her arms wrapped around herself as she felt goosebumps run down her arms. Her eyes widened at the realization. The figure watching her yesterday was Mr. Huntley. Her suspicion was confirmed.

She forced the horrified feeling away and set herself onto her task. She made sure not to miss a single spot on the carpet with the vacuum. The coffee table was soon spotless, and she quickly emptied his paper shredder and trashcan.

Evie ignored the desk, per Mary's orders. It was scattered with papers and different files. The computer was large, taking up a large section of the wooden furniture. Even if Mary hadn't ordered her to, Evie would never have touched it. Her final task was the bookcases. They stretched from wall to wall and were packed to the brim with dusty tomes. Evie carefully cleaned her way down the walls and wiped each shelf carefully, as to not disturb the books.

Upon reaching the last bookshelf, Evie was distracted by a specific title. *Utopia* by William Hurt. Her hand absently reached for the book, slowly sliding it out of its spot between two massive others. Her fingers traced the words on the cover in wonder.

All the fond memories she had when she worked for Oscar Hillard rushed into her head. He was such a kind person, never fitting in with the higher-ups of the Community. He loved sharing his beautiful library with Evie from the moment she walked through his front door. As soon as his health began to deteriorate, she read to him nightly. The best joke between them was that if he didn't eat his vegetables, she wouldn't read him a chapter before bed. *Utopia* was the last book she ever read to him.

Evie loved the idea the book held for a peaceful and united society. Where everyone lived in a paradise with no debt or greed. She missed the times when Oscar would take her hand and smile at her. He always wished for that society along with Evie.

The present rushed back to her. Evie knew she needed to get back to work. Before she placed the book back onto the shelf, a small dent on the spine of the book caught her attention. She remembered accidently dropping Mr. Hillard's book on the corner of a table, causing a small dent on the bottom of the spine. She shook her head and she quickly placed the book back onto its proper place on the shelf. It was probably a coincidence.

A masculine voice echoed off the walls of the room, startling her to her very core, "Do you like my collection?"

Evie's heart pounded loudly in her chest while she turned to face the man that spoke. A shiver ran down her spine, and her face paled.

This entire time, Evie always imagined a stern old man with gray hair and a bulging figure. Most high standing members of the Community were old men who did nothing to take care of themselves. She remembered the times when some of them would visit Mr. Hillard's home. Their bellies pushed against their shirts and their faces were wrinkled and sagging. She assumed Mr. Huntley would look the same.

Oh, how wrong she was.

Elias Huntley's large frame took up the entire doorway. He was tall with impossibly dark hair and eyes. This was a man that took exceptionally good care of himself. His handsome features gave nothing of his age away, save for the slight wrinkles next to his eyes. His clothing, like his wife's, were tailored to fit him perfectly. Nothing was out of place. Not a strand of hair or even a crease on his black suit.

Evie's eyes immediately dropped to the floor and her mind raced to find the right words to say. "Sir, I'm very sorry. I shouldn't have touched your property." He took a few steps into the room.

"The only people I want touching these books are ones who can genuinely appreciate them. You seem to be one of those people. At least, I hope you are." Evie felt a flood of relief, and she let out a deep breath.

"I consider it disrespectful when someone won't look me in the eye."

Evie felt the command in his voice, and her body froze in shock. He wanted her to look at him. Her, a woman in debt who was considered the lowest of the low. Her blue eyes lifted off the floor and met his. Mr. Huntley's face seemed friendly enough, but his eyes held no emotion.

He glanced over to the bookshelf before meeting her gaze once more. "*Utopia* was an interesting read. Does it appeal to you?"

Evie swallowed. "I've read the book. I used to read it to my former assignment."

"Your former assignment was Oscar Hillard, I believe."

"Yes, sir."

Mr. Huntley nodded thoughtfully. "Oscar was an intelligent man. I'm not surprised he would have read that one as well. One thing we had in common was our love for literature. Did you enjoy it?"

"Yes, I did."

"Why?"

Evie wondered why such an esteemed man would even care about what she enjoyed reading. Well, if he wanted to know, then she would tell him.

"It…it was a nice escape from reality. I know it's fiction, but it felt good to know there was someone else out there who thought of a paradise where everyone could live together with no conditions or suffering."

Mr. Huntley was quiet while he considered her words. His expression, however, gave nothing away of his thoughts or feelings.

"And do you think such a paradise could ever exist?"

Evie inhaled before she spoke confidently. "No. Not in this world and not with the people currently living in it." Her own words made her feel hopeless and disappointed.

There was silence as the two seemed to regard each other. Evie did not lie, but a voice inside of her told her that she should have.

Evie felt it was time to break the silence. His gaze had begun to make her feel uneasy.

"Mary told me you were at a meeting and instructed me to clean the room. I apologize—"

He cut her off with a dismissive wave of his hand. "There's nothing to apologize for. My business finished early."

Evie nodded shyly. "Please excuse me then, sir."

She went to grab for the basket and vacuum when his voice stopped her.

"Just a moment," Mr. Huntley said as he stepped over to the bookcase closest to her. He reached for a book on the top shelf and held it out to her.

"Read this."

She took it and looked at the cover. *The Disorder of Humanity* by Thomas Lane. The book looked incredibly old. The spine had a large crease down the center of it and the pages looked discolored.

Evie looked up to Mr. Huntley, unsure of what to say.

"Read it. We can discuss what you think about it another time."

Evie nodded, her eyes going wide in surprise and confusion. "Thank you, sir."

She carefully placed the book under her arm while grabbing her cleaning supplies. Out of the corner of her eye, Evie could see Mr. Huntley's eyes follow her out of the room.

Evie exited the hallway and left the vacuum and cleaning basket on the floor to quickly take the book to her room.

As she placed the book on her side table, her confusion and surprise only grew. *"Why would he want me to read this? What's the point?"*

She wouldn't have time to start tonight. It would have to wait. But she would have to make it a priority, as Mr. Huntley had given her a direct order. Quickly, she placed the book on her small nightstand and went to clean the rest of the house.

As soon as Mary arrived back at the house, she brought Evie several different planters of flowers. She was sweating and cursing under her breath, likely at the weight of the items in her arms.

"Take these damn things before I toss them outside!" Mary seethed, thrusting them into Evie's open hands. "I swear, I never want to go to that damn flower shop again!"

Evie took hold of the planters and watched Mary hunch over, desperately trying to catch her breath.

"What happened?"

Mary scowled. "Just tired of the pricks at the marketplace. The only way I can get them to even look at me is to remind them of who I work for! And I've never been to the flower shop, so as soon as they saw my bracelets, they tried to kick me to the curb! I had to drop Mr. Huntley's name just to get them to sell me the flowers! You'd think they wouldn't care who goes in so long as people are buying their shit!"

Mary finished in a huff before stalking inside the kitchen, continuing to mumble angrily under her breath.

Evie had long dealt with extreme prejudice at the marketplace because of her bracelets, but that was only when making personal purchases. Before she could enter any store, the owner would always demand to know who she was shopping for. Herself or her current contract owner. Unless it was for her contract owner, she was turned away.

Quietly, she went out to the garden to plant the flowers. Evie made it look as elegant as possible in the short amount of time she had been given, but she wasn't happy with the final outcome. Mary could only carry so many flowers, and there were many bare spots in the beds. Hopefully, she would be allowed to either buy more flowers to fill in the gaps or some seeds to grow from scratch. Evie was certain that she would feel the pain of an electric shock after the party tonight. Mrs. Huntley would likely not be pleased by the sight of the garden.

As soon as she was done with the flower beds, Evie and Mary hurried to change into their nicer uniforms for the evening. Both women matched, as they wore their knee length black dresses and white aprons. Mary helped Evie tie her hair into a tight bun on the top of her head, then both women set to task of getting the food ready for the party.

Evie jumped when the doorbell rang.

"Mrs. Huntley will get it," Mary said quickly before Evie could go. "She's always the one that greets the guests. In about fifteen minutes, we'll start serving food and drinks."

Evie nodded and continued to wash the pots and pans while Mary finished cooking. An elegant tray of shrimp cocktails was soon ready along with tomato bruschetta on toasted bread points and barbeque meatballs. The sight and smell of the food made Evie's mouth water.

With a final wipe of her brow and a sigh, Mary said it was time for them to finally go serve at the party, which had grown louder by the minute with laughter and voices.

The entertainment room was full of chuckles and light-hearted conversation when they entered. Its lights were dimmed, and several groups of people scattered throughout the room, holding glasses of wine. Women wore elegant gowns with glittering jewels carefully assorted along their bodies while men wore black suits and ties. Large gold watches shone on their wrists, glistening in the light of the chandelier above their heads.

Mary carried around the trays of appetizers while Evie went around the room pouring wine into every empty glass that was thrown in front of her. None of the guests acknowledged the two of them, and Evie believed they were all too trapped in their superiority to spare even a simple thanks or nod in acknowledgement of their presence. After a few rounds of delivering food and drinks, Mary and Evie stood against the wall.

Evie couldn't stop her eyes from wandering around the luxurious space before them. Mrs. Huntley happily laughed with several other women on the other side of the room. She looked absolutely stunning with her blonde hair swept up into an elegant knot atop her head with a large emerald necklace glistening at her neck. Evie wanted to vomit in disgust. It was such a waste of money to her. Perhaps if this were a perfect world and this social gathering wasn't built on money and the pain of others, Evie might have enjoyed a party like this.

But this wasn't a perfect world. Not by a long shot.

Mary gave a slight nudge to Evie with her elbow.

"In the far corner. All those people are on the council," she whispered, nodding in the direction she spoke of.

Evie glanced over to see four old men and one woman where Mary had gestured. All of them laughed at each other's conversations while elegantly sipping their drinks. Her eyes settled on the old woman sitting in a large armchair, one who seemed completely dressed down compared to all the other ladies in the room. She wore a simple dark blue dress with no jewelry. Her gray hair was tied in an elegant braid. Next to her chair was a large walking cane.

Evie leaned over to whisper in Mary's ear, "That woman is on the council too?"

Mary gave a slight nod.

"I didn't think women could be on the council," Evie whispered, her eyes still glued to the old woman.

All laughter seemed to pause for a moment, and everyone's eyes were drawn to the door on the far-left side of the room.

Mr. Huntley had finally made his appearance. He still wore the same suit he had on earlier. He actually looked completely under-dressed compared to everyone else, but Mr. Huntley did not seem to care.

"Elias!" one of the men exclaimed, drunkenly stumbling forward.

Mr. Huntley gave a polite smile, but it did not reach his eyes.

Evie leaned in closer to Mary. "How much longer do we have to stand here?" she asked softly.

"Not too much longer. We still need to make a couple more rounds around the room. After that, we can leave the wine on the table and go to the kitchen to start cleaning up."

Evie nodded, watching the guests make fools of themselves trying to get to Mr. Huntley.

Before they could move from their spots on the wall, Mrs. Huntley came barreling over to stand in front of Mary.

"We were supposed to have a piano player come here tonight! Where is he?"

"I haven't seen or heard from him, madam," Mary said, her brow creasing with confusion.

Mrs. Huntley stomped over to her husband, leaving Mary with a sour look on her face. Mrs. Huntley furiously whispered to her husband while Mary finally nudged Evie.

"Come on. A couple more rounds of drinks and we can start cleanup."

Evie nodded and grabbed the bottle of wine that sat on the small table beside her. Mary already had a large tray of appetizers in her hands when a loud voice startled them both.

"We already have a piano player here."

Evie looked up to see Mr. Huntley staring right at her from his side of the room. It was obvious his wife was seething with anger, but she tried to keep her face straight for the sake of appearances.

"Darling, I don't think it's proper to have her stop serving our guests. She's already occupied—"

Mr. Huntley wasn't listening. He slipped through the chatting guests over to where Mary and Evie stood. Evie began to shake when his dark eyes looked into her blue ones.

"You are trained on playing the piano, correct?"

Evie nodded and had to fight the urge to look to the floor in embarrassment. Mr. Huntley demanded eye contact earlier, so naturally she would do as told. Mrs. Huntley's wishes would have to be ignored when such a figure loomed over her, powerful and serious. And now both of these people stood in front of Evie. In any case, as the one who signed her contract, Mr. Huntley's orders took priority.

"Elias, it's fine. We will make do without it tonight," Mrs. Huntley told him in a hushed tone. She couldn't manage to hide the desperation in her voice. Mr. Huntley spoke in a natural volume. He did not seem to care if others heard him or not.

"No. You demanded a piano player. The one you hired did not show. Now, you will have to make do with the one in front of us."

Mrs. Huntley's face turned red in anger. "But—"

One glance from her husband stopped her from speaking further. His face finally showed a hint of aggravation. Even Evie was scared.

Mrs. Huntley bowed her head in defeat, and Mr. Huntley turned back to Evie. As fast as the anger had appeared, it was now gone. He gestured over to the piano in the corner of the room.

"Play for us."

Not a request. An order.

Evie slowly turned and placed the wine bottle back on the small table before walking carefully across the room. None of the guests paid her any mind. None of them had any idea what she was going to do and none of them seemed to care. Evie slowly sat on the elegant black bench and lifted the cover up to expose the pristinely kept keys. She felt the eyes of Mary, Mrs. Huntley, and her husband follow her every move. Evie had no doubt that Mrs. Huntley was hoping this performance would be a failure. It would give her a reason to finally send Evie back to the Distribution Center.

Evie closed her eyes and lifted her fingers over the keys.

She tried to imagine Mr. Hillard sitting next to her, smiling while she played. Her fingers glided smoothly over the keys as she played the last song she had ever performed for him. She had no need for sheet music as many songs were embedded into her memory. Mr. Hillard's piano wasn't nearly as expensive or as elegant as this one, but both Evie and Mr. Hillard knew the price behind the instrument didn't matter. It was always about the person playing it. She kept her eyes closed while she continued to focus on the music. In her mind, she played for her former friend. Evie wanted to dedicate her songs to him and not these disgusting people.

She performed several different songs. All of them she played with the memory of her dear friend in mind. Once she had finished the final note of her last song, she opened her eyes. Evie turned slightly to see everyone in the room was staring in amazement. Mary looked proud. Mrs. Huntley looked furious. Mr. Huntley looked intrigued.

Evie didn't know why, but the intensity in his eyes scared her.

She jumped when the guests began clapping, not expecting such a response. But they weren't turning and clapping for her. No, they were clapping for Mr. and Mrs. Huntley. Mrs. Huntley turned and immediately appeared to be a gracious hostess once more. Several men and women were congratulating them on having such a talented piano player on their staff.

Evie took the opportunity to slip off the bench and return to Mary. She suddenly felt very uncomfortable being in the room. Before both women could slip out of the room, a heavy pat on her shoulder made her freeze.

"Well done."

The touch physically disappeared within seconds, but the feeling of Mr. Huntley's hand stayed with Evie as she made her way to the kitchen with Mary.

As soon as both women entered the room, they took a breath of relief.

"I told you," Mary said, shaking her head. "I told you it would happen. You're a trophy now. It's not your talent. It belongs to them now."

Evie nodded, her face growing grim as that realization fell upon her. "I know. So, do we need to go back and serve people again?"

"I'll go back in. They should just want wine now. Stay and get a head start on the dishes."

Mary returned to the entertainment room while Evie began doing as she had been instructed. She was thankful Mary had told her to stay in the kitchen. She didn't want to be surrounded by any more of those people.

As soon as she finished washing the large pile of dirty pots and pans, Mary entered the kitchen with a tray of dirty glasses.

"They are all drunk as hell in there! Another hour or so and they should start leaving."

Evie took the tray from Mary and turned back to the sink. "Mary, how often did you say the Huntleys host parties here?"

"Almost every other weekend, hun. And they're Mrs. Huntleys parties, not Mr. Huntleys. Hell, most of the time he doesn't even make an appearance at them."

By the time the women finished cleaning the kitchen, they could hear the clatter of guests stumbling down the hall and opening the front door. They were finally leaving. When she and Mary entered the entertainment room, both women let out a loud groan. Empty wine bottles and glasses were scattered throughout the room. The women began cleaning when the sound of someone clearing their throat caught their attention. Mrs. Huntley had entered the room. Both women dropped their eyes to the floor and waited to hear her speak. Evie began to shake when she saw the expensive stiletto heels appear in front of her on the floor.

"Not a bad job tonight, little Dog."

Evie opened her mouth to thank her when pain coursed through her wrists, forcing her to drop to the floor. For several moments, she writhed in pain until Mrs. Huntley finally released the button on the remote. As Mrs. Huntley leaned over her, she began to shake.

"I showed my garden to the council tonight. I *never* want to see it look so empty again!" the woman hissed.

Evie slowly rose to her knees. Her voice was ragged when she attempted to speak, "I'm sorry, madam, but—"

There was another blast of pain and she fell back to the floor.

"I'm sorry? Are you trying to say something?" Mrs. Huntley did not hold back her sarcasm.

Evie frantically shook her head and the pain finally stopped.

"Good. On Monday, Mary will get more flowers. It better look good for the next party, or this remote will break from how hard I press this button!"

There was one final dose of pain before Mrs. Huntley left the room. As soon as she was gone, Mary lunged forward and wrapped her arms around Evie.

"Hun, I'm so sorry! I should have gotten more, but that's all the shop would let me take! I swear, I didn't think this would happen!"

Evie sat on her knees for several minutes and sobbed while Mary stroked her hair. "Why does it seem like I'm the only one doing something wrong?" Evie cried.

"I'm sorry, hun. I would probably get shocked too, but Mrs. Huntley doesn't have my remote. Only Mr. Huntley does. I don't know why, but I'm so sorry."

Evie took several deep breaths and stood. "Let's just hurry up and get this done." It was well after midnight when they finally finished cleaning the entertainment room. Evie's heart pounded the entire time. Paranoia of constantly being in pain had taken over.

Mary finally took a deep breath and looked up at the large clock on the wall.

"You know what today technically is?" she asked with a small smile.

Evie thought for a moment, then the corners of her lips turned up. It was Sunday, her one day off.

Mary laughed at her realization. "Go get to bed; I know you want to. Get some sleep, then go out and see your family."

She didn't have to tell her twice. Evie happily thanked her before rushing out of the room. The hope of seeing her loved ones made her forget about the pain she'd endured earlier in the night.

Once she reached the second set of stairs, a large figure came out of the hallway. Evie almost ran into him in her haste to get to bed.

"You are off on Sundays, yes?" Mr. Huntley asked.

Evie nodded and tried to avoid looking away from his eyes. The intensity that was in them earlier had remained.

"Good. You've done well tonight. Enjoy your day, but don't forget to read the book I gave you."

"Yes, sir. Thank you."

Evie carefully walked around him to go up the other set of stairs. She felt his gaze follow her until she was out of his sight. It made her quiver and feel anxious. Running into him had taken the excitement out of her. She practically sprinted into her room and threw her uniform off.

Evie climbed into bed and tried to forget about the look in his eyes. Instead, she forced herself to focus on seeing her brothers and sister in a few short hours.

Chapter 4

Evie managed to get some sleep, but she was awake and ready to leave just before the sun had risen for the day. Last weekend, she wasn't able to see them due to her being held by the system after the death of her former assignment. She had been forced to stay in the Distribution Center until she was assigned to the Huntleys. They wouldn't even let her tell her older brother what had happened.

But not today. Today, she would finally see them.

She crept down the stairs with her small bag over her shoulder. Mary came out of the bathroom, dressed in a plain blue nightgown. She was yawning, still not quite awake.

"What the hell are you doing up this early?" she exclaimed at the sight of Evie coming down the stairs.

"I want to spend every second I can with my family," Evie told her with a large smile.

Mary grinned back at her. "Have fun. I know it's a day off for you, but Mrs. Huntley wants the front door locked by ten tonight. Please be back before then."

Evie nodded and continued down the stairs to the front door. She opened the door and carefully shut it behind her, trying not to cause too much noise. As soon as the door was closed, Evie took a deep breath and ran. She knew exactly where to go. The Huntleys' house was a lot closer to the Laborers' Unit than her previously assigned house.

The streets of the Community Board Unit were lined with beautiful brick sidewalks and flowers. As soon as she exited the area, the surroundings quickly changed to a simple cement sidewalk and plain grass. In the distance, she could see the large factory of the Laborer's Unit.
The houses finally disappeared, and she was running on a large gravel road.

Evie finally reached the open gates of the Laborer's Unit. Large apartments surrounded the large factory inside. A factory that produced large machinery and other construction needs for the Community. Most of the laborers shared a small apartment with several others.

She made her way down the road of the unit and saw a familiar figure coming out of one of the buildings.

"Ryder!" Evie ran towards him. He barely had his arms out and ready for her when she tackled him into a hug.

Evie and Ryder shared the same blue eyes and soft brown hair. His smile was just as wide as hers when she wrapped her arms around him, but it wasn't easy for Evie. He was a head taller than her with muscles that clearly showed he had worked in hard labor for the majority of his life.

It was several moments before they broke apart, but both were still smiling.

"You didn't show up last weekend. Where were you?"

Evie's smile faded. "Mr. Hillard died. I was at the Distribution Center for a few days. I've been reassigned."

Ryder took a breath and gave Evie another small hug. Evie had always spoken to Ryder about how kind the man was. "I'm sorry, Evie. Come on. Let's go get BB and CC. We can talk later."

The walk to the Children's Unit wasn't much farther. The road they walked on was still one of gravel, and large fences surrounded the area. The large white vans of the Harmony Group would randomly drive up and down the roads in the area. They were known to make patrols throughout the Community as a whole, but their patrols around the several units were much more frequent. They were constantly searching for delinquents to send to Medical Waste.

When they reached the unit, several children were already outside. Many of them were heading to the rundown playground just around the corner. The school itself was as large as the Laborer Unit's factory and served for educational and housing purposes for minors in debt. Evie always shuttered at the sight of it. The building was made of dull gray bricks and a fading black rooftop. There was no sign of warmth in the area. Not even grass seemed to grow around it.

As Ryder and Evie approached the building, two children came outside. As soon as their eyes landed on Evie and Ryder, they ran right into Evie's open arms. The twins had the same brown hair of Evie and Ryder, but they shared the brown eyes of their father, the lover Emily had before Evie was turned in. Surprisingly, BB looked so much like Ryder while CC seemed to take after Evie. Both Evie and Ryder were thankful. The last person they wanted to think about when they looked at the twins was their mother or her lover. It was bad enough for them that their mother took no effort into giving the twins real names. Both Ryder and Evie knew the effort wasn't made due to their mother seeing them as nothing more than another check from the Community.

She remembered the day she saw them for the first time. Evie was forever thankful for being at the Distribution Center the day they were turned in. For twelve years, Evie wondered about her siblings. She had known her mother was pregnant with twins from one of her many lovers, but she was never told any news of them. Her mother refused to tell her any information about the babies except that she was pregnant with more than one child.

Evie was getting ready to leave the Distribution Center with her personal purchases when she saw her mother enter the building. She desperately wanted to run and scream at the woman. Scream, cry and perhaps even hit her a few times. The only thing stopping her were the two crying children that entered with her. Evie hid around the corner and watched as her twin brother and sister were traded for a paycheck. Silent, cold tears ran down Evie's face as the children were led away and her mother happily left, not bothering to look back.

The following Sunday, Evie and Ryder had camped outside of the Children's Unit and waited for them to come out so they could introduce themselves. Both children were immediately happy and embraced them. Evie wasn't sure if they truly believed they were all related or if the children just desperately wanted to know they weren't alone in the world.

In present day, Ryder and Evie walked hand in hand to the small playground and sat down at one of the benches.

"Evie, where were you last weekend?" CC asked, her large brown eyes fixated on her sister.

Evie gave her a small smile. "That nice man I was working for passed away. I had to stay at the Distribution Center until I got reassigned."

"Are they as good to you as the last guy was?" BB asked.

"They…they aren't bad. Not nice like Mr. Hillard was, but they are alright."

Both twins seemed pleased by the answer and Evie let out a breath. Ryder raised his brow at her, knowing she wasn't quite telling the truth. Evie gave him a look and quickly mouthed words to him, making sure BB and CC didn't notice.

"We will talk later."

Ryder nodded and turned his attention back to the twins.

The majority of the day was spent with BB and CC telling their older brother and sister about their lessons.

"They are making me learn the piano now," CC said to her big sister.

"How are you doing with it?" Evie asked.

CC raised her hands and Evie noticed the small bruises on her hands.

"I'm getting there."

Evie tried hard not to scream when she saw her little sister's hands. She remembered back to when she was a child and was forced to learn the same instrument. Women did not get a say in what they were educated in. Some girls learned the piano. Some learned the violin. So many girls would have their hands over the piano and would feel the slap of a leather strap when they played the wrong note.

The words of her piano instructor were permanently laced into her head.

"If you want to be useful, you better learn quickly. If no one wants you, you will be sent to Medical Waste! Is that what you want? No? Then try again!"

Evie pushed the thoughts away and quickly wiped the tears in her eyes away.

"Well, what about your other studies? Learning anything fun?" Evie felt awkward asking her. Learning to serve others was never a fun education. But hopefully there was one class they enjoyed.

"I'm learning how to press metal!" BB interjected. "It's actually pretty interesting to learn!"

Ryder and Evie went pale. They both knew instantly that BB would follow Ryder's path and become a laborer.

"Are you getting good at it?" Ryder asked, trying to smile.

BB nodded. "Yeah! Best in my class!"

Ryder quickly suggested they all take a walk and go get some lunch. Evie and Ryder always took turns on who added the meals onto their debt. They knew how precious money was, but they wanted BB and CC to have good memories with them while they were young.

They entered the marketplace and the smell of flowers was all around them. The streets were bustling and stores were brimming with business. They always went to the smaller food stalls for lunch rather than the fancy restaurants. Evie assumed they would be turned away before they could even step foot inside of them anyway. So many businesses discriminated against those in debt. The only reason they were allowed inside the shops was if they were shopping for their current contract owners. Evie only shopped at the Distribution Center so she didn't have to deal with their prejudice against her.

Ryder bought everyone grilled cheese sandwiches and French fries. They found a small table on the edge of the marketplace to eat and talk.

"Are the laborers working on anything new recently?" Evie asked between bites of her lunch.

Ryder swallowed his fries. "Actually, we are. Been building some ships. We're working on the metal work, and the Lumber Unit has been working on the planks for them. It's kind of weird. The work came out of nowhere."

Evie raised a brow as BB and CC continued happily eating their meals.

"As in fishing ships?"

Ryder shook his head. "Those things are WAY too big to be fishing ships."

"Where are they going to keep them?" CC asked.

"No idea. But rumor has it they're building docks around the waters of the Community Board Unit, but I've never seen them. Maybe they will station the ships there."

Evie couldn't help but wonder what they would need such large ships for.

Their days together always seemed to fly by. They took several walks around the small area and happily talked and smiled as if none of them were under their terrible circumstances. For a few short hours, they felt as if they were a normal family on a normal outing. When Ryder finally checked his watch, reality set back in.

"It's almost five. We need to get you both back."

BB and CC groaned and let Ryder and Evie take them back to their unit. Adults had a full twenty-four hours of free time, but children had to return before the sun set. Evie was sad for losing that time with them but was silently thankful to get some alone time with Ryder. Their time together was the only time they could speak like adults and not hold their feelings back.

Especially their feelings on the Community.

They all gave their final hugs to one another. Evie and Ryder waved as BB and CC sadly walked back inside their Housing Unit. The older siblings began to walk back in the direction of the Laborer's Unit.

"So…how are they really? Who are you assigned to now?" Ryder asked, his hands shoved into his pockets.

"The Huntleys. I never heard of them before, but Marcos said they are some upper-class members."

Ryder stopped walking and looked sharply at Evie. "Wait, Elias Huntley?"

Evie raised a brow. "Yeah…why?"

Ryder had a disgusted look on his face and slowly began walking again. "Lot of rumors about that guy. Lots of bad shit."

"Like what?"

Ryder took a breath. "That he's one of the guys that works at Medical Waste. Or he's the guy in charge of the Harvesters. I guess he's a huge kiss ass to the old bastards on the council."

Evie snorted. "There was a party at their house last night. It looked more like they were kissing *his* ass."

Ryder shrugged. "I don't know. And part of me doesn't want to know. But please just be careful in that house."

Evie nodded. "I will. I know as long as I do my job for them, I'll be fine."

There was silence for a moment before Ryder spoke again. "So that's the husband. What about his wife?"

Evie rolled her eyes. "She's a first-class bitch. I swear to god, Ryder. She looks so good, but everything about her is fake. Her hair, nails…all of it."

Ryder chuckled. "Are you surprised? All those upper-class women are like that."

"Well, at least I'm not alone in the house. There's another lady working there with me."

"Is she nice?"

"Yeah, she is. She turned herself in for her son. Kind of wish we had a mother like that."

The two walked in silence for a few minutes. Any words about their mother always left a sour taste in their mouths.

"Hey, so I wanted to ask you something," Ryder said out of nowhere. "If…if you ever thought there was a way we can get out of here, would you take it?"

Evie stopped walking and turned to give her brother an odd look. "What do you mean?"

Ryder looked around to confirm that they were alone. "I keep hearing some rumors about a group that helps people in debt escape. They take them to a place outside of the Community. A place where they can have lives for themselves."

Evie seemed stunned for several moments. "You can't be serious."

"I am! I know you don't get to hear these rumors, but you wouldn't believe what people are saying. It's the bonus of going to the Underground. You hear shit like this."

Evie signed. "Ryder, who the hell would risk helping us? And what's the price you would have to pay? Even if someone would help us, it could be trading one living hell for another. You want to risk taking BB and CC into that?"

Ryder began getting aggravated. "But what if it's true? Don't you want a life outside of this shit hole?"

"Not if it risks BB and CC's lives! And even if all that is true, what if we get caught? You want to see our little brother and sister thrown into the Harvester's vans and go to Medical Waste?"

They both stared at each other in aggravation. Evie took a breath, not wanting to fight with her brother.

"Ok, fine. Yes, if there was a way out safely with BB and CC, I would love that. Hell, I can't say I haven't dreamed of it."

Her words seemed to clear the air a bit.

Ryder gave her a small smile. "I know it may not be safe but…I just wanted to say we may have some hope. From the rumors, the place is called Eden. I don't know if it actually exists, but I can dream. I just want to have some fucking hope in this world." Evie nodded and gave her brother a hug. "I know. I do too." Ryder returned the hug while the sun began to set.

"What time do you need to be back?"

"I was told to be back by ten. That's when they lock the door."

Ryder stopped and gave Evie a smile after checking his watch.

"You have a couple of hours. Come with me tonight."

"To where?"

"The Underground."

Evie rolled her eyes. "Ryder, I hate that place."

Ryder grabbed her hand and teasingly began to drag her along. "Come on! It's not that bad. And Aaron will be there. He wants to see you."

Evie huffed and Ryder knew he had won. He began leading her past the Laborer's Unit and down several winding paths, ignoring the large white vans patrolling the area. They entered the most run-down part of the Community. The streetlights were dim, some poles with lightbulbs completely burnt out. The buildings were old and deserted. Several looked condemned. Evie remembered living in this general area with her mother when she was a child, but she couldn't remember which building was theirs. She was positive her mother had long moved out of this area to live in one of the upper-class neighborhoods.

They eventually reached the large metal door under the highway bridge. Two knocks on the door and they were granted entry.

The lights were dim and the music was loud. The makeshift bar across the large room was surrounded with people. People were dancing in the middle of the floor while others were standing against the walls, drinks in hand. Evie wondered how many of them were here for drug or cigarette trades. The Underground was the one place all those in debt would come to feel free for a few hours. There was no doubt that the higher-ups in the Community knew of this place, but none of them seemed to care. Evie suspected one of them was responsible for providing the drugs that came down to this place. Cigarettes were the most popular form of trading for anything they wanted in the Underground.

Evie closely followed Ryder over to the bar, scrunching her nose at the smell of cheap liquor and cigarettes. There were other private rooms that allowed the people to sneak off and either shoot up or smoke whatever drug they could get their hands on. How any of them were still able to work after that was a complete mystery. Anyone caught on drugs was immediately taken to Medical Waste.

Before they could reach the bar, a tall blonde figure practically jumped in front of Ryder.

"Hey, good lookin'," she said with a wink.

Kayla was a tall and pretty girl, but the light left her eyes years ago. Her dull blue eyes held large black bags under them and her blonde hair was thin and brittle.

Ryder took a step back and avoided her embrace. The girl smelled terrible.

"Jesus Christ, Kayla, how much have you smoked?"

As if on cue, the girl pulled out a cigarette and puffed at the stick happily.

"What? This is the only place I get to do this. Gotta get it in when I can." Kayla's dull eyes finally noticed Evie standing behind him.

"Hey, Kayla," Evie said, trying to be polite.

"Sup, bitch," Kayla replied, flicking her cigarette ashes onto the floor. "The fuck you doing here? I thought you hated this place."

"I'm here to say hi to Aaron."

Kayla smirked. "Is that all? Sure you aren't here for a hit? Randy has some good shit in the back. Or do you think you're still better than all of us?"

Evie glared at Kayla. From the moment Kayla had met Evie, she showed her dislike for her. Evie could easily remember all the times during their training that Kayla would try to steal her food and bully her in their spare time. Needless to say, both women hated each other.

Evie shot back, "I know I'm not better than everyone here. Just you."

Kayla took a step forward as if to hit Evie, but Ryder quickly stepped between them. "Kayla, fuck off. Last thing you need is a fight. You smell like a dump, and if the Harvesters catch you, your ass is taken to Medical Waste."

Kayla always had a soft spot for Ryder. Or maybe she was too drugged out to care. She gave one last glare to Evie. "One day, bitch, you're gonna be just like me. Selling your pussy for goods and looking for any way to escape this fucking hell." She flipped Evie off and stumbled through the crowd of dancers.

Evie and Ryder pitied the girl. Both of them made their way to the bar to the tall man standing against the wall, drink in hand.

"Aaron! Look who I got!" Ryder said, shoving Evie forward.

Aaron was tall with dark hair and eyes. The muscles on his chest and arms were much more pronounced than Ryder's. He has been Ryder's best friend ever since he was turned in. Both men always dreamed about one day opening a business together when they were out of debt.

Aaron's smile went wide and he scooped Evie into a hug, lifting her up into the air for a moment. They both laughed and smiled at each other as Evie's feet hit the ground.

"Evie! Where have you been?" he asked, grinning from ear to ear.

Evie returned the smile. "Getting reassigned. Working for some higher-ups now."

Aaron's smile faltered. "Did your former assignment pass away?"

"Yeah."

"I'm sorry."

Evie tried to shrug it off, but small tears threatened to spill from her eyes. "It was time. His suffering is over now."

Ryder, Aaron, and Evie spoke to each other as if they were all family that hadn't seen each other in years. That's how it always felt when they were separated. A week for them always felt like years.

"Hey, I'm heading to the bathroom for a second!" Ryder yelled over the music. He disappeared into the crowd, leaving Evie and Aaron alone.

"So…Ryder told me you guys are working on ships," Evie said, suddenly feeling awkward.

"Yeah, it's weird. And they're not fishing ships either. We just did a ton of those last year."

Evie nodded. "Yeah, that's what Ryder said."

There was an awkward silence between the two of them. After a moment, Aaron took a step closer to Evie.

"I really missed you Evie," he said, his eyes going soft.

She blushed and looked to the floor. "I've missed you too."

She felt him step close enough to her that she could feel the heat from his body.

"Evie, I've been wanting to ask you for a while… Can you please give us a chance?"

She sighed and looked up at him. "Aaron, I'm sorry but I can't. There's no future for us. You know that."

Aaron had long ago told Evie about his feelings for her. She couldn't deny that she had feelings for him as well. She remembered fondly of when they were children and the day Ryder introduced Aaron to her. Every time he would give her a flower he found growing behind the Children's Unit, she would blush. She kept them hidden under her bed until she was forced to throw them away.

But she couldn't see a future for them. Not while they were in debt. And Evie knew she would be in debt for the rest of her life.

Aaron frowned. "I told you I don't care about the debt bullshit! Yeah, we're in debt, but that doesn't mean we can't have some kind of fucking normality in our lives!"

"That's exactly what it means! I'm in debt! What's the point? You will be out long before I ever am! You're a great guy, Aaron. You can easily find someone you can have a future with."

Aaron opened his mouth to argue but stopped as soon as Ryder suddenly appeared next to them.

"You guys good?" he asked, looking between Evie and Aaron.

"Yeah. We're good, man," Aaron said, clearly aggravated.

Evie suddenly felt a rush of panic. "What time is it?"

Ryder checked his watch. "Nine fifteen."

Evie jumped in alarm. "Shit! I need to go!"

Ryder nodded. "I'll walk you."

Evie turned to say goodbye to Aaron, but he was stepping away from the wall.

"I'll walk with you. I'll take any time with you I can get. I'm done here anyway."

Evie couldn't hold back her look of surprise and felt a shimmer of happiness. Even though he was upset with her, he still wanted to spend time with her.

The three of them quickly made their way out of the Underground. The fresh air was a nice relief from the smell of smoke and alcohol. They continued conversing as they made their way to the Community Board Unit. It wasn't until a large white van pulled up next to them that they stopped talking. Their eyes grew wide at the sight of the large name stretched across the vehicle.

HARMONY GROUP

They stood tall as two men exited the van, sickening smiles on their faces.

"Identification cards," one said sternly.

All of them quickly pulled their cards out of their pockets and presented them. The second man snatched them and began scanning them with the small machine in his hand.

"Where are you three heading?"

"I'm walking my sister back to her assigned house," Ryder said with confidence.

The man nodded, then looked at Aaron.

"And you?"

"Walking with her as well. Then we are heading back to our unit."

The men smirked as they handed back their identification cards.

"Got any contraband?"

They all three shook their heads and the men chuckled.

"Time to prove it. Drop the bag and all of you raise your arms up."

Evie dropped her small bag and raised her arms up along with Ryder and Aaron. One man began patting them down while the second began rummaging through Evie's bag. Evie tensed as she felt the rough hands land on her. She gritted her teeth as he slowly ran his hands over her body. Out of the corner of her eye, she saw Aaron's face turn red in anger as the man's hands took their time running over Evie's breasts.

Evie closed her eyes as his hands began sliding up her legs. She couldn't stop herself from trembling as his hand made its way to the front of her pants.

"James, that's enough. They're clean."

The man grunted and finally took his hands off Evie. "Alright. You guys are clean. Make sure you stay that way."

Evie's bag was dropped onto the ground and the men made their way back into the van. They all scowled at the vehicle as it took off down the road.

"Fucking vultures. Looking for more people to send to Medical Waste," Aaron hissed.

Evie, Ryder and Aaron now had to hustle to get Evie back to the Huntleys' home before she was locked out for the night. All of them made it to the corner of the street with minutes to spare. She gave them one final hug before they had to separate for the night.

"I'll see you next weekend," Ryder said with a sad smile. Evie nodded and turned to Aaron, who gave her a tight hug.

"Will I see you next weekend too?" he asked with hope in his eyes.

"Only if you want to. And not in the Underground. I mean, I want to see you, but not in that place."

Aaron nodded. "Yeah, I don't really like it either. Ryder just said he would bring you there tonight."

Evie glared at Ryder while he gave her an innocent look.

"What? I couldn't think of anywhere else you guys could see each other!" Evie rolled her eyes at her brother and looked back to Aaron.

"Just meet us in the morning outside your place. You are always welcome to visit the twins with us."

Aaron gave her another smile and hug.

"I'll see you guys next weekend!" Evie said and hurried inside the house.

The front door was still unlocked and Evie carefully slipped inside. She was still unsure of when the Huntleys went to bed. She silently climbed the stairs. As she reached the third floor, Mary was heading down the stairs. Both women jumped in surprise and took several breaths.

"Jesus Evie!" Mary said, clutching her chest. "I'm not young anymore! You can't scare me like that!"

Evie tried to give her an apologetic smile. "Sorry. I didn't hear you coming."

Mary took a breath and nodded. "It's alright. Just go get some sleep. I'm gonna lock the door and head to bed myself."

Evie headed up to her room while Mary went to lock the door for the night.

Evie slipped off her shoes and climbed into bed. Before she could drift off to sleep, her eyes landed on the large black book she had on her table. She told herself she would begin reading it tomorrow and drifted off to sleep.

Chapter 5

Evie was able to get into a good schedule with Mary over the next couple of weeks. She easily became accustomed to Mrs. Huntley's weekend parties. In the evenings, she made a point to read a few chapters of the book Mr. Huntley ordered her to read.

It was taking her longer to read than she initially thought due to its long chapters. *The Disorder of Humanity* was the complete opposite of *Utopia*. It went into details of the mistakes and loss of humanity in the world and how those on top would trample over the weak. While *Utopia* was a fantasy, this book told the hard truth about the state of the world today.

One passage in the final chapter of the book really struck her:

"Greed, arrogance, and pride are the only true things that exist within people. And because of that, humanity will ultimately rot and turn to dust. Love is such a pretty picture, but what love is there outside what one has for themselves? There is none. Not so long as greed, arrogance, and pride exist in the world."

Evie agreed with the overall message of the book. The world was full of greed, arrogance, and pride. But she still believed in love. Not love in a romantic way. As much as she wished to have a romantic love, that wasn't possible, thanks to the Community. But she had love for Ryder, BB, and CC. And she would never admit it out loud, but she had love for Aaron as well. She would always have a place for him in her heart.

Evie was thankful she hadn't run into Mr. Huntley. The majority of his time was spent either in his study or out of the house. Mary made it clear to Evie that Mr. Huntley did not like to be disturbed unless it was absolutely necessary. She was able to finish his book and hoped to either ask Mary to leave it on his desk or maybe she could place it there while he was out of the house.

Over lunch one afternoon, Evie found herself curious about Mr. and Mrs. Huntley's marriage.

"Mary, why doesn't Mr. Huntley have any children? This house is big enough. And after all those years with those women, I'd think he'd have had some by now. Unless he doesn't want any," Evie asked, poking her food with her fork.

Mary shrugged while chewing on her sandwich. "I assume he doesn't want any," she admitted after swallowing. "He just never seemed like the kind of man that wanted kids. And do you *really* want to imagine what kind of a mother Mrs. Huntley would be?"

Evie shuddered. "Or how the kids would turn out." Both women laughed.

Evie was able to keep the garden under control and enjoyed being outside for large portions of the day. Her biggest aggravation was finding cigarette butts from Mrs. Huntley all over the garden. One morning, Evie was in the back garden pulling weeds. She heard the back door slam shut and Mrs. Huntley walked along the garden path. Evie immediately stood tall and lowered her eyes to the ground.

"Good morning, madam," she greeted politely.

Mrs. Huntley gave no response as she smoked her cigarette and flicked the ashes onto the stone walk path. Her eyes scanned over the flowers until her gaze landed on a small weed at the far end of the garden bed.

"How long does it take to pull weeds? Are you so weak that it takes you forever to finish my garden?" the woman snapped.

Evie took a breath and tried to control her anger. "I just started for the day, madam. I promise to get it done as fast as I can," she said through gritted teeth.

Mrs. Huntley puffed smoke into Evie's face. "See that you do." The woman dropped her cigarette butt onto the ground and went back inside the house.

Evie was later polishing the silver in the dining room when Mrs. Huntley entered.

"Where is Mary? I want my lunch early!"

Evie stopped polishing the spoon in her hands and dropped her eyes to the floor. "I believe she is in the kitchen, madam."

Mrs. Huntley huffed and swiftly knocked the large box of silver off the table. "Polish it again, little Dog!" With that, she stormed out of the room and disappeared into the kitchen.

About ten minutes later, Mary entered the dining room appearing tired and angry.

"That woman couldn't wait ten damn minutes for her lunch!"

Evie grinded her teeth as she continued polishing the silverware. "At least she didn't knock your stuff off the table!" she muttered.

Mary placed her hands on her hips and raised a brow. "You're not the only one who gets picked on, young lady. You know the kind of shit I've had to deal with over the years? How many meals I've had to remake or how many times I've had to re-clean something? I know it's frustrating, but you aren't the only one suffering here! The only leg up I have on you is that she doesn't have my remote. Mr. Huntley has it. I'm sorry you have to deal with that pain, but you aren't the only one dealing with her bullshit!"

Evie sighed and dropped the knife on the table, placing her face in her hands. "I know. I'm sorry. I'm just so sick of her!"

Mary sighed and gently patted her back. "It's ok, hun."

On another afternoon, Evie was polishing the piano in the entertainment room when Mrs. Huntley appeared. She was dressed in an elegant blue dress with a stylish purse. It was obvious she was leaving for the day. The woman glared down at Evie.

"I don't want to see a single fingerprint on this piano. Do you understand?"

Evie nodded, her eyes on the floor. Before Mrs. Huntley left the room, her hand slapped the piano and she dragged it across the surface, leaving a large smudge.

"Get to it, little Dog." She laughed and left, leaving Evie to polish the spot all over again.

Evie was surprised that she had yet to see Mr. Huntley again, but she was thankful. Mary informed her that at least twice a week, he would leave the house and not return until later in the evening. Today was no different. Mary was the one to wish him a good day as he left the house while Evie was outside in the garden.

Evie would consider herself lucky if she kept a good distance between herself and Mr. Huntley. She could have sworn she has seen him watch her from his study while she worked in the garden. As soon as Evie returned his book, she hoped to keep her distance and continue to work hard and keep herself assigned to the house.

The last thing she wanted was to be sent back to the Distribution Center.

Elias Huntley walked down the hall followed by his two informants. They knew to keep several steps back and let him lead the way. He had been down to this facility many times and would continue to do so for as long as he lived. Elias long ago learned patience, but lately, his patience was wearing thin. He wanted this business dealt with quickly, as he had better things to do.

"Has he said anything?" he asked the young men that struggled to keep up with him.

"No, sir. Nothing," one responded.

Elias refused to let his aggravation show. He had long ago taught himself to keep his emotions hidden away. He never wanted anyone to know what he was possibly feeling or thinking. That tactic often worked to his advantage.

He finally reached the large metal door and entered. There was no need to knock. The only light in the room was situated over the shaking young man tied to a metal chair. Sweat and tears ran down his face. As soon as his eyes landed on Elias, he began to struggle against his bonds. The boy struggled against the gag, desperately trying to beg for mercy.

Elias slowly approached the boy until he towered over him. The two men behind him closed the door and waited for further instructions. They knew better than to speak before he did.

"Where did you find him?" The entire time Elias spoke, his eyes never left the captive's crying face.

"We caught him near the Underground. We believe he was in there trying to get information on the Harmony Group's patrol patterns."

Elias removed his jacket and walked to the corner of the room where a small table and chair awaited him. Rather than sit, he gently placed his jacket on the back of the chair. He then turned to the table and grabbed a pair of black leather gloves. He slid them onto his hands while his eyes scanned the many tools on the small table.

His eyes settled on the scalpel.

Elias lifted the small knife off the table and admired the blade. He was amazed that such a small thing could be so sharp and precise. The whimpering of the boy in the chair brought him out of his thoughts. Elias turned and walked back over to the captive. More sweat and tears trailed down the boy's face, then a wet stain began to spread over his groin. The panic in the boy's eyes grew the moment his gaze landed on the scalpel.

Elias brought the knife up and cut the gag off the boy. He hadn't touched his skin. Not yet.

The captive was too terrified to speak, but he continued to cry and shake. Elias carefully rolled the scalpel between his fingers, his dark eyes fixated on the cowering figure before him. His words were clear and to the point.

"Tell me about Eden."

Mary instructed Evie to clean Mr. Huntley's study while she went shopping. Evie worked fast to try and finish the room so she could leave. She still felt uneasy any time she was in there, even if he was out of the house on business. Upon finishing dusting the bookshelves, she longed to grab *Utopia*. She wanted to relive those memories she had with Mr. Hillard.

But that wasn't his book. It was Mr. Huntley's book. It wasn't her place to simply take it without his permission, and she had no intention of seeking him out unless absolutely necessary.

Evie carefully placed his large black book on his desk with a small note, thanking him for allowing her to read it. She was hopeful that it would be enough that she left the note. Perhaps he wouldn't even be interested in talking about it.

Inspecting the room one final time, Evie turned to leave. Her heart pounded out of her chest as soon as she saw Mr. Huntley casually standing in the doorway. Evie hadn't even heard the door open. His face still had an eerily calm expression, but his eyes were uneasily intense.

She swallowed and forced herself to meet his gaze, still fighting the urge to look to the floor. "I just finished cleaning the room. My apologies if I was here too long. I'll go help Mary with dinner." Evie quickly picked up her cleaning supplies and turned to leave the room, but Mr. Huntley remained where he stood.

"Have you finished the book?"

Evie nodded and gestured to the desk. "I did. Thank you for letting me read it. I'm sorry it took me so long to finish."

Mr. Huntley smirked and walked over to his desk. Evie tried to take the opportunity to leave the room, but his voice stopped her. "What did you think?"

Evie turned back to see him gently lift the book off his desk, placing the note she left on top of his keyboard.

"I thought it was good, but if I had to choose, I enjoyed *Utopia* more. However, your book was more realistic."

He continued staring at *Disorder of Humanity* in his hands. "More realistic...how so?"

Evie took a breath. "It completely relates to the world we live in today. The author was right; humanity is a dead end. Greed, arrogance, and pride seem to be the only real things humanity relies on."

He was silent for several moments, but his eyes never left the book.

"When you are free, your skills will allow you to have a good paying job for yourself. Once your debt is paid, what will you do?"

Evie was taken aback. It was a question she had not been expecting. Mr. Huntley raised his gaze back to her face. "You're doing well here. If you continue to do so, I can easily recommend you for a job with the Community board. You will be paid well and can be free to do as you wish."

Evie looked to the ground, not wanting to meet his eyes. She began shaking. "I appreciate the offer, sir, but I must decline." There was a long pause.

"You decline? That's not an offer I give lightly."

Evie took another breath and met his eyes. He didn't seem angry, just curious.

"I'll be turning myself in as soon as my debt is paid. Yes, a good job will help me. But I need to free my younger brother and sister. Turning myself in again will free them much faster than just getting a job."

He raised a brow. "How so? If you have a job, you can be both free and pay for their freedom."

Evie couldn't read his face, and that frightened her.

"Freedom isn't free, sir. I would have to pay for housing, then food and utilities. That would mean little to no money for my little brother and sister. They mean more to me than any false sense of freedom."

There was a flash of emotion in his eyes, but it was gone before Evie could tell what it was. She began to have the sick feeling that she said the wrong thing. Maybe she should have thought of a lie. But the words had already been said. It was too late to take them back.

He stared at her for several moments, then nodded. "You are correct about that. But my offer to you still stands. If you continue to do well, I will help you attain a job upon the completion of your debt being paid."

Evie gave him a kind smile. "Thank you, sir."

She finally left the room and went to the kitchen. The sick feeling from before still followed her. She should have lied. She should have said something else. Evie forced the thoughts out of her head as she began helping Mary with dinner.

Elias sat at his desk, tracing his finger over the cover of the black book on his desk. The dinner Mary brought to his study sat untouched. *The Disorder of Humanity* had been with him ever since he was a teenager. He allowed very few people to touch his property, but on very rare occasions, he gave others the chance to read the words he believed in.

Not one of them would acknowledge the truth inside it. No one until Evie.

She was the only one who, besides himself and the one who had given him the book, acknowledged that it easily represented the world as it was. Cruel and decaying. All because of the selfishness of those living in it.

Elias took a breath and leaned back in his chair, closing his eyes and trying to clear his head. He had other things to deal with.

The boy had no good information. Nothing that would lead him to finding Eden. He would need to use other tactics. The council was not happy that several children in debt had gone missing. Something must be done to contain the news, as well. The Community could not afford to let the news spread of people in debt escaping.

Elias stood from his desk. He'd had enough for the day. Before he decided to make his way to his room, a sudden flash of brilliant blue eyes entered his mind and he suddenly felt the impossible pull to take care of a need.

He left his study and made his way to his wife's room. He knocked twice, then entered without waiting for a response. He didn't need a response. This was his house, after all. To him, knocking was respectful enough.

Sara's room was large with an elegant queen-sized bed and vanity table. There was a private bathroom and sitting area with a television for her own entertainment. He never liked the idea of sharing a bedroom with anyone, not even a spouse. It was peaceful to have his own space, and no one was allowed to enter it without permission. Not even Mary was allowed in to clean it; he took care of that himself. Elias made Sara's room comfortable enough to make her happy. It pleased his previous two wives as well.

Sara had been sitting on her couch watching television. Upon his entry, she turned her head to look at him. "Is something wrong Elias?"

He slowly walked over to the couch and removed his suit jacket, laying it on the back cushion. He walked over from behind the couch and gently stroked her shoulder. Then, his hand slowly slid down and stroked her breast. Sara knew what he wanted. She rose, turned off the television, and made her way to him.

They did not love each other. But Elias did not think that this was relevant in their marriage. He married her because her father was an assistant to the council. He provided Elias with many usable resources. In return, all he wanted was for his daughter to be provided for. It was easy enough. She was able to enjoy Elias's money and status, and he kept his word to provide for her.

No, there was no love. But that didn't mean they didn't enjoy fucking each other every once in a while.

Sara's hands slid over his chest and she began to unbutton his shirt. She was wearing only a small silk robe. Easy enough to remove. His hand grabbed the sash holding it together and pulled it away, letting the robe fall open. Sara was a beautiful woman, but to Elias, everything was artificial. She colored her hair, wore artificial nails, and used makeup to enhance her features. His other wives were just as artificial.

She leaned up to his face and kissed him. He returned the kiss but felt nothing. If a kiss pleased her, then so be it. Elias would return the small gesture despite the fact that she smelled of cigarette smoke. He found it disgusting. She went to remove his shirt completely, but he stopped her, taking her hand and leading her to the bed. He wasn't ashamed of his body. It would simply be annoying to explain every mark and scar on his back and arms. Elias had a need to be met. His clothing didn't need to be completely removed for it.

Sara slid onto the bed, her eyes heavy with lust. He followed, climbing on top of her, and quickly adjusted himself and unbuckled his belt. He allowed Sara to do the rest and completely release him from his pants. His hand slid up between her legs and began stroking her. She moaned and arched her hips. He wasn't selfish when it came to sex. He would give Sara the same release he wanted. Just before she could climax, he took his place completely on top of her and thrust himself inside of her.

She moaned and he allowed her arms to wrap around him. Elias closed his eyes and worked to fulfill his need. He was not gentle; that wasn't his way. But he wasn't striving to hurt her, either. Sara was enjoying it as much as he was.

Elias opened his eyes for a moment and was surprised. Sara's artificial blonde hair was suddenly a natural rich brown color. He stopped thrusting long enough to lift himself up and look into her face. Brown eyes were replaced with blue ones and no makeup was on her face. It was a natural beauty to him. Nothing artificial.

Looking into those blue eyes, his thrusting increased. An unfamiliar feeling began rising in his chest. Normally, he would want to hurry and finish satisfying himself. Now, he had a longing to make this last. A rush of heat made Elias suddenly sit up and completely remove his shirt. He wanted to feel her skin against his. Lowering himself back onto her, the woman's blue eyes seemed to widen in surprise and excitement. Her arms wrapped back around him as he continued pumping wildly into her.

Elias felt her arms tighten around him as his movements increased. Normally, this did not excite him. This time, he enjoyed the feeling of the woman holding onto him tightly while she gasped and moaned beneath him. He was losing himself completely in his desire to satisfy her. His hands grabbed her legs and forced them to wrap completely around his waist.

The young woman moaned in pleasure and Elias couldn't suppress a moan as well. He balanced himself on his elbow while his other hand wrapped around her throat.

"Tell me you're mine," he commanded, his movements growing faster.

She was panting and shaking beneath him. "I'm yours," she moaned.
His grip grew tighter, not cutting off her air but asserting complete dominance over her.

"Say it again!"

"I'm yours!"

His lips found hers and he gave her a dominating kiss. Kissing during sex was not normal for him, but he had the sudden urge to do so. She was whimpering and getting ready to climax.

"Elias, please!" the young woman cried out.

He closed his eyes and his climax hit him hard. Her voice saying his name pushed him over the edge. He thrust as long as he could, trying to make it last. When the feeling was over, he collapsed on top of her, trying to catch his breath. It usually didn't take him this long to recover. He raised his head to look into her blue eyes again, but they were gone. Instead, he was looking into the brown eyes of his wife. The fantasy was over.

He raised himself off of her and stood to adjust his clothing.

"Who is she?" Sara demanded from the bed.

He lifted his head to see his wife sitting up, glaring at him. "What are you talking about?" Elias asked, buckling his belt.

Her eyes narrowed and she gritted her teeth. "Evie... You said her name! You said her name while you fucked me!"

Elias was actually surprised. He wasn't aware he had said anything.

She pulled her blanket up to her chest and seethed in rage. "I thought you were a man of honor! You said I was the only woman you would ever be with!" He simply stared at her, his face expressionless again.

Sara breathed heavily, looking down at her hands that were gripping the blanket. "Are you going to replace me? You said I would be the last! You said you didn't want to marry again! You promised my father you would take care of me!"

Elias had heard enough. He picked up his shirt from the floor and quickly put it back on, carefully as to not expose his back and arms to her. "You have nothing to worry about. I apologize for disrespecting you," he said while grabbing his jacket.

He began walking to the door, but Sara jumped in front of him.

"Just tell me who she is! Is she on the committee? The wife of a council member? Who is it?" Sara breathed heavily and Elias simply stared down at her.

He wasn't surprised that she didn't know who Evie was. She never cared to remember the names of anyone in debt. Not even those who worked in his household. She probably only remembered Mary's name due to how long Mary had been in the house.

"You don't need to worry about that. As long as you don't do anything foolish, you will always be provided for."

Elias stepped around Sara and left her room, ignoring her screams of frustration as he disappeared to his own room.

The following morning, Evie wiped the sweat off her face as she finished mowing the front lawn.

The flower beds were her next project, as many weeds had begun to grow from the soil. She began pulling the weeds when a large black car pulled up in front of the house. A few moments later, Mr. Huntley exited his house and smiled down at Evie. In his hand was a small luggage bag.

She gave him a small smile in return, not wanting to be rude.

"Good morning, sir."

"Good morning. The flowers look lovely. Mary already knows, but I'll be back in a couple of days."

Evie nodded. "Have a good trip, sir."

His eyes lingered on her longer than necessary before turning and making his way to the black car.

Evie couldn't stop herself from watching the vehicle roll down the road. Curiosity about his role in the Community began to enter her mind. She only witnessed Mr. Huntley show up to one of his wife's parties, and she felt the respect he commanded with only his presence.

She pushed the thoughts away as she finished attending to the flowers, ready to go inside and have lunch.

Sara paced her room, smoking cigarette after cigarette. Shortly after their engagement, Elias had told her that he had no interest in other women. That he would have honor and loyalty towards her so long as she performed her duties as a wife. Sara never had a problem having sex with him at his demand; sex with him was always satisfying. He always strived for her to enjoy it as much as he did. But now she thought of him as a man just as terrible as the others in the Community. So many high-standing members of the Community had affairs and traded wives around. Elias promised her that he wasn't like that. He told her that she was the last woman he planned to marry.

"Lying bastard. Best sex we've ever had and he was thinking of another woman!" she thought bitterly.

Now her position was in danger. He could easily break his promise and replace her. She couldn't allow for that to happen. Sara couldn't deal with the shame of being his third rejected wife. Rumors were spread that his other two wives were foolish and annoyed him to no end. She deliberately kept her distance from him to ensure he would have no reason to separate from her.

From outside her bedroom window, Sara heard the sound of a car door open and close. She made it to the window in time to see the large black car begin driving down the road. He was gone.

Perfect.

Sara carefully made her way down the hall. She could hear Mary and the Dog speaking in the kitchen. They were likely eating lunch.

She crept down the hall to her husband's study. He kept everything of importance in that room. If she found nothing, she would go to his bedroom next. She was sure she could find some kind of information that could lead her to finding his mistress. If whoever it was ended up being a high-status woman in the Community, perhaps her father could help her. Maybe he could make the woman disappear. If she was of lower status, then she could deal with it herself. The smallest of accusations could lead any low-standing person to Medical Waste.

Elias always kept his study unlocked so it could be cleaned by Mary whenever he was gone. Everyone in the house knew not to go poking into his business, anyway. Sara would not be afraid to touch his things today. She would look, then carefully put everything back to the way it was.

The desk was the best place to check first. Elias had neat piles of papers and files all over the place. Sara knew she wouldn't be able to get into his computer, as it would probably be password protected, and he would know if someone tried to log on.

She carefully looked at several different papers but found nothing. The information on them meant nothing to her. She saw none with the name of Evie on any of them. Next, she carefully opened his desk drawer. Several files were neatly placed inside.

Her fingers carefully flipped through the files, trying to find something. *Anything.* Towards the back of the drawer, the woman's name finally flashed in front of her eyes. Snatching the file out of the drawer, she glared at the cover.

On the top tab, it read:

NUMBER-SIX-SEVEN-SEVEN-FIVE
BIRTH NAME: EVIE HARMOND

The number sounded familiar. She opened the file and her eyes bulged at the small picture inside.

The Dog. It was the Dog.

No, she never bothered to ask about the girl's real name. It didn't matter to her. But now the insult ran deeper. Her husband was thinking of the lowest of the low while having sex with her, a woman of high status. Not only that, but she could be replaced by a woman in debt to the Community. She forced her trembling hand to place the file back in the drawer and closed it shut. As angry as she was, she didn't want to feel Elias's wrath of someone touching his things.

Sara stormed out of the study and went into her room. The remote to the Dog's bracelets were sitting on the small bedside table. She quickly grabbed it and stormed out of the room. As soon as she reached the staircase, she jabbed her finger on the button. Within seconds, she heard the cries of pain coming from the kitchen.

It was time to put the Dog down.

Evie and Mary had finished their lunch. Evie washed the dishes as Mary grabbed the cleaning supplies out of a small cupboard in the kitchen.

"I really hate cleaning that damn oven, but it's long overdue to be done," Mary grumbled.

Evie gave her a small smile. "I can always do it; I don't mind. I'll do the oven and you can clean the bathroom."

Mary looked like she wanted to protest, but after a moment, she nodded.

"Yeah, it's probably better if you do it. It's way too hard for me to get on my knees and scrub that thing."

Evie finished the dishes and grabbed the cleaning supplies, ready to start on the oven. She took a step towards the oven when searing pain began to shoot through her wrists and arms. The cleaning supplies spilled all over the floor and Evie cried and writhed in pain on the floor. Mary gasped and tried to help Evie sit up.

"What's wrong? Evie, talk to me!"

Evie heard the kitchen door slam open and another burst of pain set in. This time, it came from the swift kick she received to her stomach.

"You think you can replace me? You fucking little whore!"

Mrs. Huntley's finger pressed the button on the remote again and Evie screamed. It was made worse when Mrs. Huntley gave her another kick. This time, to her chest.

"Mrs. Huntley, stop!" Mary all but screamed.

The pain in her wrists finally stopped, allowing Evie to suck in a breath of air. Her stomach and chest burned and her face was red and wet from tears.

She could faintly hear Mrs. Huntley yelling at Mary.

"You! Stay out of this! Don't you say a fucking word of this to anyone! Not to the Community or my husband!"

Mrs. Huntley turned back to look at Evie who was curled into a ball on the floor, moaning and crying in pain.

"Get up to your room and stay there! I don't care what it takes! You are leaving this house! Do not come out of that fucking room until you are leaving this house permanently!"

Evie moaned in pain as she slowly stood and limped over to the kitchen door. Tears flowed down her face as she forced herself to her room. Mrs. Huntley was behind her the entire way, screaming at her. About halfway up the first set of stairs, she screamed in pain as Mrs. Huntley pressed the button on her remote. Her chest burned for air and her stomach felt raw when she crawled up the stairs.

Mrs. Huntley continued to scream several obscenities Evie had never considered herself to be.

Whore. Degenerate. Homewrecker.

The profanity and insults stopped when Evie reached the stairs to her room. Mrs. Huntley slammed the door closed as soon as Evie entered the stairwell. Her body gave out as she reached the bed and she cried in pain, wondering what she did wrong.

Chapter 6

Evie had no idea how much time had passed. After a while, she suffered from hunger pains along with a large bruise on her stomach from Mrs. Huntley's kick. At random times, Evie felt the searing pain in her wrists from Mrs. Huntley pressing the button to the remote. Evie no longer could hear her own screams. Her throat was too sore and raw to make any noise above a whimper.

For the first time since Evie came here, she was relieved that the attic grew cold at night. Sleeping on the cold bed gave the pain in her stomach some relief. When the cold made it impossible to sleep, she forced herself to dress in layers.

Evie thought she was dreaming when she felt a violent shake on her arm.

"Evie!" came a harsh whisper.

She forced her eyes open to see the concerned face of Mary.

"You need to hang in there," Mary whispered as she passed Evie a water bottle.

She snatched the bottle and tore the lid off. The rush of cool water in her aching throat felt like heaven. She moaned in relief as Mary's hand rubbed comforting circles on her back.

"I got you a few more too. And a sandwich." Mary placed the small paper bag on the floor next to her bed. "I'll get you something else as soon as I can. Mrs. Huntley keeps randomly pacing the halls. I think she's trying to catch you if you try and sneak out of here."

Evie felt tears fall down her face. "What did I do, Mary? She called me a whore! What did I do wrong?"

Mary shook her head. "You didn't do anything. I don't know what's wrong with her. The woman has lost her damn mind."

Evie groaned and glanced out the window. "What day is it?"

"It's Saturday morning. Hun, you just have one more day to make it. You can do it."

Evie gave Mary a confused look. "Is the Community taking me back tomorrow?"

Mary shook her head and gave her a small smile. "No. Tomorrow is Sunday." Evie raised a brow, and Mary's smile grew larger. "Your day off, hun. You have twenty-four hours for yourself. She can't keep you up here."

Evie took a breath of relief and sunk her head back into her pillow.

Mary kept rubbing her back and talking quietly. "I have to go. Leave early tomorrow morning. Get to the Distribution Center and get some food and water to keep up here. I know you have to pay for it, but you have to make sure you're okay up here for a bit. I have no idea when that bitch will calm down."

Evie nodded in understanding. "Does Mr. Huntley know? Is he letting her do this?"

"He isn't back yet. I don't think he would have ever let her do something like this. As soon as he gets back, I'll tell him."

Evie snorted. "I doubt he would care. I just want to be out of this house, Mary. I don't want to be here anymore."

Small tears continued to fall down Evie's face as Mary continued rubbing her back, trying to comfort her.

"I don't blame you. Not at all. You can go to the Distribution Center and request a transfer, but that's a bigger fine on you. Just get yourself some food and water. You can sneak downstairs at night to go to the bathroom. As soon as he comes back, I'll tell Mr. Huntley. He will end this."

Mary gave Evie a final pat on the shoulder before quickly leaving the room. Evie had no hope that Mr. Huntley would help her.

"There's no way in hell a high-standing member of the Community is going to give a damn about how I'm being treated."

She ended up eating half of the sandwich Mary brought her shortly after she left and saved the other half for nightfall. The only hope she had was knowing that she could leave the room in the morning.

Time began to drag on her again. Throughout the day, the pain in her wrists would randomly torment her. Mrs. Huntley must have been pushing the button whenever she felt like it.

After what felt like an eternity, Evie opened her eyes to see the morning sun peeking in through her small window.

It was Sunday.

Evie forced herself up and chugged the last bottle of water Mary gave her. She pulled on her regular clothes and grabbed her bag, making sure her charge card was inside. Once she felt ready, she slowly climbed down the stairs and out of the room.

As soon as she stepped out of her room and into the main house, she felt relief wash over her. The air seemed to clear and she could truly breathe again. Evie forced her feet to move down the stairs and towards the front door. Before her feet could leave the final step, she was suddenly staring into a pair of glaring brown eyes.

"Didn't I tell you to stay up in your room? What the hell do you think you're doing?"

Evie took a breath and raised her head, daring to look into Mrs. Huntley's eyes.

"It's Sunday, madam. I'm going to visit my family."

Evie could see the hatred in the woman's eyes. Mrs. Huntley reeked of cigarette smoke and whiskey. The woman had no choice. She stepped aside, but not before giving a final glare at the pale young woman. "You come back and go straight up to the attic! I never want to see your face again!"

Evie left the house, feeling the glare of Mrs. Huntley from behind her as she did. Once she had taken a step outside, there was another blast of pain in her wrists. With a small cry, she hurried away from the door. The remote only went so far. As soon as she was far enough from the house, the jolts stopped.

Normally, she would be running to go see her brother. But Evie's legs felt heavy, and she had to force herself to keep moving. It took her much longer than normal to reach the Laborer's Unit.

As Evie rounded the corner, she could see Ryder impatiently pacing in front of the gate. Seeing him seemed to give her some strength. She quickly made her way towards him, crying out his name.

Ryder turned and had an instant look of concern. He ran towards her and caught her in his arms. Evie sobbed into his chest as he held her close to him.

Mary frantically worked on the dishes, desperate to keep herself busy. Evie had been shut up in her room while Mrs. Huntley was attempting to drink herself to death. Mary gave Mrs. Huntley meals, but the woman didn't touch them. All she did was mutter under her breath and yell at Mary to keep her mouth shut. However, Mary witnessed no attempt of Mrs. Huntley calling the Distribution Center to have Evie sent back or even send her to Medical Waste.

After a couple of hours, Mary heard the front door open and heavy footsteps made their way through the house. Mr. Huntley had returned.

Relieved, Mary took a breath. But now a new anxiety filled her. Throughout the years, Mr. Huntley had always treated Mary with respect and was always gracious for her hard work, but she still knew her place in his home and in the Community. She had to be careful on how she addressed this situation.

Mrs. Huntley had passed out in her room a couple of hours ago, finally exhausting herself with her constant drinking and paranoia.

Mary's hands shook as she poured coffee into the large cup. She placed a small plate of shortbread cookies next to the cup on the small tray. Mary knew Mr. Huntley enough to know he would be in his study. Her legs felt heavy as she went up the stairs, carefully balancing the tray in her hands.

When she finally reached the door to his study, she took a deep breath and prayed he was in a good mood. Although, he probably wouldn't be after this. She gave a gentle knock and heard his approval for entry. Mary entered with the small tray to see Mr. Huntley sitting at his desk, papers scattered all over the place.

"Welcome back, Mr. Huntley."

"Thank you, Mary," he said politely, not looking up from the report in his hand.

Mary tried to steady her hands as she gently placed the tray on the corner of his desk.

"There's something you wish to discuss with me."

It wasn't a question. It was a fact. Mary couldn't help but smirk. "You see right through me, sir." Mary took a breath and stood tall. His eyes didn't leave the paper, but she knew he was listening. She was amazed at how well he could multitask in such a way. "Sir, I'm very sorry, but I need to speak to you about Mrs. Huntley. She has been very…unlike herself since you've left."

His expression didn't change. "I'm afraid she was upset with me before I left. I apologize for you suffering the consequences of that." Mary began to shake again.

"Sir, it wasn't me who suffered the consequences. It was Ev-Dog. It was Dog who suffered."

He raised a brow, still not looking up from his paper. "Dog? We do not have a dog, Mary."

"That's what your wife demanded we call the young woman who was assigned to this house, sir."

Mary felt her heart pound heavily in her chest. His face hardened, but he still didn't look up to face her. "Her name is Evie. Never address her as such again."

Mary took in a heavy breath.

"I understand, sir. I'm sorry. But your wife has taken her anger out on her. Evie could be in danger if this keeps up."

Mr. Huntley's entire face seemed freeze for several moments. Then, he sat straight up in his seat and slowly turned to face Mary. Anxiety filled her chest, and her legs began to shake. There were only exceedingly rare occasions when she witnessed Mr. Huntley overcome with anger. The man was an expert at keeping his feelings hidden. Not this time.

Mr. Huntley was infuriated, and Mary knew it.

"What has she done?"

Ryder forced Evie to go to the marketplace before going to see BB and CC. He watched as Evie charged several bottles of water and some snacks to her card, a furious expression on his face. On the way to the Children's Unit, Evie finished a large bottle of water and devoured a bag of potato chips.

Ryder was enraged and didn't hide it.

"You need to go to the Distribution Center and file a report. They aren't allowed to do this shit. They will be fined, and you will be reassigned with no penalty."

Evie snorted. "They won't do anything about it and you know it. It's not abuse to them. She just gave me the order to stay in my room. And there's no way to prove she hit me by the time they do their *investigation*." Evie's hands made a sarcastic gesture at the word 'investigation.'

Ryder wanted to protest, but they had reached the Children's Unit. BB and CC were running at them, arms waving around while they expressed how angry they were at how late their older siblings had been. Evie was able to keep a brave face as they apologized for their tardiness. Ryder and Evie walked them to a picnic table to sit and talk.

"Aaron's not coming?" Evie asked Ryder.

"He worked late last night. We all did. Had an emergency to deal with. He said he'd catch you later. It was a rough night for everyone."

Evie nodded in understanding. She couldn't begin to imagine the long hours and hard labor they had to endure.

"Evie, are you ok?" CC asked, looking concerned.

Evie could only imagine how terrible she must have looked. She forced a smile on her face. "Yeah, I'm ok. I've had a rough couple of days, but I'm feeling a lot better now." Ryder rolled his eyes, and Evie cast him a glare.

After several hours, it was finally time to say goodbye. BB and CC ran back into their housing while Ryder began leading Evie back to the marketplace. The water and snacks from the morning had long been consumed. Now, Evie needed to make sure she would have enough food and water to make it through the next week. She was sure that Mrs. Huntley was still intent on keeping her in the attic until she could be re-assigned.

After her shopping, the sun began to set for the day.

Evie took a breath. "I need to get back. I don't want to push my luck and have that bitch lock me out of the house."

Ryder had a hard expression, but he understood. "Please promise me that if nothing changes, you'll go to the Distribution Center. File the complaint. Hell, request a transfer! Anything to get out of there."

"I can't do it, Ryder. It's a huge fine on me if I do. I can get through this. I promise, I'll be fine."

Ryder rolled his eyes. "You really need to learn how to do something for yourself every once in a while."

They began making their way to Mr. Huntley's house, carrying Evie's purchases. Before they reached the roads that led to the Community Board Unit, heavy footsteps could be heard from behind them.

"Evie! Ryder!"

Both turned and saw a flushed looking Aaron. He stopped running and began panting, trying to catch his breath. Evie felt a large smile spread over her face at the sight of him, even if he was sweating and lightly swearing.

"I've been looking for you guys all over the place!"

"Sorry man. I thought you would be too tired to do anything today."

Aaron glared at Ryder before giving a soft smile to Evie. "I will take any chance I get to spend time with you."

Evie's face turned red and Ryder smirked at his sister.

"Hey, why don't you walk her home?" Ryder suddenly said.

Evie's head snapped to her brother's face and she saw a devious smile there. Aaron straightened and grinned at Evie.

"I would love to."

Before Evie could say anything, Ryder placed the bags he was holding onto the ground and gave his sister a quick hug. "You'll thank me for this later," he whispered in her ear.

Evie didn't even get the chance to glare at her brother. He quickly clapped Aaron on his shoulder before running off down the road. There was an awkward silence between the two of them before his eyes landed on the bags on the ground and in her hands.

"What are the bags for?"

Evie bit her bottom lip, trying to think of an excuse. She didn't want Aaron to know what had happened to her. "Mrs. Huntley has been acting like a bitch. She's been threatening to keep me in my room and all that. Just getting some snacks in case she actually does it."

Aaron raised a brow but swiftly grabbed the bags that were on the ground. They began making their way through the unit.

"Have a good time with your brothers and sister?" Aaron asked awkwardly.

"Yeah. It would have been better if you were with us."

The words left her mouth before she could stop them. Out of the corner of her eye, she saw Aaron's head snap around to look at her. She tried to keep a steady pace, ignoring his burning gaze. Her face was flushed with embarrassment.

"Well...I would love to see you again next Sunday."

Evie cleared her throat. "I would like that."

She had no idea why such words were coming out of her. For so long she had pushed her feelings aside. Now she couldn't stop herself from speaking such affectionate words.

There was silence between the two of them as they approached the Huntley household. As soon as she stood in front of the large gate to the house, she dropped her bags to give Aaron a goodbye hug. Aaron was faster than her. Her bags were already dropped to the ground and he swiftly pulled her into an embrace before her bags even touched the ground. Her head laid against his chest, his heart beating loudly in her ear. Her arms moved on their own, wrapping around his waist. She closed her eyes and leaned against him, enjoying the warmth from his body. Evie desperately wanted time to stand still. She found herself longing to stay in the safety of his arms.

His head shifted, and she lifted her head to look up at him. His eyes were already looking down at her. His breath warmed her face and she found herself looking at his lips. Lips she desperately wanted to kiss.

"Do it. Do something for yourself for once. Take a step towards your own happiness."

The unknown voice whispered such pretty words. Words she wanted to listen to. Before she could raise herself up onto her toes to reach him, a jolt went through her and she saw the faces of her siblings in her mind. Evie gently raised her hands to his chest and stepped away from him. In the end, she couldn't do it.

"I-I have to go," she stuttered.

He sighed, clearly disappointed. "Yeah, me too."

She grabbed her bags and gave him a small smile. "I'll see you next Sunday, right?"

"Yeah, I'll see you then."

Before anything else could be said, he quickly took off down the road. Closing her eyes, she tried to forget the look of sadness that fell on his face before he left. Ignoring the tears in her eyes, she made her way into the house.

Evie heard nothing when she walked in the front door. She was tense, anticipating Mrs. Huntley jumping out of a corner to scream and order her to go back to her room. Even Mary couldn't be heard from the kitchen.

As she walked through the house, she tried to brace herself for the pain the bracelets would inflict on her.

Her legs were tired as she went up the stairs and to her room. The bags in her hands were heavy, and she prayed they would last her until next Sunday. Finally, she forced herself up the final set of stairs to her room. The light was on. Evie figured she accidentally left it on in her tired stupor from this morning.

Once she entered her room, she dropped her bags on the floor. Yawning, she felt ready to simply fall onto the bed and try to sleep.

Evie looked up and felt a jolt of panic in her chest. Goosebumps ran down her arms and her mouth went dry.

Mr. Huntley was sitting on her bed, staring right at her. How long he had been waiting was unknown, but he was clearly patiently waiting for her to return. Seeing him in this room was bizarre, to say the least. His large frame seemed too small for it.

Evie stood tall in respect and tried to remain calm. Perhaps he was going to inform her of when she was being returned to the Distribution Center. But why he would need to be in her room to tell her that was beyond her.

"Good evening, sir," she said politely.

He held his gaze on her for several moments before he spoke. "I apologize for the suffering you endured while I was away. There is no excuse for it. My wife has gone too far."

Evie wasn't sure what to say. She simply nodded. His gaze never left her face, and she began feeling uncomfortable.

"I must ask you to stay up here a little while longer. Mary will bring you meals. I need to take care of these issues with my wife before you are free to roam the house again. I hope you understand. She also no longer has the remote to your bracelets."

Evie nodded again and felt instant relief. "Thank you, sir."

His eyes flickered to the bags on the floor, then back to her face. "I'll make sure you are compensated for your purchases. You never should have felt the need to buy them."

He finally stood and the room felt even smaller. Evie took a large step back to allow him to pass. Mr. Huntley slowly made his way to the door but stopped to stand in front of her.

"I hope you can forgive me, Evie."

She gave him a small smile. "I don't blame you at all, sir. Thank you for helping me." He began to step away towards the stairs to leave, but Evie's voice stopped him.

"Sir… Did I do something wrong?"

The question had burned inside her from the moment she was forced to stay in the room while writhing in pain. His eyes seemed to soften at her question.

"Not at all. The fault is mine. Please don't think about it anymore."

Evie took a sharp breath and dared herself to ask her next question. "Sir, why did she do this to me?"

There was a hard silence between them. Evie had no idea what Mr. Huntley was thinking. His eyes didn't move away from hers.

"I'm afraid she was upset with me before I left. She took her anger out on you. It never should have happened."

Evie closed her eyes and began shaking again. "Mr. Huntley...your wife accused me of trying to replace her. She called me a whore and a homewrecker."

Her eyes opened and she had to fight the urge to step away from him. It dawned on Evie just how close he was to her. The intensity of his gaze was beginning to scare her. Her heart pounded in her chest and she forced herself to maintain eye contact with him. His expression was soft, but his eyes didn't glance away from her face for even a moment.

"You don't need to worry about such things, Evie. Get some rest. I promise you this won't happen again."

He left down the stairs before Evie could try and ask him more questions. As soon as she heard the door close, she let out a breath she didn't realize she was holding. She dropped to the floor and almost cried in relief. It was over. Or rather, it would be soon. Evie wouldn't have to report anything to the Distribution Center. She grabbed her bags and placed them next to her bed. A knock at the door made her jump and a few moments later, Mary came up the stairs with a large tray of food and a smile on her face.

Evie returned the gesture as Mary set the tray down on the bed.

"You told him, didn't you?" Evie asked.

Mary huffed. "Of course I did. You think I would let that crazy bitch keep you up here? Mr. Huntley won't tolerate her bullshit. If something happens to you, his status takes a huge hit. One nice thing about being Community property."

Evie was silent for a few moments as Mary lifted the lid off the large dinner plate. The wonderful smell of roasted chicken, potatoes and vegetables filled the room.

"Mary...he said he had to take care of issues with his wife. What will he do?"

Mary shrugged. "I have no idea. This hasn't happened before. She's still passed out in her room. He hasn't even seen her yet."

"He said she doesn't have my remote anymore. If he hasn't seen her yet, then—"

"I snatched it when she was asleep," Mary said with a large grin. "No way in hell was I going to let her keep it with Mr. Huntley finally back home. He's holding onto it now."

Evie couldn't stop herself from giving Mary a tight hug. "Thank you."

Mary happily returned the hug. When they finally stepped away from each other, both women were smiling.

"Eat, then go take a shower. Hopefully, you can come back to work tomorrow."

Mary left the room and Evie devoured the plate of hot food. Her cooking was always delicious, but it seemed as though she took more effort to make this meal good for Evie.

Evie fell asleep that night with hope for better days ahead.

Chapter 7

Elias patiently waited in his study for his wife to finally wake up for the day. Mary had the simple instructions to tell his wife to join him once she had her breakfast. He guessed the woman was probably sleeping off the last of the liquor she had drank the previous night.

Finally, at eleven in the morning, he heard the light sound of knocking.

"Enter."

She walked inside, her eyes red and slightly swollen. Her hair was a tangled mess and she wore only her silk robe. Sara looked at her husband with disdain.

"Good morning, darling," she said blankly.

Elias got up and walked in front of his desk and casually leaned against it, facing her. She stood tall with her arms crossed over her chest. They were silent for several moments, regarding each other.

"I told you not to do anything foolish."

Sara rolled her eyes. "I'm so sorry I kept the dog in the kennel."

"How did you know what her name was, Sara? According to Mary, you have been calling her 'Dog' all this time." Elias already knew the answer. No one had ever gotten away with lying to him. He saw Sara's body tense up.

"I'm sure you already know." She held her head high, but he could see her lips trembling slightly as she desperately tried to not seem afraid of him.

There was another moment of silence while the two glared at each other.

"You came into my study without my permission, then you went through my things…and you almost killed the woman in my service," he sneered at her.

Sara scoffed. "We both know no one would care. You just care about your little pet." Finally, she clenched her fists and gritted her teeth. "How could you…with the lowest of the low! How could you fuck her—"

"I haven't fucked her. Not yet," Elias said simply.

Sara stared at him, dumbfounded.

"Then why? Why her? What's so special about that little brat? How could you even *think* of her while being with me?"

He was done with this conversation. It was time to get to the point.

"I called your father last night and told him what you've done. He understands why this marriage needs to end. He has a room ready for you. You will be moving back to live with him. By the end of the week, I'll have our divorce finalized."

Sara's legs began to shake and her lips began quivering. "Okay, fine! You can have her! I don't care! Just don't do this to me! I'll never be able to show my face to anyone again!" She began to cry, muttering under her breath, "Your third wife...I'll be the third rejected wife... replaced by Community property!"

Elias went to sit behind his desk again, his expression growing hard. "I've paid your father a decent sum. So long as you don't do anything foolish with the money, you will be able to take care of yourself for many years."

Sara fell to her knees. "Please, I'm begging you! I'll do anything! You can have her! Fuck her whenever you want! I won't even speak to her anymore! Please don't send me back to my father!"

Elias sat straight in his chair, staring at the broken woman on the floor.

"I told you long ago you shouldn't care what everyone thinks or says about you. You are hurting yourself while you think this way. You could have easily made something of yourself, yet you chose to follow the same path of all the other wives in the Community. You allow those other women to gossip and hold down your potential. Stop caring about the opinions of others."

Sara wiped her tears and stood, glaring at him. "It's so easy for you to say! The only reason they don't speak about you is because of your position in the Community!"

"I've had plenty of things said about me behind my back. The difference between you and me is I don't allow it to bother me."

"No, you just make them disappear!"

The room was eerily quiet for several moments. Elias had no expression on his face. His emotions were impossible to determine.

"Pack your things. Your father's car will be here within the hour."

Sara had lost and she knew it. She stormed out of the study and slammed the door behind her.

Elias returned to his paperwork as if nothing had happened.

Mary made sandwiches for lunch. They sat on Evie's bed while they ate, and Evie was more than happy for the company.

"So, you'll be able to come back to work later today," Mary said between bites.

Evie sighed. "I'm happy to get out of this room, but I'm not looking forward to dealing with Mrs. Huntley again."

"You won't. She's going back to living with her father. He told me this morning when I delivered his breakfast."

Evie almost choked. "Seriously? She's leaving him?"

"Nope. *He's* leaving *her*. She is going to be ex-wife number three."

Evie stared at Mary for several moments. "Is…is it my fault?"

Mary shrugged. "I think it was only a matter of time. At this point, I doubt he's going to marry again. Serves her right for being such a gold-digging bitch."

Evie went back to her lunch, wondering what would happen now that Mrs. Huntley would be gone. "So, when is she leaving?"

"No idea. Mr. Huntley just told me her father would be here and she's leaving today. The woman is a crying mess."

Evie almost felt sorry for her. Almost. Mary gathered their plates and paused before going back to the kitchen.

"I'll let you know when she leaves. Mr. Huntley wants me to see him after she's gone. Probably to talk about what he expects of us now."

"What was it like before he was married? Is he strict about getting things done?"

Mary laughed. "Good lord, no! Don't get me wrong, he still wants us to keep a cleaning schedule, but he isn't nearly as strict. Mrs. Huntley was always the one to have so many chores for us every day. And now there will be no parties for us to prepare for."

Evie smiled as Mary left the room. Though, she didn't quite believe that Mr. Huntley wouldn't marry again. She was sure it was only a matter of time before he found another pretty face to bring into his home.

Hours seemed to drag on. The room was ungodly hot but having the bottles of water helped her against the heat. Several times, she carefully poured a little water in her hands and wiped her face to keep cool. The idea of leaving the room to go to the bathroom still made her uncomfortable, unless she absolutely had to.

Evie wasn't sure how much time had passed but finally, she heard the door to her room open and Mary came up the stairs.

"She's gone."

Evie let out a breath of relief.

"Mr. Huntley wants both of us in new rooms on the second floor. He says there's no need for us to have such small rooms in this large house."

Evie was taken aback. "Are you serious?"

Mary nodded. "Yeah. I didn't believe it either at first. But he said he wanted us in rooms on the second floor. And you're not gonna believe what room you're getting." Evie gave her a confused look and Mary laughed. "You're getting Mrs. Huntley's old room."

Evie's heart began to pound hard and her stomach churned as a sharp jolt of anxiety shot through her.

"Why?" she asked quietly.

Mary shrugged and smiled. "I think it's an apology. I'm getting one of the guest rooms. He wants us to get settled into our new rooms tonight. I'll move into mine after dinner. Get moving and we can talk about our new cleaning schedule later."

"Mary, don't you want the room? You've been here a lot longer than me. I can take one of the guest rooms. Please, switch with me." Evie felt Mary deserved it, but she also felt uneasy taking the room of his soon to be ex-wife.

Mary shook her head. "No, you take it. After what she did to you, it should be yours. And if he's ever stupid enough to marry another one of those spoiled brats in the Community, then enjoy it while it lasts."

Evie's heart continued to pound while she grabbed the few items she had. Her legs shook as she climbed down the stairs. She had never been in Mrs. Huntley's room. Mary was responsible for that, and Mr. Huntley wanted no one to enter his room.

She stood in front of the elegant white door, her hands shaking as she grabbed the door handle. Evie took a breath and forced herself to enter. It was large and more beautiful than she'd expected. Both the bed and vanity table were massive and dripping with elegance. It even had its own small sitting room with a large television. The couches were ivory with a floral pattern and the small table was a deep mahogany. The walls were a light blue, making the room look brighter.

Evie took a breath and tried to calm herself. She hoped Mary was right and that this was nothing more than an apology, but she didn't feel right accepting the room. She wanted to either take the second guest room or even Mary's old room on the third floor.

Evie turned and jumped in surprise. Mr. Huntley was standing in front of her.

"Do you like the room?" he asked, leaning against the doorway.

Evie took a breath and tried to find the right words. "I appreciate your offer, sir, but I would really like to take the other guest room or Mary's old room. I don't feel right taking it."

"And why is that?"

"I...I just don't need this large room to myself, sir. Maybe Mary would like it?" She tried hard not to insult him or make it seem like she was spitting on his generosity.

He smiled and the uneasy feeling coiling inside her stomach grew more intense. Something about his smile gave her chills.

"I want you to have it. I have no intention of bringing anyone else into my home. And Mary's new room is right next to yours. You can both use this room as you please."

Knowing that Mary could use the room as well didn't make her feel any better about the new living arrangements.

He took a step back into the hall and continued to smile at Evie.

"Enjoy your new room."

Mr. Huntley then turned and entered his own room, which was right across from the one she now stood in. Evie's stomach ached in anxiety for the rest of the day.

Elias walked into the Community Council Building with several files tucked under his arms. The young woman who sat at the front desk immediately stood in respect.

"Good morning, Mr. Huntley. The Council is ready for you."

Elias gave her a polite nod but did not slow his pace while he crept deeper into the building. He approached the large white double doors where two men were stationed outside. The Harmony Group patrolled and safeguarded the entire building. It had been a long time since anyone was stupid enough to try and attack members of the council or destroy the building, but the Harmony Group took no chances.

He didn't acknowledge the men as they opened the doors for him.

There was no hesitation in his steps as he strolled in. The moment he was inside the room, the men closed the doors behind him. Elias quickly took his seat at the round table and gently placed the folders in front of him.

"Good morning, Elias," the council head, Jareth, said politely.

He nodded in turn. "Good morning, Jareth. Council," Elias said, acknowledging the others sitting at the table.

Jareth had been the head of the council for many years. His combed hair was completely white and his thin frame made him look feeble, but he spoke with a strong voice that rang with authority.

As the five council members opened their folders, Jareth began addressing everyone in the room.

"As you all know, we have now had an obscene amount of people in debt go missing. Over two dozen adults and three dozen children over the course of the year. Now word has reached us that Eden could have infiltrated our borders again. There is only so much we can do to contain this information. Word of Eden is now spreading in the Community. We need to abolish this false hope immediately."

The other council members in the room nodded while Jareth turned to address Elias directly.

"We placed the Harmony Group in your hands, Elias. What are you doing to contain this?"

Elias's eyes did a quick scan over the people in the room.

"Currently, I have my connections in the Underground spreading the word that the adults were taken to Medical Waste. Since the children were slowly taken over time, my connections are also spreading the word that the children were freed and taken to schools across the Community. This way, we instill the fear of Medical Waste and give them the hope of freedom as well."

Jareth nodded.

"Excellent. However, we still face the issue of Eden. What plans do you have to capture them?"

Elias lazily began passing his folders around the table.

"I believe Eden is using their own connections in the Community to learn the Harmony Group's patrol patterns and are using that to their advantage. I have ordered for the patrol patterns to change daily. They will also patrol on foot and check identification cards more frequently. We are still unaware if Eden had the ability to falsify Community issued cards, but I am working on a solution to that as well. I do know that Eden has found a way to remove the shock bracelets so we cannot track those they take. We need to develop a new way to track those in debt."

Jareth nodded. He opened his mouth to speak but was stopped by the councilman on his left. "What are you doing about Eden coming into the Community, Elias? It's your responsibility to ensure that outsiders cannot enter our borders! How are you going to fix your mistake?"

The room immediately grew quiet, and Elias's eyes slowly made their way to Councilman David. The councilmen had thin brown hair, a scraggly beard, and hard brown eyes. His large figure could barely fit in the chair he was sitting in.

As soon as Elias's dark eyes landed on him, David realized his mistake. David may be on the council, but he made the dangerous mistake of forgetting how much power Elias had in the Community.

Rather than be angry, Elias was amused.

"*My* mistake, David? Remember, the council was the one that demanded more patrols within the Community and not around the borders. Not to mention that I just recently got approval to finally build ships to patrol the waters, as I requested years ago. Remember, you are the ones that disregarded the need for security around the borders, not I."

David looked down to the table in shame and Jareth chuckled. "You're right. We were reckless in that decision. The council made a grave mistake in interfering with your decisions regarding the Harmony Group. You have our apologies. The council will leave all decisions concerning the Harmony Group to you from now on."

Elias offered Jareth a polite nod. The councilman proceeded to open a new folder and extracted a piece of paper.

"We have one more topic to discuss. Contraband in the Underground has gotten out of control."

Everyone at the table opened the appropriate folder while Jareth continued to speak.

"Contraband continues to rise and is now causing a problem within the units. It's a good distraction to those in debt, but now it's interfering with business within the Community. It has also led to the deaths of several people in debt in various units."

Elias had not bothered to open the file concerning the contraband. He was already well aware of the situation.

Jareth lifted his head to address him again. "We have never had a problem with the business in the Underground, Elias, as it is a good distraction for those in debt. But the drugs are getting out of control. Do you have a solution to this issue?"

Elias nodded. "I do. I have a plan that will be executed as soon as possible. I am working with my head of the Harmony Group. Ultimately, drugs will always be a problem. But at least I can make it disappear for a while. And with luck, we will also dissolve the false hope Eden gives to those in debt."

"Good. We leave everything in your hands, Elias."

With that, the meeting was done. Elias wasted no more time with these people. He quickly stood and made his way out of the room while the others went on with small talk.

Before Elias could reach the doors to head to his vehicle, a voice called out to him, "Elias, just a moment please." Elias turned to see councilwoman Edith walking to him. It was a slow movement, as she needed her cane to walk. "Can I invite you to my office for a few minutes? It's been so long since you and I have gotten together and had a conversation."

Elias smiled at her. "It would be my pleasure." He kept pace with her slow walking as she led him to her office.

Edith's gray hair was up in an elegant bun on top of her head. She always wore elegant business suits rather than a typical skirt or dress that all the other women in the building wore.

"I heard about your divorce. My sympathies. You don't seem to have much luck with happy marriages," she said once they entered the room.

Elias smirked. "I suppose not. Luck doesn't seem to be on my side at the moment."

Edith slowly went to her small sitting area and Elias joined her. They both lounged back in the seats and smiled at each other. Elias had known Edith since he was a boy. He had considered her as his only true equal in the Community. He owed everything he had to her.

She sighed. "Well, I hear the poor girl refuses to be seen in public. It's a shame these women only see their value for who they marry. I wish they would fight to rise in the ranks rather than simply marry to make their way in the world."

Elias smirked. She was correct. Women could easily make their way up the ranks of the Community as easy as any man could. Edith was one of few women who chose to do so. But most chose the path to marry and let their husbands do the work. And it was those women who made others feel ashamed for their failed marriages.

Edith gave Elias a small smile. "So, are you to remain a bachelor or are you interested in another connection? Councilman Theo has a daughter. She's a lovely girl. Not quite as spoiled as Sara was. He's also in charge of the Farming Unit. I'm sure he can provide you with goods that would interest you for your…personal side business," she said with a smirk.

Elias chuckled. "Thank you, but there's no need for that. I have plenty of my own connections. I don't need to marry for them anymore. And I already have my eye on someone."

Edith raised a brow. "Oh? Someone I know?"

"No. She's a woman from…let's say, humble beginnings."

Edith sat back in her chair, giving Elias a curious look. "She's in debt?"

Elias smiled. "Not for long, I'm sure."

"And what's so appealing about her? What's so special about her, Elias?"

He was quiet for several moments, his eyes resting on a small painting on the wall. "I had her read the book you gave me. I've had so many people over the years read it. Only you and I ever believed the truth inside of it. No one until her." His eyes met Edith's again, a smile forming on his face. "So many people have hope for this world. But not her. It's surprising and refreshing to find someone like us, Edith. I'm tired of empty marriages. I want someone I can finally connect with. I'm tired of being alone."

Edith considered his words as she looked him over. Finally, she grinned. "Well, as long as she makes you happy, you have my blessing. You're powerful enough that no one will question it or criticize you for it."

He smiled and stood from his seat.

"Have you proposed to her yet?" she asked.

"Not just yet. There's one more thing I want to find out before I fully commit to my decision."

"And what is that?"

His smile grew wider. "I'll tell you after I decide."

Edith smirked as he made his way to the door. "Mysterious, as always. You do love keeping people in suspense. In any case, I hope she makes you happy."

Elias gave one last smile before turning to leave. "I have no doubt she will."

He swiftly left the building without another word, ready to return home.

Chapter 8

For the next couple of weeks, things were much more relaxed in the house. Mary and Evie kept up with the basic household work, but both were happy to feel like they could breathe without Mr. Huntley's now ex-wife breathing over them. Mary and Evie also enjoyed watching the television in her new room. It took quite a while for Evie to get used to the large space and sleeping in such a soft bed.

Ryder was happy to hear things were getting better for his sister. Evie never told him about Mr. Huntley giving her his ex-wife's old room. It still didn't feel right for Evie to have it. Several times she convinced Mary to sleep in that room for the night while she slept in Mary's new bed. Mary continued to be the one to serve Mr. Huntley his meals and clean his study.

As soon as Mr. Huntley's dinner was served, Evie and Mary would take some time and relax in Evie's new room. They enjoyed having the time to enjoy a movie or television show. For that small amount of time, Evie felt as if she was free.

The current commercial playing advertised for the highest rated college in the Community. She didn't know why, but it sparked a question that Evie wanted to ask. "Hey Mary?"

The older woman turned her head to look at Evie.

"If you weren't in debt, what would you do?"

Mary looked to the ceiling in thought. "I don't know. I used to work at the marketplace before I turned myself in."

"But isn't there something you dreamed of doing? A career or goal you have?"

Mary was thoughtful again before a small smile played on her face.

"I would love to have my own little café. Just coffee, pastries and maybe some sandwiches. Nothing big or fancy. A little business to call my own."

Evie smiled. "I would love to work for you someday."

Mary smirked and looked back at Evie. "What about you?"

Evie shrugged. "I don't know. I've been in debt since I was twelve. I haven't been able to do anything I could possibly have an interest in."

"Well… maybe you should think about it. I know you want to turn yourself back in when your debt is paid off, but maybe someday you will get to have a life of your own and fight for your own dreams."

Evie was silent after that. She was convinced she would be in debt for the rest of her life. But the idea of having a life outside of servitude would be a dream come true. It's a shame she just had no idea what kind of dream job she would love to have.

On one Sunday evening, Evie was begrudgingly walking next to her brother as they made their way to the Underground. Ryder had been pestering Evie to go with him and try to enjoy life as a free adult for one night. Evie would go, but she was adamant on not touching a single cigarette or a drop of alcohol.

As they rounded the corner of the street, Evie felt as if cold water had been thrown over her. A heavy feeling was spreading in her chest. Ryder took a few steps forward before noticing his sister wasn't following him.

"Evie? What's wrong?"

Evie's eyes darted around the area. "Ryder…where are all the Harvester's vans? I haven't seen a single one tonight."

Ryder began to scan the area as well. Their nightly patrols ran like clockwork. Tonight, something was wrong.

"Let's keep moving," he simply said, taking her hand.

She continued to follow him as they rounded another corner and the entrance of the Underground came into view. Before they crossed the street, Evie froze again.

"Ryder, please don't go in there! Something is wrong!"

She couldn't explain her feelings. But the closer they got to the Underground, the more her body began to shake and her heart pounded painfully in her chest.

Ryder seemed to resist the urge to roll his eyes and turned to his sister. "Evie, I'm sure everything is fine! Let's just—"

Evie grabbed the front of his shirt and almost shook him in frustration. "Please listen! I can feel it! We can't go in tonight!"

Ryder stared into Evie's panicked eyes for several moments until he finally took a breath and gently removed her hands from his shirt. "Okay, we won't stay. At least let me go grab Aaron. He really wanted to see you tonight."

Evie released a breath and nodded. Ryder quickly ran inside and she decided to step away from the street and sat on the grass to wait. Out of the corner of her eye, she noticed movement. From down the opposite road, five large white vans suddenly came to a screeching halt in front of the Underground entrance.

The names on the vans were noticeably clear:

HARMONY GROUP

In a panic, Evie scrambled to hide behind the bushes as the van doors suddenly burst open and several men jumped out, covered head to toe in riot gear, holding large guns and batons. Evie covered her mouth with her hand to keep herself from screaming as the men broke down the door to the Underground and rushed inside. Almost as soon as the men entered, the sound of screaming and gunshots could be heard. Instinctively, Evie jumped up to try to find her brother and Aaron, but she was suddenly thrown back to the ground as swarms of people began running out of the Underground.

Screaming and gunshots still filled the air as people in debt scrambled for their lives. Evie screamed for Ryder and Aaron, hoping she would find them.

"Evie!"

She turned to see Ryder and Aaron running straight for her. Without missing a beat, Evie turned and began sprinting with them down the road. From behind them, the sounds of yelling and screaming could be heard. Evie took a risk and glanced behind her. She would never forget the sight of sobbing men and women being thrown into the large vans. The horrible noises didn't cease until they were near the Community Board Unit. They were well away from the scene now. Evie, Ryder, and Aaron were on their knees, trying to catch their breath.

Evie looked to her brother, who held up a finger to her.

"Don't...say...a fucking...thing!" he managed between his panting.

Aaron gave Ryder a confused look before looking at Evie. She simply shook her head and slowly stood.

"What happened in there?" Evie asked when she could finally breathe properly.

Aaron stood and helped Ryder to his feet. "It was a fucking raid. They were trying to grab as many of us as possible. Trying to take people to Medical Waste." He avoided her eyes, as if ashamed.

Evie thought for several moments. It explained why they hadn't seen any patrols earlier in the evening. They were preparing for the raid.

"But...why? Why would they do this now?" Evie cried. "The Community has never cared about the deals in the Underground before!"

Ryder stumbled over to his sister and wrapped an arm around her. "I have no idea. But we should count our blessings. We almost got caught. We were able to push through them."

Aaron walked over and the three of them hugged each other tightly.

Evie sniffled, holding back tears. "Swear to me that neither of you will go there again! Swear it!"

Aaron gently rubbed her back. "We promise Evie. We promise."

Both men silently escorted Evie back to Mr. Huntley's house, then quickly ran back to the Laborer's Unit. Both took great care not to be seen by any passing vehicles.

Conner knocked hard on the front door and waited patiently. Within moments, the door opened and Mary quickly greeted him.

"Good morning. I'm here to see Elias Huntley. He is expecting me."

Mary nodded. "This way, sir."

Conner followed behind the woman, holding the stacks of folders under his arm as he walked. He had seen her several times over the years while he worked for Mr. Huntley. While Conner had never had any formal conversation with Mary, he knew she was smart enough to know her place and treat him with respect.

Mary knocked on the door to the study.

"Come in."

Mary stepped inside, leaving Conner in the hallway. "Sir, there is someone here for you."

She stepped aside and allowed Conner to enter the room. Mary respectfully closed the door behind her while Conner went and stood in front of Mr. Huntley's desk.

"Good morning, sir," he said politely.

Mr. Huntley was standing by the window, staring outside. Conner wasn't sure what he was looking at, but Mr. Huntley's gaze didn't falter. Whatever he was looking at held his attention.

"Good morning, Conner," Mr. Huntley spoke without breaking his gaze.

Conner stepped forward and gently placed the files on Mr. Huntley's desk.

"The raid last night was successful. We apprehended over two dozen people. Over half of them were tested positive for drugs or had other dangerous contraband in their possession. They were sent immediately to Medical Waste. There were also about a dozen casualties. All were found dealing or intoxicated at the time."

"What contraband was found?"

"Mostly drugs. But we did also find cigarettes, condoms, and pocketknives. Everyone with drugs and knives were also sent to the facility."

"And the others?"

"Awaiting interrogation. We are trying to see if any of them have information on Eden. The others we apprehended are in no condition to be interrogated."

Not once did Mr. Huntley move from his spot in front of the window.

"Good. Drugs will be scarce for a while, but we both know they will be back in the Underground within a few weeks. Then, the same system starts over. Once things get out of control again, we'll take things from there."

Conner nodded. "Understood. We were able to find footage all over the Community of the people who escaped the Underground. The Harmony Group awaits your decision on what to do with the footage."

Mr. Huntley finally stepped away from the window and made his way to his desk. As he took his seat, Conner couldn't help but wonder what held his attention outside of the window.

Mr. Huntley gracefully began looking through the many pictures. "Is there any evidence that those who ran had contraband or were intoxicated?"

"We won't know unless we find them, sir. We have plenty of information to capture them. Most of them are from the Laborers and Lumber Units. But we also discovered some in the Domestics Unit. A couple of them work in the Community Board Unit." Mr. Huntley listened while flipping through the photos. Conner took a breath before his next sentence. "One of the suspects is the young woman you have assigned to your house."

He seemed to freeze for several seconds as if processing what Conner had said. "Where is the footage?"

"Second folder down, sir."

Mr. Huntley swiftly opened the second folder and flipped through the photos. He quickly found what he was looking for.

"I have tapes in the car, as well, if you want to see the video footage."

Conner watched as Mr. Huntley's eyes scammed over the photos of the young woman and two men either running down the streets or collapsed on the ground. He seemed almost mesmerized by the photos.

"Sir, I have two men waiting outside. With your permission, we can detain her and the other men she was with. Both are confirmed to be in the Laborer's Unit. Interrogations will be quick."

Conner's words seemed to snap him out of his current thoughts.

"That won't be necessary. Don't waste time tracking down the ones that escaped unless there is clear evidence of drug dealing or using. They will spread the word to others in their unit. The news will keep them from doing anything stupid in the Underground. For a while, at least."

Conner nodded. "Then there are several other suspects we can detain. We have no evidence that this woman or the men she was with were associated with the drug dealing or that they were using the substances. We only have reports on the two men trading cigarettes for alcohol."

"But nothing about the woman?"

"No, sir. Number six-seven-seven-five has no known history of trading or even drinking in the Underground."

Mr. Huntley seemed to already know the answer before Conner spoke. He simply nodded and closed the folder after pulling out his pictures of interest.

"Begin tracking down everyone that has a confirmed history of trading in the Underground. Do not send them to the facility until after they are interrogated. We need information on Eden. Tell them we will be willing to make a deal if they provide any useful information."

Conner nodded as Mr. Huntley stood.

"I'll follow you out to get the tapes. Everything will need to be reported to the council. There is a party tonight. I can speak to one of the Council heads then."

He swiftly walked out of his study and Conner took the opportunity to quickly look out the window. All he saw was the garden where number six-seven-seven-five was pulling weeds out of the flower beds. Nothing of interest.

Conner shook his head and followed Mr. Huntley out of the room.

Evie felt as if she was in a daze the entire morning. The events of the previous night kept playing over and over in her head. She was in constant fear for her brother and Aaron. The Harvesters could easily find them. Not only them, but herself as well. The street cameras all over the Community could lead them to find anyone who had fled that night.

She spent most of the day trying to push the negative thoughts out of her head. Evie was certain she would see them next Sunday.

Evie and Mary were washing the lunchtime dishes when heavy footsteps suddenly entered the kitchen. Both women turned to see Mr. Huntley. It was odd for both of them to see him in the kitchen.

"Can I get you something, sir?" Mary asked. Evie continued doing the dishes while Mary addressed him.

He had a small smile on his face while he addressed both of them. "I'm afraid I have to attend a social gathering tonight. You won't need to worry about my dinner."

Mary nodded in understanding, and his gaze fell on Evie.

"I'll need someone to attend with me tonight. Evie, you will be joining me."

Evie almost dropped the plate she was holding into the sink. Mary looked just as shocked as Evie did.

"I'm sorry, sir?" Evie asked, hoping she either misheard him or he was joking.

"You'll be accompanying me tonight. There are appropriate clothes in your room. Be ready by seven."

He exited the room. Both women looked at each other, still not quite believing what he said. Once dishes were done, they quickly went up the stairs and into Evie's room.

On the bed was an elegant black dress. Evie picked it up and she could barely feel the weight of it in her hands. Next to it was a pair of simple black heels with a gold chain necklace.

Evie looked at Mary and began trembling. "Why is he doing this? Has he done this before with anyone else?" she quietly asked.

Mary shook her head and took the dress from Evie, inspecting it very carefully. "No. I have no idea what's going on in his head."

"Mary, I can't do this. I don't want to do this! Something doesn't feel right!"

Mary quickly placed a hand on Evie's shoulder. "Evie, breathe! It's one night! Just go. Maybe he really just wants the company."

Evie resisted the urge to roll her eyes. Mary was desperately trying to calm her down and say anything to make her feel better. "It's just one night, hun. Hell, you should go and see what life on their side of things is like."

Evie looked back to the dress in Mary's hands. "Please tell me that isn't one of his ex-wives' old dresses."

Mary shrugged. "I haven't seen it before, so probably not. Not a single wrinkle on it. I bet you it's a brand-new dress."

Both women forced themselves to go back to work, though it was hard for Evie to concentrate on anything properly. When it was six, Mary made Evie stop cleaning to go shower and get ready for the evening. After her shower, Evie sat at the vanity table and looked at the several types of makeup splayed out before her. All of it was brand-new. It looked completely foreign to her.

Mary went into the room and began helping Evie with her hair, pulling it back and out of her face. "Part of me always wanted a daughter," Mary admitted while playing with her long brown hair. "I always imagined doing her hair just like this."

Evie gave her a smile, but her words didn't make her feel any better about the situation.

Mary finished braiding her hair before turning to the makeup.

"I've never worn makeup before," Evie admitted.

"I have, but it's been a long time," Mary said, looking over the options.

"I don't want to wear any. I don't need it."

Mary sighed. "I know you don't, but you don't want to insult Mr. Huntley by not wearing any. It looks like he bought all this for you."

Evie bit her bottom lip in frustration. She desperately wanted to put her foot down. She didn't ask for any of this and didn't want any of it. "I don't want to wear it ..." Evie said softly.

Mary sighed again. "Look, we don't have to use all of it. Just the little things will be enough. Maybe some lipstick and eyeliner."

Evie clenched her teeth, but she gave in. Mary quickly helped her and when Evie looked in the mirror, she didn't recognize herself. Even with the simple makeup and hairstyle, she looked like a woman of high status, not Community property. None of it felt right to her. The dress was sleeveless and knee length, and the light fabric made her feel naked. Mary found a black shawl in the closet that Evie could wear. The heels felt foreign on her feet. She was thankful they weren't too high; otherwise, she wouldn't have been able to walk properly.

Mary finished placing the gold necklace around Evie's neck and looked at the clock on the wall. "It's time."

Evie sighed and stood up from the vanity table. Mary led her downstairs where Mr. Huntley was waiting by the front door. He looked elegant in a black suit and tie. His eyes landed on Evie and he smiled.

"You look lovely."

Evie blushed and dropped her gaze to the floor. "Thank you."

Before she could make a step towards the front door, he reached into his pocket and produced a large jewelry box. "Before we leave, I have something for you."

Evie's heart pounded as he opened the box to reveal two large cuff bracelets. The smooth gold easily reflected her image. He gently placed each bracelet on her wrists, and she immediately understood why he got them for her. They covered her Community bracelets.

He placed the box back in his pocket and placed his hand on her back, leading her out the door. "We will return later tonight, Mary. Please don't wait up for us."

Evie cast a worried look over her shoulder to Mary who tried to give her a reassuring smile. Mr. Huntley led Evie to the elegant black car parked in front of his home and opened the door for her. She carefully went inside, and he closed it behind her. Evie felt her heart pound in her chest when Mr. Huntley entered the car on the opposite side and they took off.

Evie's hands were clasped tightly in her lap while the car drove. She kept her eyes nervously on the floor.

"Sir, where are we going?" She didn't see the harm in asking.

"A council member is having a party at his house. I have business to discuss with him."

"Mary said you hated parties."

"I do," Mr. Huntley simply said.

"You don't seem like the type of man to go to anyone you have business with." Evie didn't look at him, but she felt his eyes on her.

"And what kind of man am I?" His voice was perked with curiosity.

Evie took a breath. "The kind of man that makes people come to you for business."

There was brief silence in the car before she heard him laugh. "I suppose you're right," he said, highly amused.

Finally, she forced herself to look up at him. "If I'm right, why are you going to this party?"

He stared at her for several moments but made no effort to answer her. The car suddenly came to a stop, and Mr. Huntley gracefully exited, leaving her question unanswered. He opened the door on her side and helped her exit the vehicle.

The house was almost as large as Mr. Huntley's, although it didn't look nearly as intimidating. He led her to the front door with his hand on her back. With one knock, the door swiftly opened. Evie was met with laughter and loud conversations. As soon as they entered the house, Evie was greeted by a young man.

"May I take your shawl, miss?" he asked politely.

"No thank—"

Before she could finish, Mr. Huntley gently took it off her shoulders and handed it to the young man. She hoped to keep it on all night for comfort. Evie was led into the next room and was astonished by what she saw. The party that Mr. Huntley's ex-wife once had at his home was nothing compared to this. Men wore their finest clothes and women wore glittering jewels and flashy makeup. People laughed loudly over the piano music playing from the corner of the room. There was even a small dance floor in the center.

"This way," Mr. Huntley said quietly into her ear.

Evie followed close behind him. She felt completely out of place and wanted to leave as soon as possible.

They approached an older gentleman that laughed with several other men. "William," Mr. Huntley greeted, approaching the group.

The man in question swiftly turned to Mr. Huntley and gave him a wide smile. "Elias! I feel so honored! You actually accepted my invitation!" The old man's eyes fell on Evie, who likely appeared just as uncomfortable as she felt, though she tried to keep her face straight. "And who is this?"

Evie held her breath as the man stepped in front of her.

"Who is this lovely young lady? The next Mrs. Huntley?"

The man grabbed her hand and gave it a slobbery kiss. Evie had to fight the urge to snatch her hand away and wipe it on her dress.

"William, we have business to discuss," Mr. Huntley said, his expression like stone.

The old man nodded at him, then turned to wink at Evie. "I'm sure I'll be seeing you later." He turned to leave while Mr. Huntley faced Evie.

"I'll be back shortly. Stay and enjoy the party."

Evie opened her mouth to speak, but it was too late. Mr. Huntley and several others left the room from a side door. She looked around and felt sick. In no way did she want to be left alone. In the corner, she saw a table of food and drinks. Evie walked along the wall to get to the corner, hoping they would have some water. When she reached the table, her stomach churned. The table was filled with appetizers along with bottles of wine and champagne. No water was in sight. Evie groaned and began to head over to the opposite wall where the windows were to get some air.

"Excuse me," a giggling voice said from behind her.

Evie turned and saw three young women, all in elegant gowns and jewels covering their necks, wrists, and fingers. Their hair was clearly colored blonde. Their brown eyes and eyebrows gave it away. But unlike Mr. Huntley's ex-wife, these women did not make it look elegant, and the color did not fit any of them at all.

"Didn't you come here with Elias Huntley?" one of them asked. Evie nodded, and the girls giggled. "I didn't expect him to move on so soon!"

Evie wanted to argue that she wasn't with him in that way, but she was still Community property, and she was in a room full of high-standing members. She needed to be careful.

"Please excuse me. I need some air."

Evie tried to turn away, but a hand on her arm stopped her. "No, we need to know! Is he worth it?"

Evie looked at the woman with utter confusion while gently removing the hand on her arm. "I'm sorry?"

The girls giggled and continued drinking their champagne.

"Well, you're going to be his fourth wife, right? It's obvious the man just moves from woman to woman after a while. Poor Sara is a wreck and won't even leave her house. Aren't you the one he left her for?"

The women laughed at Evie's horrified expression.

"Is it worth being the fourth wife? I mean, we know he's filthy rich. Is he a good fuck too? Is that it?"

Evie felt sick, but she gritted her teeth and clenched her fists. She couldn't stop the words. "You're all disgusting."

The women stopped laughing and looked at Evie in surprise.

"You are all disgusting! Is that all that matters to you people? How much money a man has? How good he is in bed? What is wrong with all of you?"

While the women scowled in anger, Evie took the opportunity to rush away. She heard them calling for her, but their words were ignored. She was able to make it to the other side of the dance floor before a large figure approached her from behind.

"Hey, don't I know you?"

Evie whirled around and was faced with a very overweight and elderly man.

"I'm sorry, but we've never—"

"No! I know you! I've seen you before!" The man's slurred words gave away that he was drunk. His face was bright pink with a large smile that sent chills down Evie's spine. "Yeah, you were at Elias's house! Elias Huntley! I never forget a pretty face!"

The man stumbled towards Evie, and she quickly took several steps back, frantically looking around for an escape.

"You were that pretty little piano player!"

She began to panic as he got closer.

"You have very talented fingers! What are you doing here? Are you here to play for the party?"

Evie began to shake. "No, I'm here with Mr. Huntley. He went—"

The man lunged forward, and Evie felt his arms wrap around her waist. "So, how much for a night?"

Evie frantically began pushing him away. "Sir, let me go! I am here—"

"Come on, how much? You can come to my home on your day off! Two packs of cigarettes for just a few hours! And if I really like you, I'll make it three!" he said with a wink.

Evie felt a rush of rage take over her as the man's hands grabbed her backside. Without hesitating, Evie raised her hand high and slapped the man across his face. He stumbled back and clutched at his cheek, which was now a bright red. Evie's handprint could not be missed.

Her feeling of rage was now replaced with fear. Realization had set in. She had just slapped a high standing-member of the Community. As the man gaped at her, Evie realized the music had stopped and everyone was staring at her.

The man's look of astonishment dissolved into one of anger. "You slapped me! You little bitch!"

Evie took a step back as the man pointed at her.

"Someone call the Harmony Group! This whore in debt dared to put a hand on me!"

The guests in the room began gasping and murmuring to each other. Evie began to feel dizzy and her legs began trembling.

"It's over... I'm going to Medical Waste... I'm going to die..."

The man lunged forward and grabbed her arm. "Maybe I'll ask them to go easy on you if you get on your knees for me right now!"

Evie felt tears fill her eyes. She opened her mouth to speak but a large hand suddenly grabbed the man's wrist and forced it from her arm. She looked over her shoulder to see Mr. Huntley standing tall behind her.

The man blinked several times in surprise before he spoke. "Elias? What are you doing? This whore placed her hands on me! Everyone saw it!"

Evie continued shaking as Mr. Huntley gently placed his hands on her shoulders. "I'm sure they did. I saw it as well." Evie felt a wave of panic as the man began to smile. "But I also saw you assault her first, Manny."

Evie looked up at Mr. Huntley in shock. He was glaring intently at Manny, who was now opening and closing his mouth rapidly. He seemed to be fighting for the right words to say. "S-she's in debt! It doesn't matter! She's Community property—"

"Wrong!"

Evie jumped at the sound of Mr. Huntley's commanding voice. It was hard and loud, making it easy for everyone in the room to hear him.

"Evie is mine. I own her contract. You put your hands on what is mine." Mr. Huntley stepped around her and stood only an inch away from the cowering man. "How is your wife, Manny? And your two sons? Are they well? Do they still enjoy living in the Community Board Unit?"

Mr. Huntley leaned down to speak directly into the old man's ear.

"Please remember they can all disappear at any given moment. All it takes is one phone call. And I will make sure you watch it happen."

Manny let out a high pitch squeal and rushed out of the room.

Mr. Huntley turned and gave a hard glare at the crowd around them. The audience that formed seemed to have gotten the hint. They quickly separated, and the music began to play again. Evie could still hear murmuring and see party members casting her evil looks. The facade was gone. They all knew what she was now.

Everything in this room made Evie sick. It was such a waste. A waste of food and a waste of money. The high members of society hated her for being in debt, yet she was turned in because of the selfishness of her mother. But that did not matter to them.

All that mattered to them was that she was in debt. And that was all they needed to know about her to be able to condemn her.

A large hand on her arm brought her out of her thoughts and made her jump.

"Are you alright?" Mr. Huntley asked.

Evie nodded. "Yes. Thank you for defending me, sir."

Mr. Huntley turned slightly and glared in the direction that Manny had run off to. "I do not tolerate sexual assault."

Evie was surprised. She did not once think that a man of high standing would care about anyone in debt.

"Are we leaving now?" she asked, sounding hopeful.

"Not yet. There's one more thing I want to do before we leave."

Evie was confused until he took her hand and began leading her to the dance floor. She began to panic and even tried pulling away. "Please, sir, I don't know how!"

He continued guiding her to the floor and gently held her close to him. "Just follow my lead."

She felt clumsy as one arm wrapped around her waist and the other held her hand. His height made her feel even smaller. Evie felt his eyes on her while she tried to focus on his tie.

"I apologize for leaving you alone. I did not think that Manny would be foolish enough to touch you."

Evie shook her head. "It isn't your fault. Thank you for standing up for me. I'm sure I would be heading to Medical Waste if it wasn't for you."

She looked up in time to see him smile down at her.

"I would never let that happen."

Evie looked back to his tie and blushed.

"Now tell me…before the situation with Manny, were you enjoying yourself? How did you like the party?"

Evie hesitated, not wanting to lie but also not wanting to tell the truth. "It's…an interesting experience."

He outright laughed at her response. "Never lie to me, Evie. Tell me the truth. What do you see in this room?"

Evie glanced around at the other dancing couples. Many people were still casting her evil looks. With a quick look to the corner, she saw the three women from earlier glaring and whispering to each other.

"It's a waste," she muttered.

"A waste?"

She didn't hold back her words. Her anger and frustration from the night was pouring out now. If he wanted the truth, Evie would give it to him.

"It's a waste. There's so much wasted money here. On things that mean absolutely nothing. The food, the alcohol, all of it.

"And how does it feel being around these people?" His question was asked with no anger or aggravation. Rather, he seemed to be pushing her to let out all her feelings on the matter. "I feel sick. These people are disgusting."

"Why?"

She gritted her teeth. "Because they only care about themselves and are only in their position because of the people that were turned in!"

Evie didn't realize she was beginning to raise her voice, but it was too late. The words had come out of her mouth. Evie wasn't sure if others around them could hear her.

They were already casting her ugly looks. Perhaps her words didn't matter to them anymore.

When she looked up to face him, she was surprised to find that he wasn't angry at all. No, the man was smiling.

"I appreciate your honesty."

"You aren't angry?" Evie felt stupid asking but couldn't stop herself.

"Not at all. Can I tell you a secret?" He leaned down close to her ear and his breath was hot on her face. "I feel the exact same way." She couldn't hide the shocked expression on her face as he lifted his head and smiled down at her. "These people are a waste of skin. They waste their money on things that mean nothing when it all ends for them."

Evie continued to stare at him in surprise and he laughed. "Did you expect me to say something else?"

Evie forced herself to look away. "You seem to fit in well with them," she mumbled.

"I know how to play the part. I only let them see what I want them to see. They don't know the truth of anything about me."

Evie tried to steady her breathing. "So, am I seeing the real you, or is this another farce you put on for people?"

He chuckled. "You see the truth, Evie. And you tell the truth. You truly are a wonder."

Evie gazed back up to his face. "Why did you bring me here?"

"To see if you felt the same way I did. To see if you could see these people the way I see them."

She wasn't expecting that answer and wasn't sure how to respond.

"You are the most selfless person I have ever met. You allow yourself to suffer for your loved ones. You fight your way through the pain of being in debt to secure a future of freedom for them. You are a rare treasure in this world, Evie."

Evie swallowed and tried to keep breathing. This was all building up to something. She could feel it. "Sir, please tell me what you want from me."

Mr. Huntley's eyes seemed to darken, but his smile was still there. "Do you remember the offer I gave you a few weeks ago?" She nodded. "I have another offer for you."

Evie began to feel dizzy. She didn't know if it was from the dancing or because of the situation that was unfolding in front of her.

"How would you like to see your older brother go free? For his debt to be paid?" Evie felt her blood run cold and her heart pound in her chest.

"I can free him," Mr. Huntley said. "I could free him, and he could go on to pay off your younger brother and sister's debt."

Evie swallowed. "And what do you want in return?"

His smile seemed to grow as he leaned down and whispered in her ear, "Marry me."

Evie swore her heart stopped for several moments. She wasn't sure she heard him correctly. "Sir?"

"Marry me. I'll pay off your debt and your brother's debt. He will be free to work and free your younger brother and sister. You will be free and live in comfort for the rest of your life."

Evie felt dizzy and tried not to fall. She couldn't believe this was happening.

"Sir, we hardly know each other!"

"I know enough about you. I know that you are a strong and beautiful woman. You feel the way I do about this corrupt society. We are the same. Your selflessness and incorruptibility is a rare thing in this world. And I want it, Evie. I want you."

Evie forced herself to breathe and steady herself. His arm around her tightened and her heart pounded loudly in her ears.

"I've waited a long time to find someone like you, Evie. Think it over."

The rest of the night seemed to flash by. Evie soon found herself back in the car and heading to Mr. Huntley's house.

Her mind didn't allow her to sleep that night.

Chapter 9

Evie was in a daze as she walked to the Laborer's Unit. Mr. Huntley's offer kept running through her mind. She had the opportunity to free her older brother, but that meant another type of ownership over her. Rather than be Community property, she would directly be Mr. Huntley's property.

She approached the Laborer's Unit and walked over to Ryder, who was waiting for her in front of his housing unit. As soon as he saw her, he knew something was wrong.

"You ok?" he asked.

Evie nodded. "Let's go get BB and CC. We can talk later."

Ryder knew not to push her. At least not yet. He tried to make small talk as they went to the Children's Unit. Evie tried to concentrate on speaking to BB and CC about their classes and training, but her thoughts continued to wander.

Finally, the sun began to set for the day, and it was time for the children to head back to their housing. They all said their goodbyes and Evie walked with Ryder out of the unit.

"Want to come back with me to the Laborer's Unit? Aaron wants to see you."

Evie nodded and Ryder sighed. "Evie, what's wrong? You're acting weird."

She took a breath. "Mr. Huntley offered to pay off your debt. He said he would pay it off so you can be free to pay off BB and CC's debt."

Ryder narrowed his eyes and gave his sister a sideways glance. "And what does he want from you?"

She closed her eyes, not wanting to see Ryder's response. "He wants me to marry him."

There was silence, and Evie opened her eyes to see Ryder wasn't walking next to her. She turned to see him a few steps back, looking perplexed.

"Are you serious?"

She nodded before averting her gaze to the ground. Ryder rushed to Evie and grabbed her shoulders.

"Please, tell me you're joking. Tell me you're fucking with me."

Evie shook her head. "I'm not. I'm dead serious. He wants me to marry him. He said he'd free you so you can work to free BB and CC."

"Evie...you can't do it! You hardly know this guy! And he hardly knows you!"

"I know, ok?" she snapped, burying her face in her hands. "I know! Something about him is wrong! But he offered, and how the hell am I supposed to turn that down?"

Ryder gently grabbed her chin and forced Evie to look at him. "Evie, listen to me. I'll be fine! I can take care of myself. I know you want to be free too, but don't sell yourself like that. Because this time, it's with no opportunity for freedom. It's until you die."

Evie looked back to the ground and Ryder let out a breath.

"Come on. Let's go see the guys."

They walked in silence until they reached the Laborer's Unit. Several men were gathered around outside of the housing unit. The weather had a slight chill to the air, but the shirtless men didn't seem to mind. Evie assumed it was a relief as their bodies were covered in sweat from the day's work. All of them were well toned, proof of the hard labor they have done for most of their lives. They all seemed to be laughing and having casual conversations. Ryder walked straight over to Aaron while a few guys went to Evie to say hello. She wasn't friends with all of them, but she knew them through her brother and Aaron.

"Evie! How have you been?" Danny was tall with dirty blonde hair and dark blue eyes.

His muscles showed his hard work as a laborer. Evie always thought he had a kind face.

She offered him a small smile, trying to be polite. "I'm good, Danny. Good to see you again."

Danny opened his mouth to speak but stopped and cast a glance behind her.

Evie felt a tug on her arm and she turned to face Aaron. She gave him a smile, but he didn't give her one in return.

"You okay?" she asked, not even bothering with a greeting.

"I need to talk to you."

He began leading her away from the group. Evie looked over her shoulder to see Ryder going to speak to Danny and the other men in the small group.

Once they were far enough away, Aaron turned back to her. "Ryder said Huntley asked you to marry him."

Evie's head whipped around to the group of men to glare at Ryder. Amongst the group, her brother was trying not to meet her gaze. Evie sighed and turned back to face Aaron.

"Yes, he did. He said he would pay off Ryder's debt."

"Are you going to take the offer?"

"It's…a tempting offer."

Aaron inhaled a sharp breath. "Please don't do it. Please, Evie…"

Evie raised a brow and gave him a curious look. "Aaron, no offense, but this has nothing to do with you. You're my friend, but this is my family we're talking about."

"You know I never considered you just a friend!" he snapped.

"And I told you it could never happen! You know I'm planning to turn myself back in as soon as I work off my own debt! I'm sorry, Aaron, but I can't do this!"

Evie began to turn away, tears flooding her eyes. Aaron grabbed her hand, and she was instantly spun around. Aaron's arms wrapped around her, and before she could comprehend what was happening, his lips crashed into hers.

Her mind was spiraling in several different directions. His kiss made her feel warm and alive in a way she had never felt before.

Aaron broke the kiss and looked back into her eyes. "I'm sorry…I've been wanting to do that for a long time now."

Evie blinked several times while Aaron pulled her into a tight hug.

"I wish we could have a normal life. I wish I could have taken you out on a real date. Maybe dinner. Maybe a walk under the stars. I would sell my soul to have a normal life with you."

Evie's arms slowly wrapped around him. Tears were still in her eyes, but she tried to blink them away. "I'm sorry. Life will never be that way for us," she said sadly.

He pulled back to look at her. "Please don't do it. Please…I know you want to turn yourself back in for the money. God, you don't know how to do anything for yourself." Aaron grabbed her hands and held them tightly in his. "I want to help. I think I'm almost done with my debt. Choose me, Evie. I'll turn myself back in too."

Evie's eyes widened as he continued speaking.

"I'll do it. I'll put the money towards freeing BB and CC. Ryder can finish his debt and get a regular job to help. Please…"

He was begging her at this point. Evie tried not to sob.

"I can't ask you to do that. I can't let you do that!"

Aaron pulled her into his arms again. "I want to! Please, marry me. No, we can't have a fancy wedding. Hell, we can't even legally marry while in debt. But I don't need a piece of paper for that. I wish I could get you a ring. I swear, I'd get you the largest diamond ring I could find."

Evie lightly laughed and leaned against him. "Diamonds are tacky and a waste of money. I'd never let you waste your money on one."

Aaron smiled at her. "We can do something with the people we care about. Fuck a traditional wedding. We can do something for us. Just us. Ryder can give you away. BB and CC can be in the ceremony."

Evie grinned back. "I'm trying to imagine myself walking down a gravel aisle in front of the Laborer's Unit. Then a reception at the Underground."

He continued smiling. "Please, choose me, Evie. Please…"

Evie fought with everything she had not to say yes. Putting aside Mr. Huntley's offer, she couldn't let Aaron do that. He was so close to being free and being able to have a life out of this nightmare.

She took a step closer to him and smiled. "If I could ever marry anyone, Aaron, it would be you. It would always be you." She gave him a kiss on his cheek and turned to walk away, not daring to kiss him on the lips in case she changed her mind. Evie quickly started heading back to Mr. Huntley's house.

"I'll never give up on you, Evie! I swear, I'll never give up on you!" Aaron called.

Evie couldn't stop herself. She began to run, tears running down her face.

"Evie, wait!"

It was Ryder. He was running after her. She didn't stop running until he grabbed her arm and forced her to turn and face him.

"What's wrong? Talk to me!"

Evie sobbed and looked into her brother's face.

"It's not fair! None of this is fair!" She cried into her brother's shirt while he wrapped his arms around her. "Aaron asked me to marry him! I wanted to say yes! I want to say yes so badly, but I can't make him do that for me! I can't let him turn himself back in! Nothing is fair in this life! Nothing!"

Ryder stepped back and gently placed his hands on either side of her head, forcing her to look at him.

"Evie, you need to stop this! Stop thinking you have to do everything yourself! Jesus, don't you deserve some happiness too? No, you can't live together and have a 'happily ever after' like those high-standing bastards can. BB and CC will be fine. They can stay in training and use those skills when they get out. But Aaron loves you! I know you love him too! I can see it every time you look at him. Please, think about yourself for once!" He wrapped her into a tight hug.

"Please, Evie. Do something for yourself for once. Don't marry that guy. You can't have a traditional wedding with Aaron, but he loves you. He won't own you like Huntley will. Please, think about it."

Her brother wiped the tears off her face and walked Evie back to Mr. Huntley's house. They gave each other a final hug, and Evie entered the house. She made her way quickly to her room, hoping she wouldn't run into Mr. Huntley.

Once inside, she fell asleep crying.

Over the next two days, Mary noticed Evie was not herself. She would constantly ask Evie if she was alright, but Evie would simply nod and return to work. Evie was, however, successful in avoiding Mr. Huntley. Mary continued to serve his meals and clean his study.

After another day of seeing Evie upset, Mary had seen enough. Before Evie could retire to her room for the night, Mary stopped her from leaving the kitchen.

"Alright, what's the matter? And don't you dare say it's nothing. Something is wrong."

Evie stared at Mary in defeat. "Mr. Huntley asked me to marry him."

Mary's eyebrows raised in surprise as she listened to the girl's every word while Evie hunched over with her head in her hands.

"He asked me the night of the party. He said he would free my older brother and he could work to free my younger brother and sister."

Mary was silent for several moments. When she opened her mouth as if to speak, Evie continued.

"On Sunday, a man I really care about told me he loves me. Well, actually, I love him too," she said with a small smile. "He begged me not to marry Mr. Huntley and to marry him instead. He said he would turn himself back in with me to free BB and CC."

Mary sighed deeply. "Well, I won't lie to you. I had a feeling he wanted to ask you. I mean, the dress, the room…I just hoped I was wrong about it. But what do you want? What would make you happy?"

Evie looked down to the floor. "I want to free my brothers and sister—"

"No, what do you want?" Mary snapped. "Jesus! Yes, you want to free them. But what about you? Don't you deserve some happiness too? Who will make you happier?"

Evie snorted. "I have no idea how I can answer that. I don't exactly get the chance to have a normal dating life with Aaron, and I don't know anything about Mr. Huntley. His money doesn't mean anything to me."

"Then what's stopping you from choosing this other man?"

"I don't want him to feel like he has to sacrifice for me. And now I have the chance to at least free one of my brothers. But I don't want him stuck turning himself back in for BB and CC, either." Evie buried her face in her hands while Mary's brows scrunched together, seemingly in thought.

"Hun, I think you are one of the most selfless people I have ever met. But you need to stop and think about yourself for once. Make yourself happy and let others help you for once in your life."

Evie was still torn on her decision. "I really need to be alone. Thank you, Mary."

She heard Mary huff in aggravation, but she ignored it and went up the stairs to her room.

Just as she rounded the corner on the second floor, a voice stopped her.

"Hello, Evie."

A chill went up her spine and she turned to see Mr. Huntley coming out of his study.

"Hello, sir," she said respectfully.

He slowly walked closer to her until he stood right in front of her. "Have you considered my offer?"

Evie took a deep breath and tried not to look away from him.

"I'm still considering it, sir. It's a serious offer I need to think about."

Mr. Huntley stared at her for several moments, his expression impossible to read. His hand slowly raised to her face and she tried not to flinch as he gently tucked a strand of hair behind her ear.

"I'm a very patient man, Evie. But there are certain times when my patience is tested." Evie tensed and couldn't hide the fear in her eyes. Was that a threat? He leaned down, his breath brushing her face. "Don't make me wait too much longer."

Mr. Huntley's statement sounded gentle, but Evie could feel the command in his voice. He finally entered his room, and Evie released the breath she was holding in. She forced her feet to move and entered her own room before dropping onto her bed and staring at the ceiling.

Evie's head was spinning. Never once did she think she would be stuck in this situation. Ever since BB and CC had been turned in, all she ever wanted was to buy their freedom. If she took Mr. Huntley's offer, Ryder would be free to try and work off BB and CC's debt. As a laborer, his skills would easily help him get a good job. He would make much more money than she would out of debt. But that meant basically selling herself to Mr. Huntley.

What bothered her the most was his demand of her in return for Ryder's freedom.

Why would he want to marry her? Mr. Huntley called her a treasure and told her that he had waited for someone like her. Why? Why was she so special? He knew nothing about her on any personal level.

Then, there was Aaron. She couldn't deny that she had feelings for him. He was a good man and always treated Ryder, BB, and CC as if they were his own family. He was also turned in by his own parents, like her and her siblings. Aaron more than understood the pain of being thrown away for money.

With a sigh, she closed her eyes.

Evie knew a life with Aaron wouldn't change much of anything in her current situation.

She would only be able to see him once a week and have to share that time with Ryder, BB, and CC. The times they could possibly be intimate would force them to trade cigarettes for condoms along with finding a private place to be alone. And God forbid if an accident happened and she became pregnant while in debt.

Then there was a possible life with Mr. Huntley.

He divorced his previous wives due to becoming tired of them. How long would it be until he did the same to her? In no way did she want to become one of the arrogant and delusional high-standing members of the Community. She felt completely alone and out of place at the party Mr. Huntley had forced her to attend. Evie knew that's exactly how she would feel every day is she married to Mr. Huntley.

A couple of cold tears leaked out of Evie's eyes. *"When will I ever get a chance at something for myself?"*

As if struck by lightning, she bolted right up in her bed.

Ryder was right. All her life, she thought about everyone but herself. Didn't she deserve something good in life? The Community had taken everything from her. All her life she had no freedom and was subjected to serving high members of the Community who treated her like she was nothing. But she wasn't nothing to Aaron. Mr. Huntley saw her as something to own. But to Aaron, she was a woman to love and respect.

Evie jumped out of bed and quickly put on her sneakers. She needed to hurry, as she didn't have much time. As quietly as possible, Evie left the bedroom and crept down the stairs.

Upon reaching the last set of stairs, she almost ran into Mary.

Mary jumped at the sight of Evie. "What are you doing up this late? Get to bed!"

Evie smiled, side-stepping her. "There's somewhere I need to go! Don't bother waiting for me. Lock the door. I'll be back before it's time to work!"

She rushed to the door but stopped when Mary called down to her.

"What in the world are you doing?"

She turned and gave Mary a large smile. "Thinking about myself for once!" Evie didn't hear her response as she sprinted out the door.

She ran as fast as she could down the road leading to the Laborer's Unit. If she didn't make it in time, it would be sealed for the night. Then, she would be locked outside until morning and forced to find a place to hide until she could go back to Mr. Huntley's house. Evie considered it to be a blessing that there were no Harvester vans patrolling the area; otherwise, she may have been caught.

Her legs were aching in pain by the time she reached the unit. Evie breathed a sigh of relief when she saw the open gates. She forced herself to hurry inside and begin to frantically look around. A crowd of laborers slowly made their way into their housing units. Evie prayed she could catch him in time.

As she ran towards the group, Evie began screaming for the one she was looking for.

"Aaron! Where are you?"

The group of men turned to see Evie, bent over and panting. Her lungs burned, but she forced herself to continue calling out. "Please, I'm looking for Aaron!"

"Evie?"

A large figure moved through the crowd, and she smiled at the sight of him. Aaron was shirtless and covered in the sweat of a hard day of work. Ryder stepped up behind him, appearing just as concerned, but Evie paid him no mind.

She was here for Aaron.

Both men came forward, but Evie summoned the last of her energy and ran right for Aaron. He barely had time to open his arms to catch her as she practically tackled him. He stumbled back a few steps, just barely stopping himself from falling to the ground.

"Jesus Christ, what are you—"

He didn't have the chance to finish. In a flash, Evie rose up on her toes to reach his face. In an instant, she pulled him in for a kiss. All those around them froze and watched in awe at what was unfolding in front of them. Even Ryder was unsure of what his sister was doing.

Aaron was in complete shock when she finally pulled away from him. He stared at her, mouth agape, and tears stung her eyes. She ignored them. She ignored all the other men around them. Even her brother.

All she saw was Aaron.

"Evie, what are you—"

She cut him off again. "I choose you!"

There was another stretch of silence as Evie wrapped her arms around Aaron. Her head was against his chest and she could hear his heart pounding. The sweat on his body didn't bother her at all. She never wanted to let him go.

"I choose you! I want to be with you in whatever way I can be! For once in my life, I want some happiness of my own! I want happiness with you!"

For a short while, all she could hear was his heart beating against her ear. Without warning, he grabbed her chin and gently made her look up at him.

"Say it again," he said low, so no one else could hear.

Evie did not whisper. She didn't care who listened in. "I choose you! I want happiness with you!"

They stared at each other for several long moments. Neither of them noticed those around them smiling at the sight.

"Aaron…I love you."

He didn't wait a second longer. His arms wrapped back around her and he lifted her up with ease. Aaron's lips found hers, and Evie was more than happy to respond, kissing him back. The crowd burst into cheers and applause. Ryder was also grinning from ear to ear, happy to see both Evie and Aaron together at last.

Aaron and Evie pulled away from each other, both of them unspeakably joyous. He held onto her as if he never wanted to let her go. Evie smiled, feeling true happiness for the first time in her life.

More cheering and even whistling swarmed the two of them as Evie held him close to her. Aaron grew aggravated. He turned to snap at the group of smiling men. "Jesus, guys, can we get some privacy?"

Finally, the workers dispersed, leaving them alone. Ryder gave his sister a smile and she happily returned the sentiment. Before the last of them entered the building, one of the men stepped back outside.

"Hey! You guys need this more than I do!" The man tossed a small pack towards them before walking back into the building.

Aaron and Evie looked down. It was a condom.

She blushed while Aaron shook his head. As soon as all the men were gone, he turned back to Evie. "What made you decide?"

She took a breath before answering. "I just want to do something for myself for once. Ryder was right about BB and CC. They can learn their skills and use them once they are free. I want some happiness for once in my life. I want to be with you."

He smiled down at her. "I can't give you everything he can, Evie. Huntley has a lot more to offer you."

Evie shook her head. "I don't care. I don't want to be owned by anyone. I want to be with someone I love. I just want you."

Aaron's expression softened, and their lips met once more. Soon, the kiss became deeper. His hands ran down her back, and her hands ran up his chest. Evie pressed herself harder against him, and he moaned.

Before another move could be made, a loud sound made them both jump. Two men had just closed and locked the gate to the Laborer's Unit.

Evie giggled, blushing. "Guess I'm stuck here for the night."

Aaron pulled her close again. "I have no problem with that."

He bent down to kiss her neck, but she pushed on his chest slightly. "We can't stay out here like this. Someone will see."

Without hesitating, Aaron threw Evie over his shoulder and turned towards the large storage building next to the housing unit.

"Don't forget the condom," Evie said with a laugh.

She'd meant it as a joke, but Aaron quickly grabbed the small package off the ground and, for a moment, she felt as if she could fall. He quickly took off towards the large building, heavily breathing the entire way. The door was easily pushed open and he slammed it shut behind them.

Evie couldn't see a thing. There was not a single speck of light inside the building. Aaron was breathing hard as he ran through. He must have known exactly where to go. Turning on the lights wasn't an option. Someone could see the lights from outside and possibly discover them. After several turns, Aaron gently placed Evie on the ground, and she heard a door open. He led her though the darkness by the hand, his grip soft and sure. Without warning, he turned and gave her another hard kiss.

Evie was then gently laid down on a soft surface. She assumed it was a storage room for the housing units. Probably blankets and pillows. Evie didn't get the chance to think about it further, as she felt Aaron's weight on top of her. His lips found hers, and his hands traveled over her body. She closed her eyes and enjoyed the feeling.

His hands and lips didn't leave her body for a moment and gently, he removed her clothes. Once she was completely bare to him, she took the opportunity to lift her legs up and he was between them. She heard a loud groan of pleasure. After his pants were removed, she heard the small package being opened.

Evie tensed for the pain, her eyes closing and her head turning to the side. She had a brief education on sex in school, and it was only to tell the girl how painful it was and how they would be punished if they became pregnant while in debt.

Aaron gently turned her head to look at him. "Evie...do you want this?"

She took a deep breath, then nodded.

Very slowly, he pushed himself inside of her. She hissed in pain and tried to stop the tears from falling. Evie didn't know what to expect for her first time. Pain ripped through her abdomen while Aaron tried not to move. She could hear his heavy breathing and moans.

"Y-you ok?' he asked between breaths.

She wrapped her arms tightly around him and nodded.

"C-can I move?" She felt him begin to shake. It was obvious he desperately wanted more.

She nodded again and braced herself for more pain as he slowly began to move.

Aaron's every move and touch were done in an attempt to make Evie feel pleasure. He was trying to make her feel the same amazing feeling he did. After a few moments, she could feel the pain slowly dissolve and heat began to rise inside of her.

She moaned as his movements increased. Her arms tightened around him and he picked up his pace. He panted and thrusted harder. Within minutes, she felt her body fill with heat and her climax hit her hard. Aaron was quick to follow, his groan echoing through the room.

By the end of it, both were equally satisfied.

Aaron held Evie tight in his embrace as they slept. Evie would trade the large comfortable bed at Mr. Huntley's house for the small storage room if it meant she could always be with Aaron. Throughout the night, she heard his heartbeat as she laid on his chest. His fingers would randomly trace patterns on her skin while he slept, making her smile.

For the first time in her life, Evie felt selfish, and she had no regrets.

Chapter 10

After an unknown amount of time, Evie's eyes fluttered open, and the sunrise shone through the small window in the room. She was finally able to see enough of the room, and she had been right. The room stored extra blankets and pillows for the housing units. Several shelves lined the dull gray walls. Aaron was happily sleeping right next to her, still snoring. Evie loved how peaceful he looked while asleep. Unfortunately, she had to wake him up.

"Aaron? I need to get going."

He groaned and forced his eyes open. When he saw her face, his own broke out into a huge grin. "Can we just replay last night really quick?"

Evie smiled back. "I wish we could, but I have to get back to Mr. Huntley's house."

They both slowly stood and began to dress. Evie ignored how sore she was. Work was going to be tough today, but she didn't care. It was all worth it. Before she could turn to face Aaron, he came up behind her and wrapped his arms around her.

"Marry me this Sunday. We can do something here. Or at the Children's Unit. I don't care where."

Evie smiled, leaning closer into his embrace. "I don't need all that. Not a ceremony or a ring. I just want you."

He smiled against her neck. "I want one. With BB and CC there. Ryder can give you away. Yeah, it will be lame as hell. But I want to have something. Maybe I can come up with some kind of ring for you."

Evie gazed up into his eyes. "If that's what you want, then I'll wait."

They had one more deep kiss before Aaron led her out of the building. The space was lined with shelves and many boxes of unknown contents. The walls were the same dull gray as the room they exited and it was obvious the building was old. He peeked out of the door and looked towards the gates.

"The gates are unlocked. You can get back to the house now." Aaron turned back to Evie.

"You won't get in trouble for being out like this, will you?"

She shook her head. "I left after work was done, and I'll be back in time to start for the day. I should be fine as long as I hurry."

"Do you want me to walk you back?"

Her gaze grew softer. "I'll be fine. You need to start work before I do."

He smiled. "I'll make sure to tell Ryder about Sunday. We'll figure something out."

The mere thought gave her butterflies. "I can't wait."

They shared one final kiss, and Evie took off back to Mr. Huntley's house. Evie knew she had to hurry, but she didn't feel as rushed as she had last night. Her fear now was that Mary may not have unlocked the front door yet.

By the time she reached the house, her lungs were burning. Very slowly, she tried to open the front door. She gave a breath of relief to find it unlocked. Evie quietly crept inside and made her way to the kitchen. The large clock on the wall read six-fifteen. She was late. Evie hoped Mr. Huntley was still asleep.

Evie opened the kitchen door to see Mary over the stove top, no doubt cooking Mr. Huntley's breakfast.

The woman didn't look up from her cooking. "You're fifteen minutes late."

Evie gave her a wry grin. "I'll take whatever punishment you give me. It was worth it."

Mary lightly laughed as she flipped the eggs.

"Does Mr. Huntley know that I was gone?"

"I doubt it. He usually wakes up around now, so I think you got here just in time."

Evie nodded in understanding. "I'll go get changed and hurry back."

"You better. Just because you met up with your new boyfriend last night doesn't mean you get to slack off today."

Evie couldn't stop herself from blurting out her next words, "You mean fiancée."

Mary's head whipped around to look at Evie, but she had already disappeared up the stairs to her room, giggling.

Evie changed quickly into her work clothes. She was thankful she was able to get back downstairs before she saw or heard any evidence of Mr. Huntley being awake. She knew at some point that day she would need to confront him. As she tended to the garden, Evie tried to think of the right words to say to him. She felt that he was a man that was never told no.

After lunch, Evie decided it was time. She needed to be brave and face him.

Trembling, she gently knocked on the door to his study.

"Come in."

Evie took a deep breath and entered. She forced herself to stand tall as she stood in front of his desk. Mr. Huntley was bent over, scribbling away at some paperwork. "Sorry to disturb you, sir. But I have made a decision on your offer."

Mr. Huntley paused his writing and gracefully placed his pencil to the side. He sat up straight in his chair and faced her head on, his eyes flashing with an emotion she couldn't quite place. Evie swallowed.

"I appreciate your offer, but I won't be able to accept it."

She saw a muscle twitch on his jaw, but otherwise, he remained stoic and unmoving.

"And why is that?"

She considered her words carefully. "I can't leave it up to my brother to pay off my siblings' debt. I can't let him do it alone. I truly appreciate your offer, but I need to help free them as well. I won't let him deal with that burden alone."

The more she thought about it, the more she realized that she would have turned down Mr. Huntley's offer even without Aaron's feelings for her. She wouldn't let Ryder do it alone. A life of comfort wasn't going to temp her to leave all the burden on Ryder to free them. She was going to work with him to free BB and CC.

And now she had Aaron to help her, as well.

There was a long silence as Mr. Huntley considered her words.

"I'm not sure what to say. I'm not used to being rejected. And now twice by you."

Her heart continued to pound in her chest. "I mean no offence. I really appreciate the offer…but I can't do that to my brother. I'll still be turning myself in to help free them from debt."

He said nothing for a while, and she felt goosebumps slowly rise on her arms.

Finally, Mr. Huntley stood. He continued staring into Evie's eyes as he slowly made his way towards her. She forced herself to stand tall and not look away. His lack of expression scared her, as she had no idea what he could be thinking.

Mr. Huntley was now only a few inches away from her. Then, very slowly, he raised his hand and tucked a loose strand of hair behind her ear.

"And there's nothing I can do to change your mind?"

Evie took a step back. It was a risky move, but she needed space. "No sir. I appreciate your offer, and I will continue to work hard for you. But I can't marry someone I hardly know."

He took a step forward, making her blood run cold. "That would change over time, Evie. We'll have plenty of time to get to know each other."

She inhaled and took another step. Her fear of him was slowly fading. She wasn't sure why, but she was thankful. "Maybe, but I also won't marry someone I don't love."

He didn't step forward this time, but Evie could have sworn his eyes had grown darker.

"Is there someone else?"

Evie blinked. She hadn't expected that question. "I'm sorry, sir?"

Mr. Huntley took another step closer to her. She clenched her fists in frustration of him invading her personal space.

"Is there someone else? Is that why you turned down my offer?"

A shiver ran down her spine, and her palms began to sweat. What would he do if he found out about Aaron?

"No, sir. I'm rejecting your offer because I feel it's what's best to help my family."

He raised a brow. "So, there is no other reason for you rejecting me? No one else you are rejecting me for?"

Evie swallowed. She wouldn't lie to him, but she wouldn't tell him about Aaron either.

This wasn't about Aaron. It was about her family.

"No, sir."

Evie could have sworn she saw a flash of anger in his eyes, but it was gone before she could be sure. He took a step away from her and gave her a small smile.

"I see. I appreciate your honesty. Thank you."

He made no gesture to indicate so, but Evie could tell she had been dismissed. She gave him a polite smile and a nod before leaving his study.

Evie didn't realize until she was back downstairs that she was shaking. Her legs felt heavy and goosebumps ran down her arms. She took a deep breath and went to help Mary in the kitchen, trying to ignore her body's reaction to leaving the study.

For the next few days, Evie felt a smile on her face almost every moment of the day and she could hardly sleep from her excitement. It was Friday. In two days, she would have her abnormal wedding with Aaron. She even found herself humming while working in the garden and cleaning the house.

In the evening, Mary and Evie worked to finish cleaning the kitchen, both ready to retire for the night. It was then that a voice startled them.

"Good evening."

Both women jumped at Mr. Huntley's voice. Neither of them had noticed him entering the kitchen. His face wasn't cruel or judgmental towards Evie for her rejection of him; rather, a small smile played on his lips.

"Evie, I know this is last minute, but I need you to accompany me again tonight." Her stomach coiled with worry, and she felt anxiety rise in her chest.

"I'm sorry, sir. I wasn't aware you had plans tonight," Mary stated, setting down the plates she had been scrubbing. "When do you need to leave?"

Mr. Huntley's eyes never leave Evie's, even while Mary spoke.

"Immediately. There's no reason for you to change. Please, come with me."

Mr. Huntley said the words like a complete gentleman, but Evie felt the command in his voice. She gave one last pleading look to Mary before turning to leave the kitchen with Mr. Huntley.

With his hand on her back, led her out of the house. A large black car was waiting for them on the other side of the gate. Ever the gentleman, he opened the door for Evie then made his way to the opposite side to enter the vehicle.

Evie's heart pounded in her chest. Something was terribly wrong. She was sure of it.

"Sir, is there business you need to attend to?" Evie was desperate to break the silence.

"Yes," he said simply, continuing to look through the car window.

Evie noticed they had exited the Community Board Unit and were making their way towards the most run-down part of the Community. The building looked worn down due to years of abandonment. Windows were either broken or boarded up with planks of wood.

"Can you please tell me why I'm accompanying you again?" she asked politely.

"All will be made clear very soon."

Evie was confused, but she didn't dare push the matter.

Finally, the car stopped in front of a large black building. Vines and several other weeds grew around the building, yet the windows and doors appeared to be in good condition. It towered over the black car, the night sky making it look darker than it was.

Mr. Huntley exited the car and assisted in helping Evie out of her seat. Next, he led her inside the formidable structure in front of them while the driver remained in his seat.

The paint on the walls was faded and peeling. It was obvious that no one had inhabited the building for many years. The musty smell filled her nostrils and almost made her feel sick. Mr. Huntley guided her down several hallways and finally opened a large metal door at the end of a narrow corridor. Her legs trembled, and she didn't move from her spot in the hallway.

"In here, please," he said politely.

Evie took a breath and entered the room. Mr. Huntley followed behind her and she flinched when the metal door closed behind them. The room was small with a mirror stretching across the far wall. A single lightbulb lit the room from the ceiling.

The room was suffocating, and Evie fought the urge to run back outside. She had no idea why Mr. Huntley could possibly bring her to this building.

Mr. Huntley made his way to stand in front of her, his large frame leaning against the mirror. His face had no expression, making Evie tremble. He gave no hint of what he could be thinking.

"Evie…the one thing I despise the most is lying. No matter how hard the truth is, it's all I ever want to hear."

Evie clenched her fists, trying to steady herself.

His eyes suddenly narrowed, and she knew the point of this trip was finally here. "I will ask you one last time… Was there someone else you rejected me for?"

Evie felt a sudden flash of rage through her body, making her next words come out sharp and biting. "I told you my reason, sir. That answer will not change."

Mr. Huntley raised a brow. "Is that so?"

Evie stood up straight, refusing to let him intimidate her. The quiet in the room was suffocating until he finally spoke again.

"While telling a lie may be what seems like the best solution, the truth is the only thing I will ever allow."

Evie's brows furrowed in confusion as Mr. Huntley raised his hand up and flipped a small switch against the opposite wall. A light lit up from behind the mirror and he stepped aside.

It was a one-way mirror. Aaron stood on the opposite side of the room, looking confused and angry.

Evie gasped, staggering forward to rest her fingers against the cool glass. Already, tears stung her eyes, threatening to overflow. She swallowed hard, willing her legs to stop shaking.

"Sir, please… I-I didn't …" She didn't have the strength to finish her sentence.

"Evie, you need to learn this lesson very quickly. I do not tolerate lies."

Once again, his hand went to the side of the wall where he pressed a small button. A loud buzzing sound echoed in both rooms, and the door to Aaron's room opened. Three very large men entered the room. Without any warning, one man stepped forward and punched Aaron, the blow splattering blood from his lips.

Evie screamed and pounded on the glass as the other three men approached Aaron. He fought as hard as he could, but there was nothing he could do against three men that were just as large as he was. He was outnumbered. Their attacks were fast and brutal, landing on his face, torso and legs. More blood came. When he finally collapsed to the dirty floor, they continued. Kick after kick tore into his abdomen, making him scream in agony.

Evie shrieked, trying to hold back her sobs. In a panic, she turned to Mr. Huntley and grabbed his jacket, "Please, make it stop! I'm sorry! Please, just make it stop!"

Mr. Huntley stared down at her for several seconds before lazily lifting his hand to press the button again. As soon as the buzzing sound went off, the three men backed away from Aaron. Evie released Mr. Huntley's jacket and turned back to the mirror. Aaron was curled up on the floor, trembling in pain. His nose was clearly broken, and he was wheezing, still spitting blood. There was no doubt that they probably broke several bones in his body. Her heart sank.

Evie placed her head against the glass and closed her eyes, sniffling. She felt Mr. Huntley step up behind her, his warmth seeping into her and making her cringe. She hated him, and she'd never forgive him.

"Now, he will recover. It will take some time, but he'll be able to return to work. However, what would happen if his spine was broken? If he broke his leg or arm beyond repair? What happens, Evie, when an injury won't be worth fixing? When an injury no longer allows him to work off his debt?"

Evie lifted her head and pressed her forehead against the glass. Aaron was still curled up on the floor and the three men appeared ready to finish what they had started.

She felt Mr. Huntley's breath on the back of her neck. "What happens, Evie?"

Evie could only whimper out her answer, "...Medical Waste..."

He towered over her small frame and placed his hand on her shoulder, steadying her. "Do you know what happens at Medical Waste, Evie?"

She buried her face in her hands and sobbed.

"It starts with blood extraction. They take all the blood they can and save it for the hospitals. Then, they check and see if anyone in the Community needs an organ transplant or bone marrow. Nothing will go to waste." Mr. Huntley bowed his head down to speak right into her ear, his voice hollow and sinister. "And they don't waste money on things like pain relievers and numbing agents. They wouldn't waste those things on Medical Waste subjects."

He stood straight again but left his hand on her shoulder, sending unpleasant shivers down her spine.

"Now, will you ever lie to me again, Evie?"

Evie clenched her fists and leaned her head back against the glass. "No...I swear on my life...I won't lie to you..."

His hand on her shoulder tightened. "It isn't your life you're swearing on, Evie. It's his... and your brothers' and sister's lives."

Evie felt a terrible stab of pain in her chest. Now it was a threat against her entire family. Not just Aaron.

His hand finally let go before he raised his finger to the button again. Evie gasped.

"No!" she screamed, turning and grabbing his hand. "Please, I promised you! Please, leave him alone! You've done enough!" Evie let go of his hand and grabbed onto his jacket again. She sobbed into his chest while he stared blankly down at her. "Please…please, stop this…"

There was a long silence in the room. While still looking down at her, Mr. Huntley raised his hand and pressed the button again. Panic coursed through her at the buzzing sound. She turned and looked into the window.

The three men swiftly came to Aaron and gently picked him up off the floor. They carried him out of the room before the door slammed shut behind them.

"He will be taken to the hospital. It's a shame so much money in medical bills will be added onto his debt."

The way Mr. Huntley spoke to Evie almost caused her to lose the contents of her stomach. He spoke as if they were having a casual conversation about the weather. Not about him possibly killing her family or ruining their lives.

Evie continued shivering against the glass, and Mr. Huntley came to stand closer. "Never lie to me again." With that final warning, he turned and left the room. The door was open and ready for her to follow behind him.

Evie sobbed and pressed both hands against the window. "I'm sorry…Aaron, I'm so sorry."

Chapter 11

Evie couldn't make herself get out of bed Saturday morning. She found herself running back and forth from the bathroom to vomit. When there was nothing left in her system, her stomach ached in pain. The more she thought about the previous day's events, the more her hatred for Huntley grew. The man was no longer Mr. Huntley to her. Calling him Mr. Huntley implied respect.

To Evie, he was simply Huntley.

She had no idea how much time had passed until Mary knocked on the bedroom door. Time was going by in a flurry of worry, and she was trying to forget the nightmare she was living in.

"Evie?" Mary opened the door slowly, letting some light into the large room. "Evie, where are you?"

She flipped on the light switch and saw Evie curled up on the floor.

"Evie?" Mary quickly came over and knelt over the shaking woman. She grabbed her shoulder and gave it a hard shake. "Evie, wake up! What's wrong?"

Evie groaned and forced her eyes open. She had forgotten that she'd laid on the floor rather than return to the bed after her last trip to the bathroom. "Mary...what time is it?"

"It's seven in the morning. What's going on with you? Are you sick?"

Evie shuddered and turned away from Mary. "Please don't make me work today...I can't do it...I don't care what he does to me..."

She began softly crying again, and Mary immediately knew Evie wasn't sick.

"Hun, tell me what's wrong. What happened? Is this about Mr. Huntley taking you out last night?"

Evie nodded and began sobbing harder. Her face grew puffy and her eyes stung. "He...he had Aaron beaten within an inch of his life! Huntley claimed I lied to him about choosing Aaron over him. But I would have turned down his offer with or without Aaron! And he almost killed him!" Evie yelled onto the floor while Mary rubbed her back gently.

"Was he taken to the hospital?" Mary asked quietly.

Evie nodded, rubbing her eyes.

"It's okay, hun. I'll take care of things today. I'm going to bring you up some soup."

Evie shook her head. "I'm not hungry."

"I don't care. You're eating it," Mary chided, giving her a flat look. "You can't make yourself sick like this. You need to eat to keep your strength up. Remember, tomorrow is Sunday. Build yourself back up and go see your family."

Mary rose from the floor and forced Evie onto her feet.

"You can't stay on the floor. Get into bed, at least. Mr. Huntley is in his study already. If he asks, I'll tell him you're sick."

Evie snorted. "I don't care what he thinks. I don't care what he does to me."

Mary had no words. Evie was practically pushed into bed before the woman swiftly exited the room.

Mary was true to her word and brought soup, but it went ignored until she physically couldn't stop herself from eating it. The soup had long since turned cold, but she didn't care. Her mind wouldn't stop replaying Aaron's torture as he was beaten within an inch of his life. All because of her. And now, he was facing even more debt. She wasn't even sure it would be possible for him to be free from the Community anymore.

Evie didn't realize how much time had passed until Mary brought her dinner.

"Evie? How are you feeling?"

She had stopped crying hours ago and was now sitting in the middle of the bed. Her eyes were red and sore. "Like shit," Evie answered bluntly.

Mary gave her a small smile and placed the large tray in front of her on the bed. "I don't blame you." She lifted the lid off the plate and Evie was greeted with the smell of roasted pork loin and potatoes.

"Mary, please…I'm really not hungry."

The woman shook her head. "No, you need to eat. You can't keep blaming yourself for this. Eat and feel better so you can go visit your family tomorrow." She gave her a small pat on the shoulder and exited the room. Evie forced herself to eat the food, not wanting to waste it.

Evie knew she would always blame herself, but Mary was right about one thing: She needed to get stronger. She needed to feel better so she could visit her family tomorrow. She needed to continue to fight for her brothers and sister. But it would be too dangerous to see Aaron again. No, she had to stay away from him. For his sake.

After what felt like an eternity, Evie forced herself to look at the small clock on the wall. It was four in the morning. She slid off the bed and got dressed. She didn't care what time it was.

As far as Evie was concerned, it was Sunday.

Evie quietly exited the room and made her way down the stairs. Silently, she unlocked the door and slipped outside. The air felt like a blessing compared to the large bedroom she'd locked herself in for the day. The sun hadn't even risen yet, but Evie didn't care. She began slowly making her way to the Laborer's Unit. Most likely, she would have to wait outside the gates before she could get in to see her brother.

Her feet controlled where she was going, but her mind was elsewhere. Huntley had claimed that he'd done this because she'd lied to him. But was that really the reason? Was he that angry at the rejection? Evie hadn't lied about anything. She would have turned him down despite Aaron's feelings for her.

No, there had to be something else to all of this.

Evie reached the front gates and, sure enough, they were still locked. She sat back against the gate and shivered. Her mind was far away from the chill that ran down her spine and the cold air blowing through her hair. It was another hour and a half before one of the laborers appeared and unlocked the gate. He gave Evie an odd look as she stood to enter.

"Ain't it a little early?" the man snapped.

Evie ignored him and trudged inside the unit. She waited another twenty minutes before men slowly started coming out of the housing units. As soon as Evie saw Ryder, she ran right to him.

Ryder was clearly surprised to see his sister so early. He had usually been the one to meet her outside first. He gave her a tight hug after she ran into his arms. "Evie, you ok?"

She didn't cry, but she held onto him for dear life, as if he'd be gone forever. That they all would be. Evie buried her face in his chest, holding back a sob.

He wrapped his arms around her, and they stood there for several moments. "Did you hear about Aaron?" Ryder asked lightly.

Evie now felt tears come to her eyes when she looked up at her brother. "What have you heard?" she asked, still fighting the urge to cry.

Ryder sighed, pulling back to look at her. "I heard he had a bad accident. He was sent to another location to do some welding work. They took him to the hospital. I don't know any more details."

Evie couldn't hold back her tears anymore and began sobbing. She held him tighter and cried harder than she'd ever cried before. None of this felt real.

"Hey, it's going to be okay! He's strong, so he'll heal quickly. I'm sorry we can't have your wedding until then, but—"

Evie began to cry harder, her entire body trembling. "There isn't going to be a wedding!" she exclaimed through ragged breaths.

Ryder was silent for several moments. Finally, he took a step back. "Evie…what's going on?"

She continued shaking, staring to the ground in guilt. "It…it wasn't an accident. It was my fault. He got hurt because of me."

Ryder forced her face up to meet his eyes. His eyes narrowed and his teeth were grinding together. "Evie, what are you talking about?"

Evie closed her eyes and took a breath. She owed it to Ryder to tell him the truth.

"I refused Huntley's offer. I told him I couldn't leave it up to you to work off BB and CC's debt. He asked me if I was choosing someone else over him. I told him no. I wasn't lying! I just didn't want you to have to pay off BB and CC's debt alone! But somehow he found out about Aaron…and…"

Another wave of impenetrable sadness took hold of her, threatening to never let go. She bowed her head in shame.

"Huntley made me watch as he was beaten within an inch of his life! He made me watch!" Her voice was hoarse now, wavering with sobs. Ryder silently listened, not interrupting. "It's my fault… It's all my fault. Even when he heals, I can't see him again… I can't let anything happen to him."

Evie sniffled, and Ryder clenched his fists, seething with rage. He'd heard enough of his sister's crying and forced her to look up to him, his hand under her chin.

"Evie, listen to me. It isn't your fault! This is all Huntley! He's a sadistic bastard, and you need to get out of that house!"

Evie wiped her eyes and tried to take a step back, shooting him an incredulous look. "How am I supposed to do that? The only way I can get out of his house is if he sends me back."

Ryder shook his head. "No, you can go to the Distribution Center and request a transfer. Yes, it's a penalty on you, but you need to get out of that house."

Evie's instincts screamed against the idea of adding onto her debt, but she knew that might be her only choice.

"And what happens when I transfer out? What's to stop him from coming after Aaron again? He can come after you too, along with BB and CC!"

"Evie, we will all be fine! You need to get out of that house! It's way too dangerous for you to stay there." He stepped forward and grabbed his sister's hands. "Get to the Distribution Center. I'll go get BB and CC. Meet up with us at the Children's Unit. Go early so hopefully you won't be waiting all day. Ask to speak to your case worker and make him put in a transfer request."

He quickly wrapped his arms back around her.

"I'm gonna ask around a little bit and see what I can find out about Huntley. I want to see if I can figure out how he found out about you and Aaron."

Evie nodded before tearing off down the street. She was glad to get everything off her chest and speak to Ryder. But no matter what anyone else said, she would always blame herself for Aaron's injuries. Perhaps Ryder was right. Maybe if she got out of Huntley's house, it would all end. Maybe Huntley would lose interest in her and leave her and her family alone.

All she could do was try.

She ignored the sounds of the passing Harvester Vans and motorbikes as she made her way to her destination. The Distribution Center opened right at eight in the morning. Evie was the first one to walk in through the doors, and she headed straight for the front desk.

"How can I help you today?" the woman asked in a bored, monotone voice. Her thin blonde hair fell around her face, making it hard for Evie to properly see her.

"I'm number six-seven-seven-five. I need to speak to my caseworker."

The woman rolled her eyes and did some typing on her keyboard. Evie could finally see her pale blue eyes and skin. The woman looked as if she hadn't been in the sun for years.

"Your assigned caseworker is off today. You'll have to come back tomorrow."

Evie felt a rush of panic. "This is an emergency! I need to make a transfer request."

The woman stopped typing and gave Evie a skeptical look. "A transfer request?"

Evie nodded. "Yes, please. If I can't speak to Marcos, I need to speak to someone! I need to transfer out as soon as possible!"

The woman cocked her head before gesturing to the waiting area. "Take a seat. You'll see the first available caseworker."

Evie gave a nod of thanks and sat down in one of the metallic chairs. She looked up and the large plaque was still across the room. Several months ago, she was sitting in the exact same seat in which she was waiting to be assigned to Huntley's house. Now, she was waiting to try and get transferred out of it.

After waiting for about thirty minutes, her number was finally announced over the intercom. "Number six-seven-seven-five, report to office fourteen."

Evie took a breath and made her way to the room. She needed to be completely respectful and hope they could help her. Eventually, she found the office door and knocked. This time, she waited to be called into the room.

"Come in."

Hearing a phrase so often used by Huntley made a sour taste form in her mouth. Bracing herself, she entered the room to see an older woman sitting at a large desk. Her brown hair had several streaks of gray and her brown eyes had small bags under them. She gestured for Evie to take the seat across from her. "So, I hear you want a transfer?"

Evie nodded as she sat on the chair. "Yes, ma'am. As soon as possible."

"Are you aware that if you do this transfer, it will be a heavy fine added onto your debt?"

Evie took a deep breath, then nodded again. "I understand."

The woman brought out a form and began filling it out. "If you are being abused in any way, you have the right to make a transfer at no penalty to you. Do you want us to do an investigation?"

Evie quickly shook her head. "No, I just need to get out of that house."

The woman raised a brow at Evie and gave her an irritated look. "So, you want to transfer with a heavy fine for no reason at all? Are you serious?"

Evie balled her fists and tried not to snap at the woman. "I just want to transfer out of that house, please!"

The woman began shaking her head. "No, I can't let you do this to yourself. If they aren't abusing you, then you can—"

Evie exploded, her words coming out hard and fast. "I want to transfer because I work for a man who is sadistic and threatened to harm every person I care about!" She hunched over in her seat, fighting back tears. "Please…please let me transfer out of that house." she begged.

Evie slowly sat up and looked at the old woman. When she looked at Evie, her eyes were soft and looked to be full of pity. The woman did some more typing at the computer and her eyes went wide.

"You work for Elias Huntley," she muttered to herself in disbelief.

Evie was silent as the woman turned back to the paperwork.

"Sign the bottom of the sheet. It will take five to seven days for the transfer of your contract to be completed. Your caseworker will come and pick you up once they successfully find you a new assignment. And there will be a considerable fine added onto your debt once you are no longer in your current household."

Evie's hand shook as she signed the bottom of the paper. Never in her life did she think she would ever fill out one of these forms. She now believed there was no way she would pay off her debt, but hopefully her family would be safe.

She quickly exited the building once the paperwork was completed. Evie desperately wanted to see her siblings. She doubted they would be allowed to visit Aaron, but Evie didn't want to take the risk even if they could.

Evie entered the Children's Unit, and the twins were swift to run into her arms once they saw her.

"Ryder said you had to go to the Distribution Center!" BB yelled. "What happened?"

Evie smiled at the twins. "I'm trying to go to a new house. I don't like the one I'm at."

Ryder quickly walked over to them. "Hey, guys. I need to talk to Evie alone. Can you both go see your other friends really quick?" The twins gave them a confused look before walking towards the playground where other children played.

She and her brother took a seat on a small bench that was near the playground.

"Did you do it?" Ryder asked.

Evie nodded. "Yeah. She said it would take five to seven days. I guess I have to have another assignment ready first."

Ryder nodded, mulling over his thoughts. "I tried asking a few buddies in my unit before I came here, but they don't know much about Huntley. We can go to the Underground tonight. I'm sure someone knows something about him."

Evie nodded but felt aggravated. She knew it was the best place to find out information, but she still hated going to the place. Especially after the Harvesters had raided the place not too long ago.

Ryder and Evie tried to make the most of their day for the sake of their younger brother and sister. They forced smiles until it was finally time for the twins to return to their unit. As soon as the twins were out of sight, they went to the Underground.

As always, the place was packed full of people. All of them were still desperate to escape reality for a short time. There was still noticeable damage from the Harvesters, but no one seemed to care, and they acted as if the raid had never happened.

Ryder turned to Evie and had to yell over the music for her to hear. "I'm going to ask around! You try the bar!"

Evie nodded and made her way over to the corner, walking along the wall to avoid all the people dancing in the center of the room. The woman behind the makeshift bar was as close to a bartender as this place would ever have. Her brown hair was in a tight ponytail and her muscles showed she must be working in either the Farming Unit or Lumber Unit. Evie always wondered how she made time to work in the bar when she had her debt to pay off. She finally found a seat at the corner of the bar just as the woman passed two beers to the men waiting across from her. Once they'd walked away, Evie gestured to the woman. She came over quickly, her mouth already turned up into a fake smile.

"What do you want? A beer is four cigarettes. Got no wine today,"

"No, that's not what I'm looking for."

"Well, if you don't want drinks then what do you want? Nathan is dealing weed and condoms in the back."

Evie shook her head. "No, I wanted to ask a couple of questions. I need to know if you know anything about Elias Huntley."

The woman appeared taken aback. "Huntley? Elias Huntley?"

Evie nodded, leaning in close over the bar. "Please, I work for him. I know he's a dangerous man. I need to know everything I can about him."

The woman hesitated before moving closer. "Look, I want to help you out, but what's in it for me? Nothing's free here."

Evie panicked. "Please, I don't have anything now, but I can repay you. I swear, I'll get whatever you want from the Distribution Center."

The woman scoffed. "I don't believe in false promises, and you shouldn't either. Nobody like us should."

Before she could walk away, Evie grabbed her hand.

"Listen to me!" she snapped. "The man threatened everyone I care about. I don't care what happens to me. He almost killed the man I love and threatened my family! Please…I need to know who this man really is."

Evie was on the verge of tears. The bartender stared back in shock, mouth agape. Evie slowly let the woman's hand go and tried not to completely sob in public, her cheeks already flushing in embarrassment. After several moments, the bartender sighed and leaned back closer to Evie.

"I only know rumors. Most of the rumors are that he runs the Medical Waste Facility. Some say he's in charge of finding delinquents to go to the facility. Sometimes, they're delinquents. Sometimes…they aren't. Then, I heard some shit about him providing the goods we trade down here. I don't know what's real and what isn't. I doubt all of them are true, if any of them are. Way I see it, he's just some kiss-ass to the Community council."

The woman stood straight, but she continued looking right into Evie's eyes.

"If any of them are true, you'd better watch your ass. Do what he says and keep your mouth shut. If you can, transfer out. There may be a fine attached, but it may be worth it if it means you get away from the bastard."

Evie nodded and gave her a small smile. "Thank you."

The woman grinned back before turning to serve the two new men that approached the bar. Evie quickly looked around and found her brother talking to a few men in the corner. She had no idea what time it was, but she needed to go back to Huntley's house. Evie quickly went over to him and tugged on his sleeve.

"I need to start heading back," she said over the loud music.

Ryder said a quick farewell to the men he was talking to then began following Evie out of the Underground. She was thankful for the rush of fresh air. The smell of the Underground always made her sick.

They began walking towards Huntley's house. Ryder was pale and visibly shaking.

"What did you find out?" Evie asked without looking at him.

"A lot of sick shit. And after what he did to Aaron, I wouldn't be surprised if it's all true, too."

"Tell me what you heard and I'll tell you what I've heard."

He looked around, making sure they were alone before speaking. "One guy said he runs the Medical Waste Facility. Another person said he trades black market goods."

Evie shuddered at the thought. "I heard the same stuff. You think any of it is true?" Ryder was silent for several moments.

"I'd like to think that none of it is true, but we both know the Community is fucked up. I don't think all of it is true, but one thing or another is."

Evie wrinkled her nose in disgust and shivered. She wasn't sure if it was the chill in the air or the thought that she was in the service of a man that did such evil things.

They soon reached the street of Huntley's house and Ryder gave Evie a tight hug.

"Be careful. You'll be out of that house soon. Whenever I hear news about Aaron, I'll let you know."

Evie nodded and began walking to the house. Before she could take another step, Ryder grabbed her hand and forced her to look back at him.

"Evie…if there was a way out…if Eden does exist…would you take the risk? If we could get BB, CC, and Aaron out of here, would you do it?" Evie was quiet before she answered.

"Yes. If BB, CC, and Aaron could be saved from this place, I'd take the risk with you."

Ryder had a small smile on his face when his sister turned back to the house. She dreaded every step she took, but knew she had no choice. Evie had a small amount of hope that she would be out of his house by the end of the week.

Mary met her as soon as she walked into the front door. The older woman had a grim expression, but she attempted to smile at Evie.

"Did you have a good day with your family?" she asked while locking the door.

"Yeah. It's always good to see them."

Mary was quiet for several moments. Evie could immediately tell she had something to tell her.

"Mary, are you okay?"

The woman sighed and met Evie's eyes. "Mr. Huntley ordered that you serve his meals from now on. Starting tomorrow morning, you have to deliver them to his study."

Evie clenched her fists and teeth, knowing she had no choice but to follow his order. She knew it was rude to Mary, but she said nothing and made her way up the stairs.

She hoped this would be the last week she ever had to serve him again.

Chapter 12

Evie forced herself to get out of bed in the morning. She decided to speak to Mary about changing rooms permanently and was now completely against staying in the large bedroom.

Maybe she could just sleep in the attic again and Huntley wouldn't notice.

The women forced themselves to eat their oatmeal. Then, Mary quickly sent herself to cook Huntley's breakfast while Evie did the dishes.

As soon as the breakfast tray was ready, Mary handed it to Evie. "Just go in, say good morning, leave the tray on his desk, then leave with his dinner dishes. That's all you have to do."

Evie gave a small nod and left the kitchen. Her feet felt heavy and her hands began shaking, but she forced herself to keep moving. As she approached his office, Evie balanced the tray on one hand while she gave a quick knock on the door.

"Come in."

Evie entered and avoided making eye contact. She was relieved to see he was bent over his desk busying himself with paperwork.

"Good morning, sir," she said as politely as possible.

"Good morning, Evie," he replied.

Evie quickly placed the tray down and made her way out with the dirty dinner dishes. She released a breath as she walked back to the kitchen. Perhaps he had lost interest in her. Maybe she could transfer out of the house with no problems. The thought made hope blossom in her chest.

The rest of the day dragged on uneventfully. Evie successfully delivered his food with no more than the exchange of greetings. She began to relax as the day came to an end.

Before it was time for bed, Evie took a steadying breath and addressed her friend.

"Mary...can we please switch rooms?"

Mary raised a brow. "Why?"

"I...I just can't stay in that room anymore. Either we switch, or I'm going back to the attic. I'd rather you take the room. You deserve it, anyway."

Mary was silent for several moments before speaking. "Evie, please just stay in there. If Mr. Huntley finds out, he may get angry."

Evie clenched her fists tightly at her sides. "I don't care! I don't care what he does to me!"

Mary stepped forward and placed her hands gently on her shoulders. "Hun, what about your family?"

She averted her gaze to the floor. "I can't stay in that room. I can't do it."

Mary gave Evie a tight hug. "I understand. I'll take the bedroom. Don't sleep in that damn attic."

Evie hugged Mary back, now feeling guilty. "I…I applied for a transfer. I thought you should know."

Mary took a step back and gave Evie a sad smile. "I figured you would. Just hang in there until it's time for you to leave."

She nodded. "I'm sorry to leave you here. I just can't stay here anymore."

"I know, hun. I understand. Go ahead and get to sleep. I'll take the big room. We can move our stuff around tomorrow."

Evie hurried upstairs and slipped into the guest room. She hoped that Huntley wouldn't notice or care.

Friday morning came, and Evie was losing hope of leaving quickly. Maybe Monday would be the day. She went to Huntley's room with his lunch. It was business as usual. She couldn't help but be thankful for that.

As she always did, she balanced the small tray with one hand and knocked on the door.

"Come in."

Evie entered and was surprised to see Huntley in his sitting area reading a large book rather than working at his desk. His back was facing her as he lounged in the large armchair. She quickly went to the desk and left his lunch tray.

"I'll leave your lunch here, sir."

It wasn't until she turned to leave that he finally spoke.

"Have you ever read this book, Evie?"

She turned and saw he raised the large tome so she could read the title.

The Epitome of Greed.

"No, sir, I haven't."

He lowered the book and appeared to go back to reading it. "You should read it. It's very good."

Evie took a breath and tried to be civil. "Thank you, sir, but I would rather concentrate on my work."

Huntley placed the book onto the small coffee table as he stood and walked over to his bookcase, his eyes locking on Evie. "I'm sure you have plenty of time. Work has gotten much easier without Sara and her ridiculous parties."

"Thank you, but I need to go back and help Mary in the kitchen." She tried to turn to leave again.

"Is it because you believe you're leaving soon?"

Evie felt her blood run cold, and she turned to look back at Huntley. Her face went pale when she saw him holding up a piece of paper.

It was her transfer request.

Huntley gave Evie a small smile. "Did you really think I wouldn't find out, Evie?"

She forced herself to face him head on and look into his dark eyes. But she couldn't stop herself from trembling. "I don't think it's appropriate for me to stay here any longer, sir."

He smirked and looked at the paper. "And why is that?"

She felt her patience wearing thin. "I think you know why, sir."

His smirk never faltered. Huntley slowly stalked over towards his desk. "And why should I allow you to transfer?"

Evie grinded her teeth together. "I don't understand why you would want me to stay! I've refused all of your offers, and you even accused me of lying to you!"

Huntley raised a brow. "I *accused* you of lying?"

"Yes! I told you, I didn't refuse your offer because of my feelings for another man! I didn't reject you for another person! I rejected your offer so my brother didn't have to work off my brother and sister's debt alone! It was never because of Aaron!" Evie was almost yelling by the time she was done speaking.

Huntley's expression hadn't changed at all. It remained cool and calculated.

"Then perhaps I owe you an apology."

She continued to clench her fists and glare at him. It was clear he didn't regret making Aaron suffer. Any apology he made would mean nothing to her.

Without looking away, his hand reached down to the side of his desk and pressed a button. Evie heard the sound of a machine she could not see.

"In any case, I won't allow you to be transferred."

Without looking away, Huntley dropped the paper and the sound of shredding followed. The transfer request had been destroyed.

His smile widened as she glared at him. "I'm sorry, Evie, but it took quite some effort to get you into my home. I won't be letting that effort go to waste."

He switched off the machine and Evie's eyes widened. "What are you talking about?"

Huntley leaned back against his bookshelf and the two stared into each other's eyes. Hers were full of fury, while his remained cold and emotionless.

"I can't let someone as selfless as you get away from me. I never thought someone like you existed in this disgusting place. But I was wrong. And for that, I am grateful."

Evie blinked. "Someone like me?"

"Yes. Someone who sacrifices so much for others and asks nothing in return."

"I only sacrifice for my family. I don't exactly sell my soul for every person I meet."

"But still. I've been in my position for a long time, Evie. Do you know how many people I have seen betray their own family for a taste of freedom? To try and live the same wasteful life as those in power? I've seen it many, many times, Evie. You are the first who was willing to give up everything for people you love."

Evie shook her head. "You're wrong. There are many others in debt that sacrifice for the people they love."

"There is only one other person in debt that may be as selfless as you, and she's already here in my house."

"You... you mean Mary?"

"Indeed. The mother who turned herself in for the sake of her child. Another rarity. All it took was a large bribe from her previous assignment and I transferred her contract to my house." His eyes suddenly narrowed. "Unfortunately, Oscar wasn't going to part with you for any amount."

Evie's legs began to tremble. "What does Mr. Hillard have to do with this?"

Huntley smirked. "Oscar and I spoke often. Mostly about literature. He had quite the collection of books. Most of them were very rare. I often tried to buy them from him, but he wouldn't budge." He gestured towards his bookcase. "I received all of them after his death. Including that copy of *Utopia* you love so much. That was his book."

Evie looked at the bookshelf and her eyes landed on the book. It was no wonder the book had the small dent on the spine. She cursed herself for her stupidity as It should have been obvious.

"Oscar was like me," Huntley continued. "He loved rare things. Especially books. I'm sure you can imagine my interest when he spoke about the young woman who was taking care of him. One who was willing to turn herself back in for the sake of her family." Evie's eyes flashed back to Huntley. He had a sick smile on his face.

"Sadly, Oscar wouldn't part with you for any amount I offered him."

Evie's stomach dropped. "Oscar didn't die of cancer," she whispered.

"Cancer was going to take him eventually, Evie. I made his passing peaceful."

Evie's hands covered her mouth as she fought not to get sick. "How? How did you...?"

"It was simple. I had connections to the hospital. All it took was changing some of his medications. It helped him pass away easily and without pain."

Tears fell from her eyes as she remembered their last day together. Mr. Hillard was looking and acting more tired than usual. And she was the one who had given him his medication.

She began shaking. Her anger was taking over all other emotions. Evie finally looked up and glared at Huntley. "You murdered an innocent old man, you bastard!" she yelled.

Huntley continued to smirk. Her anger seemed to amuse him.

"He was the only man in the Community who treated me like a human being!" she screamed. "And you killed him just to get me to work for you? You sadistic fuck!"

His smirk slowly disappeared from his face. "You think I did this just to get you to work for me?"

Evie didn't answer. She continued to shake and cry furious tears. Huntley's eyes briefly glanced to the ceiling, appearing to be thoughtful for a moment.

"Perhaps it started that way. But soon it became more than that. Especially when I learned that you and I are the same."

Evie was immediately offended. "I am nothing like you!"

"You are exactly like me!" Huntley snapped.

Evie felt a painful jolt of fear in her chest. This was the first time he had finally shown a hint of emotion during their exchange.

"You and I are exactly alike! We both believe this world is cruel and rotting from the inside out. You are just like me in many ways, Evie. I used to believe this world could change. But it didn't take long for me to learn that the Community is a dead end. It's a cruel and hopeless place."

"The Community is cruel and hopeless because of people like you! You help bring pain to every—"

"You don't know what pain is!" His yell echoed through the room. Evie's fear of him returned instantly. His face was now scowling, and for the first time since she had met him, he looked absolutely enraged.

He continued to look right into her eyes as he slowly began to walk towards her. "Do you know what it was like years ago for people in debt? Before I worked for the position and power I have today? The pain of everyone in debt was tenfold! Physical abuse, rape, and neglect were just the tip of the iceberg. So many died as a result. Starvation, infections due to injuries, and STDs infected the entire Community. All because those old bastards thought those in debt were worse than insects and treated them as such."

Evie began to back away from him when he began getting too close to her. He stopped his movements and inhaled deep, trying to compose himself.

"As I said, you don't know what pain is. You have no idea what it was like for us those years ago before I changed everything."

Evie froze at his words. "'For us'?"

"Yes, Evie. For us. Well, I suppose I should say for me."

"You were in debt?"

He nearly laughed. "Are you surprised?"

Evie couldn't even find the words to respond. Not once did she imagine that someone with his power started as a person in debt.

"Let me tell you how things used to be," he said. "Those bracelets around your wrists? They were around our necks. The day off you get every week didn't exist. We worked twenty-four hours a day, seven days a week. No time off to see any loved ones we may have had. We were beaten for no reason. Raped whenever they wanted to use us. We suffered from infections and diseases with no health care. They didn't care what happened to us."

Suddenly, he unbuttoned the cuff of his sleeve and rolled it up his arm.

"And those numbers you are assigned? They were branded onto us."

He straightened his arm and Evie could clearly see the scars.

FIVE-EIGHT-EIGHT-FOUR.

Evie's mouth was agape as he unrolled his sleeve.

"Should I remove my shirt so you can see the scars on my back? Would you like to physically see the extent of their torture on us?"

Her arms and legs went numb but she forced herself to remain standing.

Huntley stood tall with his eyes locked onto hers.

"It's because of me those in debt have so many privileges. I made it so abusing someone in debt could result in disciplinary action. The collars became bracelets and the days off were established so they could heal. So that they had a day to see their loved ones and feel like human beings again. As soon as I got enough power, I made the changes happen." Evie finally found the strength to speak.

"How? How did you—"

"It wasn't easy," Huntley said, cutting her off. "It took many years of hardship. Many years of working under those old fools before I finally held more power than they did. Unfortunately, power does come with a price."

Evie's eyes hardened and she raised a brow. "And what did you do to get this power? Whose ass did you have to kiss to get to where you are now?"

His eyes narrowed, and his expression darkened. "Watch yourself, Evie. No, I didn't have to 'kiss ass' to get my power. Rather, it was a trade. Information for my freedom and position."

"What kind of information?"

"Information on anyone who was stupid enough to try and challenge the Community."

Evie's stomach churned so bad she nearly threw up. She tasted bile in her throat and swallowed it back down, trying to find her next words.

"What do you mean 'try and challenge the Community'?"

"Come on, Evie. Don't you ever wonder why no one in debt tried to rebel against the Community? Why you don't hear even a single whisper from anyone who planned to try to start a rebellion?"

Evie began to grind her teeth. "Because you turned them in."

"Their odds of success were slim to none. I chose the option where I knew I would succeed. And I did. Exposing the small rebellion earned me my freedom. Then, it was only a matter of pretending for a little while longer to gain the money I needed to truly start my life. Overall, I'd say I turned in over fifty people who even hinted at the idea of trying to go against the Community council."

"You sent fifty people to Medical Waste?" Evie gasped, covering her mouth.

"No, fifty people were executed. Medical Waste didn't exist until I built it a couple of years later."

Evie's eyes went wide with a sickening realization. "You...you created the Medical Waste facility?"

"The council was desperate for a solution to fix the damage they had done. So many needed blood transfusions, new organs, or bone marrow. Anyone who was sent there would have been executed anyway. I just made sure they didn't completely go to waste."

Evie fought back against another stream of nausea weaving its way up her throat. "You killed so many innocent people! What is wrong with you? You're not as bad as the council, you're worse!"

Huntley raised a brow. "Innocent people? You think everyone in debt is innocent?"

She glared at him when he casually strolled over to his desk. He opened his desk drawer and withdrew several files. After walking back in front of his desk, he turned to face Evie again, leaning against his desk while his fingers lazily flipped through the different papers.

"Let's see... Here is number four-eight-eight. Turned in when he was sixteen. Recently, he was caught stabbing his fellow lumber worker to take his cigarettes for trade. Immediately taken to Medical Waste."

Huntley tossed the file on the floor towards Evie, causing her to jump in surprise.

"Then there's number seven-four-two. She was selling herself for drugs. She was finally taken to Medical Waste after her negligence led to the death of another person at the Farmers Unit. Some poor girl was killed by a tractor after seven-four-two pushed the girl in front of it while intoxicated."

He threw the folder on the floor with the other one.

"Now, those are a couple of people you may not necessarily know. How about some family knowledge?" He began to go through the files again. "Your younger brother and sister are already on their way to becoming a problem in the Community. Both were caught stealing snacks from other children. Now, that's not an offence that would send them to Medical Waste, but it's a small start down a delinquent's path."

Huntley tossed the file down, and Evie tried not to cry. Not once did her brother or sister tell her of what they had tried to do.

"Then there is your older brother," he continued. "He traded cigarettes for some condoms. Apparently, he has been fucking a couple of women that work in the Laborer's Unit. Not to mention his drinking, of course."

Another file fell to the floor. She couldn't help the sob building in her throat.

"And how about your young man?" Huntley said with disdain. "He has been drinking on and off. No drugs, but he traded cigarettes for condoms." Another file added to the pile on the floor.

"And then there's you,"

Evie's head snapped up to meet his eyes. Huntley's face was suddenly soft, and he had a small smile on his face. He was holding up a single piece of paper.

"Number six-seven-seven-five. No trades in the Underground. No reports of theft, assault or otherwise. Just a simple work history and documentation of your training."

Rather than drop the paper on the floor with the others, Huntley gracefully turned and placed it on his desk. He met her eyes, his gaze hopeful.

"Do you think they are all so innocent now, Evie?"

Hot tears ran down her cheeks. "No, I never thought every person in debt was innocent. But all of them are desperate to escape the hell you helped to create! And if the council has a problem with contraband, why don't they stop the contraband trading?"

"Why would I allow them to stop the majority of my business?"

Evie's face went pale. It was hard for her to not collapse on the floor. "Your business?"

"Yes. But I also see it as a solution. The contraband I leak into the Underground keeps those in debt distracted enough to forget foolish ideas of rebellion. A small amount of escape in return for compliance. Why do you think the council turns a blind eye to the Underground? You're a smart woman. Don't tell me you've never wondered about that yourself."

Rage consumed her in its impossible grip, and her icy glare was murderous. Every rumor she had heard about him was true. Every one of them.

"You're a monster."

There was silence in the room as the two regarded each other. Evie's eyes were filled with hate while Huntley's eyes seemed amused.

"I believe you're the first person to ever tell me that."

"Or the first to say it directly to you," she snapped back.

Huntley smirked. "I'm happy you're being so open and honest with me, Evie. It's refreshing compared to the false flattery I'm used to."

Evie suppressed the urge to roll her eyes. "You said you wanted honesty. That's what you're getting."

She had just turned to leave when his voice stopped her.

"I have another deal for you, Evie."

She began walking to the door, desperately wanting to leave the room. "I've had enough of your deals!" Her hand was on the doorknob, but his next words made her freeze.

"You will want to hear this one."

Evie gritted her teeth, recognizing the command in his voice.

"They will all go free. All of them. Your brothers and sister will be free from debt if you marry me."

Evie turned back to give him a look of pure hatred. "I'll go ahead and decline your offer now. I'll work hard for you until my debt is paid. It won't be much longer now. Then, I'll work on freeing my brothers and sister without your help!"

She heard his cruel laughter once she'd turned to leave and spun around to see him with a large, mocking smile, his dark eyes locked onto her blue ones.

"Evie...Do you really think the Community keeps track of everyone's debt?"

The world stopped. She felt like a bucket of cold water had been poured over her head.

"What do you mean?"

Huntley walked back around his desk and casually opened another drawer in his desk, drawing out another file. "Do you want to know how much you were turned in for? How much money your mother received when all of you were turned in?" He flipped open the file.

"Your mother received twenty-five thousand dollars for each of you. I'm sorry to tell you she burned through all the money quite quickly and eventually found herself in debt. She ended up being taken to Medical Waste about six months ago due to being caught dealing drugs to help keep up her lifestyle."

Evie looked to the floor. She hated the woman but would never once wish Medical Waste on her mother. It wasn't a fate she'd wish upon anyone.

"But I suppose that is inconsequential. Your debt was twenty-five thousand dollars. With all the years you have worked, don't you think you should be finished paying it off? And if not you, your brother? He has been in debt much longer than you. Don't you think he should be free by now?"

Evie continued staring at the floor, refusing to look at him and let him see the defeat in her eyes.

"Why do you think the Community never makes a point to tell you how much is left?" Huntley continued. "All caseworkers are ordered to never tell any of their cases how much money is left for them to work off. Because the caseworkers don't know. They are ordered to tell their cases that the Community holds such information confidential and they will be immediately released upon paying off their debt."

There was silence in the room, and Evie felt as if she could crumble apart at any moment. All those years of hard work were for nothing. Not just for herself, but for everyone debt to the Community.

"But...there were people...they were freed..." Evie whimpered hopelessly.

"The Community frees people after so many years of service, long after they have paid off any debt they had. It served the purpose to give everyone hope. Hope is what keeps them working hard. They have something to strive for. Mary was turned in for the same amount and used it for her son. I guarantee you that she will belong to the Community for the rest of her life."

Evie covered her face with her hands and cried. She could hear Huntley's heavy footsteps making their way to her.

"This is the reality of the Community, Evie. You of all people deserve the truth."

She snapped her head back up when she realized how close he was. Desperately, she pressed herself back up against the door, cursing herself that she hadn't already left.

"You may not like to hear it, Evie, but you and I are exactly alike. We both know the Community is a dead end. You deserved to know the entire truth. All I have done was make sure my place is secured here. No one can touch me by any means. I'm offering the same thing for you."

Evie's heart was pounding hard and she began shaking, goosebumps running down her arms. The intensity of his eyes frightened her, and he now stood directly in front of her.

"Evie, I have waited a long time to find someone who feels the way I feel about this disgusting place. I'm tired of being alone. Marry me, and I'll make sure no one can use you again."

Huntley actually sounded sincere. His hand slowly tucked a strand of her hair behind her ear. Evie couldn't stop herself from flinching, but he made no effort to react to her response. He carefully leaned down over Evie so she could feel his breath on her face. "You have two choices. One, accept my offer and free your family from debt. Or two, refuse me and continue to work for a non-existent goal. Either way, Evie, you and I will be together for quite a while."

Evie gritted her teeth. She didn't want to leave the room as a crying mess. She wanted to be strong and show no fear to the man in front of her.

"So I marry you, and then what? How long until you get bored and move on to the next woman? How long will it take for me to become ex-wife number four and you move on to wife number five?"

Huntley stood tall again and looked down on Evie. "Don't be ridiculous." He turned and headed back towards his desk. "Every marriage I've had was a business arrangement. My first wife was the daughter of the council head at the time. She was a 'gift' to me after I finally finished turning in those foolish enough to try and rebel against the Community. I separated from her because she abused my name to get what she wanted. My second wife was the daughter of the man who provided the contraband for me to sell to the Underground. Once I had control of that, I no longer needed him, and therefore, no longer had to deal with her."

He sat back down in his chair but never lost his eye contact with Evie.

"Then there was Sara. Another marriage because I owed her father a favor. That's all my marriages have been. Business arrangements. I provided for them, and they lived in complete comfort until I was finally done with them."

His smile returned, and it was an honest one. "This will be the first marriage that I will actually enjoy."

Evie wiped her tears off her face and took a few steps away from the door while continuing to stand strong. "You seem confident that I will accept your offer."

"You're a smart woman, Evie. I'm sure you will see reason. Even if it takes a little bit of time."

Evie wanted to snap and tell him she would never accept him, but a sudden thought raced through her head. She remembered when Huntley's ex-wife beat her and forced her to stay locked in her room.

"You think you can replace me? You fucking little whore!"

Her words echoed through her mind as she looked up and glared at Huntley.

"Your ex-wife...she accused me of trying to replace her. How long have you been planning all of this?" Evie demanded.

He looked thoughtful for several moments before answering. "Since the night of the party. Remember, I took you with me to see how you felt about this society. To see if we truly are the same. And we are. As soon as you answered me, I knew I wanted you."

Evie clenched her fists and gritted her teeth. "If that's true then why did your wife throw me in the attic to die? Why did she accuse me of trying to replace her before you even separated from her?"

The corners of his mouth slowly raised into a sickening smile. "I'm afraid I let a fantasy get the better of me. From the moment you read my book, I haven't been able to get you off of my mind. You have taken over much of my thoughts. I was with Sara the night before. All I could see was your face. I'm afraid I may have slipped and said your name."

Evie suddenly felt cold. Her hands and legs shook and her bottom lip was trembling. His smile was haunting her, and she felt the desperate need to run.

He leaned forward slightly against his desk, his gaze never leaving hers. "And at the risk of sounding too improper, Evie, I have to confess to you…I've never finished so hard in my entire life."

Evie had heard enough. She turned, ready to finally walk out of the room.

"And Evie," he began, stopping her once again.

Evie shuddered and looked over her shoulder at him.

"Move back to your proper room. Tonight."

Without respond, she quickly left his study and slammed the door shut. She tried to make her way to the kitchen, fighting back the urge to vomit.

"Get to the kitchen to help Mary. Get to the kitchen to help Mary."

She told herself that over and over in her head. But as soon as she reached the final step on the staircase, Evie knew she couldn't hold it in anymore. She ran straight for the guest bathroom and vomited into the toilet. She couldn't stop herself from dry heaving. Once she was done, Evie sank to the floor and sobbed.

She knew this world was full of dark and terrible people. But Huntley was more than that. He was a monster. The worst thing for Evie was knowing that he was right. In many ways, she was like Huntley. They both knew this world was hopeless and decaying. It was horrifying how close Evie was to becoming like him. The difference between them was Evie had loved ones to fight for. Huntley must have had no one.

Evie jumped at the sound of the bathroom door suddenly opening. Mary looked down at her, clearly looking worried. "What happened? What's wrong?"

Upon seeing Mary, Evie sobbed harder. Her chest was burning and her throat was raw and sore from vomiting. Her head pounded in pain and her eyes were red.

"H-he's a monster!" Evie cried as Mary dropped to the floor, wrapping her arms around the hysterical young woman. Mary gently rubbed her back while she cried into her chest. "He killed Oscar! He killed my former assignment just to get me here! He built the Medical Waste facility! He almost killed Aaron! He's a monster!"

After several minutes of her crying, Evie forced herself to sit up and look into Mary's face. "Did you know? Did you know any of this about him?"

Mary was quiet for several moments. "I…I had my suspicions. I heard the gossip. I think I just refused to really think about it."

Evie's head dropped to look at the floor. "He…he wants me to marry him… He said he would free my brothers and my sister if I do." Evie silently began crying again.

"Why is this happening to me, Mary? Why couldn't I have my own bit of happiness for once in my life?" She buried her face in Mary's shoulder, staining her clothes with tears.

Chapter 13

Evie forced herself to work on Saturday. Mary took over the task of delivering Huntley's meals to him for the day. Evie couldn't face him. Not yet. Her mind spiraled in several different directions. The events of the previous day still made her sick. She was in the house of a monster, and Evie felt that there was no escape.

Sunday morning finally arrived, and Evie eagerly left the house. There was much she needed to tell Ryder. After crying for half of the night, she had spent the rest of it and the morning trying to put together several pieces of the twisted game she found herself playing.

"He created the Medical Waste facility. He leaks the contraband that goes into the Underground. But how did he know about me and Aaron? How does he know so much about Ryder, Aaron, and the twins? Because of his connections? Does he trade information for his contraband?"

As she made her way to the Laborer's Unit, the questions continued racing through Evie's head. She told herself she was done being a crying child over everything happening and needed to find out exactly how Huntley was getting his information.

"If I can find out how he gets his information, I can try to protect my family for the future."

The gates were open, and she arrived just in time to see Ryder walking outside. He looked as grim as Evie did. They silently gave each other a hug and began to walk to the Children's Unit.

"Our boss was finally nice enough to let some of us see Aaron. He's still in bad shape, but he's healing up good."

Evie nodded. "Next time you see him…please tell him I'm sorry."

"He doesn't blame you. I told him about Huntley."

She clenched her fists. "You don't know anything about him…" she muttered through gritted teeth.

Ryder stopped walking and gave Evie a confused look. "What are you talking about?"

She looked to the ground, not able to meet his eyes. "All those rumors we heard about him are true. All of them. He created the Medical Waste facility. And he also leaks the contraband into the Underground."

When she raised her head to look at her brother, the look of horror on his face could not be masked. He tried to close his mouth, but he continued to stare.

"He also killed Oscar. He killed my former assignment just to get me into his house."

For several moments, Ryder didn't say anything. Finally, he wrapped Evie in his arms. There were no words, really, for something so awful. She melted into him, grateful for the comfort her family provided. After a while, she pulled back and gave him a weak smile.

"Come on. Let's go see BB and CC. I need to see them today."

Ryder nodded, and they continued their walk over to the Children's Unit. There were no words exchanged, as neither of them knew what else to say. Upon seeing their brother and sister, Ryder and Evie put on their best fake smiles and prepared to give the twins a great day of visiting.

For lunch, Evie insisted on taking them all out to a good restaurant using her charge card. Ryder began to protest, but a pleading look from Evie quickly made him stop. As they began walking out of the Children's Unit, Evie whispered into her older brother's ear. "Please, let me do this."

Ryder gritted his teeth but nodded. The marketplace had a small burger shop that made all of their mouths water. They could easily smell the seasoned ground beef cooking on the grill along with the smell of fresh fries coming out of a fryer. Evie happily pushed for everyone to get the largest cheeseburgers they had and even milkshakes. Ryder outright refused, but Evie purchased one for him anyway. He begrudgingly ate the food so it wouldn't go to waste. She happily enjoyed the smiles of her twin brother and sister as they consumed their own chocolate dessert.

Normally, Evie would never spend money on expensive food, but she wanted this day to be special for all of them. And the knowledge that her debt will never be paid off stopped her hesitation. By the end of the day, the twins had large smiles on their faces as they stood outside of the Children's Unit.

She pulled them both close to her, awkwardly trying to get her arms around both of them. "I need you both to promise me that you'll behave yourselves. No stealing, fighting, or anything! If you ever need anything, let me know and I will get it for you. No matter the cost, I'll take care of it." She pulled away and could clearly see the look of surprise on the twins' faces. Evie sighed. "I know about you both getting into trouble stealing snacks."

Their eyes went wide and their faces went pale. BB looked to the ground in shame and CC had tears in her eyes. Out of the corner of her gaze, Evie caught Ryder opening his mouth to speak, but a hard glare made him stop.

"Just promise me that you will both behave. Because if you don't, Well... you know what will happen."

The twins nodded and gave Evie another small hug. They had no words when they gave a final hug to Ryder. With a final sad look, they silently made their way inside of the unit.

Ryder turned to Evie, clearly aggravated. Before he could speak, Evie raised a finger to her lips and stepped closer to her brother. "We need to talk somewhere where we won't be heard. Somewhere off the grid of the Harvesters' patrol vans and street cameras."

Ryder was thoughtful for several moments before taking her hand and leading her towards the Laborer's Unit. Neither of them said a word as Ryder led her behind his apartment building and into a small, wooded area.

"This is where some of us sneak off for some alone time. Never seen anyone but a laborer and their friends come back here."

Evie raised a brow. "Alone time but with a friend?"

Ryder cast her an awkward look. "Well...not alone time like that, Evie."

Evie immediately understood and turned red. They were going to the place where laborers would hook up with their one-night stands. Eventually, the duo found a comfortable place to sit against the building. They were surrounded by several trees and bushes, making them both feel safe and alone.

"You said every rumor about Huntley was true. Were you serious?" Ryder asked, sitting on a beaten-up log.

Evie nodded, sitting down beside him. "He told me himself. He was in debt and worked his way out by turning over everyone who was planning on rising against the council. Then, he created the Medical Waste Facility. He's also the one leaking contraband into the Underground. All the alcohol, condoms, drugs, and cigarettes come from him."

Ryder was horrified. "Then...Jesus Christ. I always wondered why they never shut that place down. I mean, it's been up for so long. I thought the council didn't know or just turned a blind eye to it for whatever fucking reason."

"They knew about it since it started. Huntley said he leaks contraband to keep everyone from trying to rebel against the council. If anyone steps out of line or overuses the stuff, they get sent to Medical Waste."

Evie looked to her brother to see him staring at the ground. He was breathing heavily as he ran a hand down his face in disbelief.

"He knows about you. Huntley knows almost everything about everyone. He knows about your trades in the underground."

Ryder's head snapped up, and he faced his sister. "What trades?"

"He knew about you trading cigarettes for beer. And you've also been sleeping with a couple girls from the Laborer's Unit." A look of shame fell over her brother's face. "He also said BB and CC have been in trouble for stealing from other children. And Aaron was trading for condoms in the Underground."

Ryder stumbled over his next words. "Evie, he was getting those for you. I swear, he wasn't—"

"I know," Evie cut him off. "I just didn't dare tell Huntley that."

Ryder's shoulders dropped and he covered his face with his hands. "Jesus Christ...I had no idea we were being watched like that."

Evie felt tears begin to form in her eyes. "There's something else you need to know," She said, fighting the urge to break down into a sobbing mess. "All of our hard work has been for nothing. I found out that the Community doesn't keep track of our debt. They release us long after we work off the amount we were turned in for. If anyone is released, it's a random luck of the draw. And it's only to give those in debt hope of being free one day."

She wiped her tears away and looked at Ryder. He was staring down at the ground. It looked as if he also had tears threatening to spill out of his eyes.

"Why... why would he tell you all this? You can easily tell everyone the truth now! Why tell you everything and risk the truth getting out?"

Evie looked at her brother, wiping more tears away. "Ryder, can you look me in the eye and tell me that everyone will believe me? People in debt are being released when the Community needs to bring them hope. That's proof enough for them. No one will ever believe me, and I think he knows that."

Ryder seemed to have no words. Somehow, Evie knew that he believed she was right.

There was silence for several moments before Evie finally spoke again. "Ryder, there are so many unanswered questions here. I want to know where he got this information. I mean, he created Medical Waste and leaks contraband into the Underground. Maybe that's how he knew about the trades you and Aaron have been making. But what about the records on BB and CC? How did he know about my personal relationship with Aaron?"

Ryder scoffed. "Not trying to sound like a jackass, Evie, but the man is a higher-up in society. It probably doesn't take much for him to figure things out. He can just pay someone for the information."

She rolled her eyes. "I know, but I want to know exactly how he's getting it! And from who. If I can find out, maybe it will help you all stay safe. Maybe it can help you all stay out of his sight for the future."

Ryder raised a brow. "And how are you going to even start looking?"

"He leaves the house at least once a week. That's when either me or Mary clean his study. Once he's gone, I'll look around and see what I can find."

"And what happens if you get caught, Evie? That could be a one-way ticket to Medical Waste!"

"Then I won't get caught! I'll be careful. I promise you I will, but I need to see what I can find out."

He sighed; his face now plastered with defeat. "I know I can't stop you, but please be careful! I can't lose you, Evie."

She placed her hand on his shoulder and gave him a reassuring smile. "I swear I'll be careful. I won't get caught. And I'll tell you everything I find next Sunday. I promise." Evie and Ryder finally noticed the sun had set and darkness surrounded them. She stood and gestured for him to follow. "Walk with me. I need to start heading back." Ryder slowly stood and they began heading back to Huntley's house.

"I'm going to take a guess and say you aren't transferring anytime soon."

It wasn't a question. She knew he had already known the answer.

"No," Evie said hotly, growing angry again. "He caught my transfer request at the Distribution Center. He destroyed it right in front of me."

Out of the corner of her eye, she could see Ryder grinding his teeth as his face turned red.

"Evie, I swear to God, if I ever get the chance, I'm going to kill this guy!"

"After all the things this man has done, I'm pretty sure you will have to take a number on that. I'm sure a lot of people have said the same thing." She tried to say it with a light tone and gave him a small smile, wanting to make it seem like a small joke, but he was clearly not listening. Her brother only grew more lost in thought.

As soon as they reached the outside of Huntley's house, she wrapped her arms around Ryder and brought him back to reality. He leaned in, taking a deep breath and letting it out slowly to calm himself.

"Please be careful, Evie. Promise me that you'll be careful!"

She pulled away and nodded. "I will. I promise. I'll see you next Sunday."

With a heavy sigh, Evie forced herself to walk into the house while Ryder took off back to the Laborer's Unit. As soon as the door closed behind her, a familiar feeling of dread took over. Being in this house felt like a prison that she could only escape from once a week. And if she wasn't careful, Evie might find herself in a situation where she may never get to leave at all. Or worse, leave this prison as a Medical Waste subject.

From the hallway, Evie could hear the sound of running water from the kitchen. She could only assume Mary was doing the dishes. Her feet felt heavy as she forced her way up the stairs to go to her room for the night. Part of her wanted to be polite and say goodnight to Mary, but she was overwhelmed with the longing to be alone.

She turned the corner and was startled when a large figure seemed to appear right in front of her. If she hadn't stopped when she did, she would have walked right into him.

Huntley gave her a polite smile. "Did you enjoy your Sunday off, Evie?"

She offered him no polite smile but tried not to glare up at him. "I did, sir. Thank you."

Evie desperately wanted to step around him and go to her room, but his large frame took up the majority of the hallway.

"Mary told me you haven't been feeling well. Do you need to see a doctor?"

His smile sent chills down her spine, but she refused to allow herself to show fear. it was obvious he was trying to tease her. Her words were curt and cold. "No, sir, I feel fine. Thank you."

"Good. Then I assume I'll begin seeing you again during the day. I requested to Mary that you be the one to bring me my meals."

Evie clenched her jaw. "Yes, sir. I'll begin that task again starting tomorrow morning. I apologize for deviating from schedule."

His smile widened, and he took a step towards her. Evie could now feel his breath on her face as he stood over her, and an unwelcome shiver ran down her spine. "Good. I look forward to seeing you again more frequently. I only get to see you when you come into my study."

Evie narrowed her eyes. "With respect, sir, you are the one who decides to stay in your study all day. And I'm always here doing the tasks I am told to do. You can easily see me outside of your study and at your leisure."

Huntley's eyes seemed to darken, and he leaned down closer to her face. "Are you offering for me to come and see you when I please?"

Her heart pounded hard in her chest and she chose her next words carefully. "You own my contract. The Community assigned me to you. You can see me whenever you demand, as my contract states."

He raised a brow. "The Community assigned you to me? Perhaps you should remember that I am the one who brought you into my home, Evie. Not the Community."

Evie took a breath and confidently met his leering gaze. "Yes, that is true. But you should remember that, at the end of the day, I'm Community property. Not yours. You own my contract and my services. But we both know that's not quite the same as owning me as a whole."

As a flash of anger appeared on his face, she fought the urge to smile. His smile had disappeared. Evie knew she'd hit a sore spot and was proud to get a small victory over him.

"Please excuse me, sir. I would like to go to bed so I'm rested to begin my day tomorrow. I want to make sure I'm up bright and early to deliver your breakfast to you."

His eyes didn't leave hers. Not even as he took a step back and allowed her to pass him. His gaze was burning into her back as she walked into her room and gently closed the door behind her.

Chapter 14

The following morning, Evie was true to her word. At seven thirty in the morning, she delivered Huntley's breakfast with nothing more than a polite greeting. His eyes were on her every time she stepped into his study. With each passing day during the week, Evie became more and more nervous. Not once did Huntley give any indication that he was leaving the house. By the time Thursday came around, Evie had lost hope and feared that she would have to wait another week to be able to go through his study.

On Friday morning, her wish was finally granted. Gently, she knocked on his door with the breakfast tray in her hand.

"Come in."

She entered and, polite as always, gave him her standard greeting. "Good morning, sir."

"Good morning, Evie."

She placed his tray on the usual spot and collected his dinner dishes. Before she could leave the room, his voice stopped her movement.

"I'll be heading out of the house for a bit later today. I have some business to take care of," Huntley said, not looking up from the paperwork at his desk.

Evie gave a polite nod. "Understood, sir. Should I tell Mary to expect you home for lunch and dinner?"

"I'm sure I'll be out of the house for lunch, but expect me home for dinner."

Evie nodded. "I'll let her know."

She turned and felt the burning sensation of his stare on her back.

Evie was sure he hadn't seen her victorious grin while she walked to the kitchen. Mary had just finished the dishes when she entered the room.

"Huntley wanted me to let you know he won't be home for lunch. He's heading out of the house for business."

Mary shrugged. "Well, that's some less work to do today."

Evie took a small breath and prepared herself to lie. "He wants me to clean his study while he's gone. As soon as he leaves, I'll get started."

Mary stared at Evie for several seconds before replying. "If you want, I'll do it. It's bad enough he's making you bring him his meals."

Evie shook her head. "No, it's ok. Just let me do it. He will be out of the house, so it's not a big deal."

Mary seemed hesitant and looked as if she had more to say, but dropped the subject.

Evie began her cleaning tasks in the entertainment room but was obviously distracted. She kept frantically looking at the clock on the wall and stopping to listen for the sound of the front door opening. Finally, at ten thirty, she heard the sound of heavy footsteps walking down the hall. She rushed to finish polishing the large piano, her heart pounding at the opportunity in front of her. Evie had just finished polishing the final spot when she looked up to see him leaning in the doorway to the room.

"Please inform Mary that I'm heading out. I should be back in a couple of hours."

She nodded and forced a small smile. "Have a nice day, sir."

With a smile, Huntley turned and swiftly exited the house. A breath of relief left her. As quickly as she could, she gathered her cleaning supplies and made her way to the study.

Evie heard the vacuum running in the hallway. She approached Mary and gently tapped on her shoulder.

"Huntley's out of the house. I'm going to get the study done and over with."

Mary simply nodded and Evie made her way up the stairs. Her feet felt heavy as she approached the entrance of the study. With a trembling hand on the doorknob, she entered the room. Her first priority was to clean the room. If that wasn't done, he would immediately become suspicious. She forced herself to use a steady pace to vacuum the floor, dust the bookshelves, and empty the trashcan and paper shredder.

Once she felt confident the room was done, she turned her attention towards the desk. Her heart pounded in her chest as she approached it. Papers were scattered everywhere. Evie was not confident enough to lift up any papers to read them properly. God forbid he notice them moved in any way.

She carefully leaned over the desk and looked over the papers she could clearly see. The ones laying on top of the desk seemed to be several invoices. Nothing that would lead Evie to the answers she was looking for. She knelt down to the bottom drawers of the desk and carefully opened the largest drawer. Inside, she found several files tightly packed. She would need to be careful and make sure all files went back to their proper places.

The tabs were easy to read. The first file to catch her interest was labeled 'DELINQUENTS.'

Very carefully, she lifted the file up and laid it on the floor, her legs folded neatly under her. It was filled with files of people in debt and listed their crimes. The first paper showed the picture of a young man with dirty blond hair and dull blue eyes.

At the bottom of the picture, the paper read:

NUMBER: FOUR-TWO-EIGHT-SEVEN

UNIT: LUMBER

CHARGES: THEFT & ASSAULT

SENTENCE: MEDICAL WASTE

The second paper down made her gasp. She instantly recognized the face of Kayla, the bully of her childhood.

At the bottom of the picture, the paper read:

NUMBER: TWO-ONE-ONE-THREE

UNIT: FARMING

CHARGES: THEFT & MURDER

SENTENCE: MEDICAL WASTE

Evie had read enough and carefully placed the file back into the drawer. It wasn't surprising to her that he had such information on those who went to the facility. He did create it, after all. Her eyes scanned over the files and caught another one of interest. 'SURVEILLANCE.'

Again, she carefully placed the file on the floor and opened it. The first paper held a map of the Community, with small dots across the map. She could only assume they pinpointed all the cameras in the Community. She wished there was a way to make a copy so she could show it to Ryder.

As soon as Evie flipped the map over, her stomach dropped. Right in front of her eyes was a large picture of her. It displayed her walking to, what she assumed, was the Laborer's Unit. The following pictures displayed her sitting with Ryder, BB, and CC while having lunch together. The next picture almost made her sick. It displayed her and Aaron passionately kissing in the Laborer's Unit. It was clearly the night she accepted his proposal.

With gritted teeth, she forced herself to place the file back into the drawer.

"He has pictures of me from all over the Community... but how is he getting them?"

She carefully looked over the tabs again and another caught her eye. 'POSSIBLE PATROL PATTERNS.' The first paper displayed a simply drawn map of the Community with several line patterns surrounding the waters on the Community boundaries. She was confused until she flipped the paper over. The other side displayed several progress reports from the Laborer's Unit. Reports of large ships being built. Memories of the conversation she had with Ryder months ago flashed in her mind.

"Been building some ships. We're working on the metal work, and the Lumber Unit has been working on the planks for them. It's kind of weird. The work came out of nowhere."

Ryder's words echoed through her head. That had to be it. They were building ships to patrol the waters around the Community.

"But why does Huntley have this? Why would this matter to him?"

Another page flip revealed yet another hand drawn map of the Community. Several lines were drawn through the streets with arrows pointing down the different directions of the roads.

On the bottom of the map, she could see the small scribble of words:

'PATROL PATTERN A'

Evie felt more confusion. The file held a lot of information on the Harvesters, their patrol patterns, and their plans to expand out into the open waters.

"Why does he have all of this? What's the point?"

After several moments of silence, her blood ran cold. There was only one reason Evie could think of as to why he had this information.

Huntley was the head of the Harvesters.

She carefully sat back and silent tears streamed down her face. It explained everything. He must have ordered them to follow her and take pictures of her. She felt completely violated.

After several silent moments of crying, another sick realization set in. He ordered the raid on the Underground. He ordered the arrest and execution of dozens of innocent people. All because of contraband he himself was selling.

Evie couldn't handle anymore. With shaking hands, she closed the file and placed it in its correct spot inside the drawer. Before she could close it, one final file at the very back of the drawer caught her attention.

'EDEN'

Her eyes went wide as she carefully placed the file on the floor.

"No, it's impossible... Eden isn't real!"

The first paper on top was a list of numbers. There were dozens of those in debt who had gone missing over the course of several months. The second paper was another list. It read:

'SUSPECTED MEMBERS OF EDEN'

Evie sat back and a wave of feelings washed over her. "It's real... Eden is real ..." She whispered to herself.

For the first time in her life, she felt true and genuine hope inside of her.

"What the hell are you doing?"

Evie jumped and her face paled. She looked up to see Mary standing over her, hands on her hips and a furious expression across her face. "Evie, what are you doing?" All the young woman could do was sit on the floor and stare up at the angry woman.

"Eden...Eden is real..." she whispered.

Mary's stance didn't change, but she raised a brow. "What did you say?"

Evie suddenly felt a rush of excitement as she leaned forward over the folder and flipped back through the papers. "It's real! Eden is real! It's all here—"

The papers were quickly snatched out of her hands. Mary was now on her knees, desperately trying to place the papers neatly back together.

"I can't believe you! I warned you! I warned you about this!" Mary shoved the file into Evie's hands. "Put it back where you found it! Now!"

Evie's hands continued to tremble as she placed the folder back into the drawer and closed it. Once it was shut, Mary grabbed her arm and forced Evie to her feet.

"Mary, I'm sorry, but—"

Evie was stopped mid-sentence by a hard slap to her cheek. She stumbled back while Mary glared at her, breathing heavily.

"Mary, what—"

"I told you! I told you not to go through his things! Do you know what would have happened if it was Mr. Huntley who found you? Do you think I want to watch you being dragged out of this house into a Harmony Group van?"

Evie felt a rush of anger and glowered at Mary. "I won't apologize! I needed answers! You can't imagine what it's like for me! For my family! You—"

"Enough!" Mary's yell filled the room and Evie jumped, startled. Mary's eyes were narrowed and she was gritting her teeth. It was clear she was infuriated. "I knew you were lying to me! I knew he wouldn't care what you did while he was out of the house! Damn you, Evie!"

She turned and began walking out of the study. "Get this room cleaned up and get out of it before he gets home!"

Mary slammed the door shut behind her, and Evie almost felt a rush of guilt. She was sorry for upsetting Mary, but she had no regrets about looking through Huntley's papers. She had found the answers she was looking for. Huntley was the head of the Harvesters. That's how he was getting his information and those pictures of her. And more importantly, Eden was real.

There truly was a possible way to escape from the Community.

She carefully gathered the cleaning supplies and left the study. Her mind was swimming with all the information she had discovered. The pain from the slap didn't even bother her. As soon as she entered the kitchen, she heard the sound of a knife tapping a cutting board. The knife was practically slamming into the vegetables.

Evie put the cleaning supplies back into the closet and sighed. She turned to look at Mary with her head high and a confident expression on her face.

"Mary, I understand you're angry. But I can't apologize for what I did. I had questions I needed answered. Please don't hate me for it."

Mary placed the knife down on the counter and looked up to Evie.

"I don't hate you, but I'm sure as hell pissed off! I warned you! Now what's going to happen if he comes home and sees something is out of place? He will notice just the smallest change on his desk!"

Evie narrowed her eyes, her blood beginning to boil once more. "Do you know what that man has been doing to me? He's been having me followed! He's in charge of the Harvesters! He had them follow me and take pictures of me and my family! That's how he knew about me and Aaron! I needed to know how he was getting that information, and I have my answer now! I'm sorry, Mary, but I don't have any regrets for what I did!"

Mary gritted her teeth and went back to chopping vegetables. "You are going to be the death of me, girl!" she snapped, her chopping pace increasing.

There was silence in the room for several moments before Evie spoke again.

"Are you going to tell him?"

Mary suddenly stopped her movement. She seemed frozen in place.

"Are you going to tell him I went through his desk? You told me once you wouldn't save me if I did something wrong. Are you going to tell him?"

Mary looked conflicted. After several awkward moments, the older woman finally sighed. "No, I won't tell him. But if he finds something amiss in his office, I'm not saving you. I'm going to tell him you were the one to clean it. He can do the math from there."

She went back to her cooking while Evie released a breath. All she could do now was hope that she had placed everything back exactly where it had been.

Evie took several steps forward until she was standing in front of her. "Mary, Eden exists! I found proof in his study!"

Mary looked up to her and raised a brow. "What? What is Eden? What are you talking about?"

"You can't tell me you haven't heard a single rumor about Eden! A group of people who help people escape! I didn't believe it at first, but it's real! There are people out there who can help us!"

Both women jumped at the sound of the front door opening and closing. Mary quickly flashed a hard look at Evie and raised a finger to her lips.

"Don't ever mention that name again! Not here or to anyone!" she harshly whispered.

Evie opened her mouth to speak but was stopped short by the sound of the kitchen door opening. Huntley entered the kitchen and gave a polite smile to both women.

"Welcome back, Mr. Huntley," Mary immediately said, standing tall.

He gave a slight bow of his head. "Thank you. My business was done earlier than expected."

Mary nodded, and Evie simply fought hard not to glare at him.

"Do you want anything for lunch, sir? I can make you something small until dinner, if you like," Mary offered.

"No, thank you. I can wait until dinner."

He flashed a smile at Evie and swiftly left the room. His footsteps could be heard going up the stairs.

Mary turned and glared at Evie. "You better pray he doesn't find anything! Like I said, if he finds anything out of place, I will not save you!"

Evie nodded and turned to head out of the kitchen. She exited the house and walked into the backyard. As soon as the door closed behind her, she fell to her knees and breathed deeply.

"Eden is real...I might be able to save my family!"

Chapter 15

Huntley gave no indication over the next couple of days that he found anything amiss in his study. Once Sunday arrived, Evie felt relief completely wash over her. As soon as she was awake, she got dressed and rushed out of the house. She was eager to get to her brother and tell him everything she had learned.

She reached the Laborer's Unit just as the gates were opening for the day. Evie ran for her brother's housing unit and eagerly waited outside. Ten minutes later, Ryder exited and greeted her with a tight hug.

"Not gonna lie, I spent the entire week worried about you. Did you find out anything?"

She nodded. "Oh yeah. We have a lot to talk about. But let's save the serious talk for later. I want to see BB and CC. Let's just try and give them a good day."

Ryder gave her a small smile and the two of them began making their way to the Children's Unit. There was a chill to the air, hinting that winter would soon be upon them. Winter was the worst time of year for everyone in debt. It affected the different units in its own way. Evie wasn't sure what happened with the Farming and Lumber Units, but it was hell for the Laborers. The snow and freezing temperatures wouldn't stop them from being forced to work outside when necessary. Food became much scarcer. That is, unless you were classified under Domestics like Evie. It was also a lot harder for the four of them to spend time together.

The Children's Unit wouldn't allow them to spend any time together inside of the building. Evie could easily remember the days where they all had to wear layers of clothing in order to bear being outside to see each other. Oftentimes, their visits were cut short so the twins wouldn't get sick.

They approached the Children's Unit and watched as dozens of children ran out of the building. After about ten minutes of waiting, Evie and Ryder became concerned. Usually, BB and CC were the first to exit the building.

"Where the hell are they?" Ryder wondered out loud.

"No idea. Maybe we can go in and ask?"

Ryder clenched his fists in anger as they made their way inside. Evie couldn't remember the last time she was inside. The lights were dim and the walls were a dull yellow. The tile floor was worn with time, and it couldn't be determined what color it was supposed to be.

They approached the front desk to see an elderly woman bent over a large book.

"Excuse me, can you help us?" Evie asked politely.

"What do you want?" the woman snapped, not looking up from her book.

"Our brother and sister are supposed to be free to visit with us today, but they didn't exit the building. We would like to ask where they are."

The woman rolled her eyes and slid her chair to the computer on the corner of the desk. "Names?"

"They are BB and CC. I don't think they have been issued numbers yet."

The woman typed, looking at the computer. After several moments, the woman sighed and rolled back to her original spot. She still did not lift her head to look at Evie or Ryder. "They are under lockdown for two weeks. They are being disciplined for fighting with other children." Ryder's eyes narrowed while Evie grew concerned.

"Why were they fighting? Was there a reason? Are they alright?"

The woman rolled her eyes and lifted her head to finally address the two of them. "Look, they are under lockdown and it's no business of yours! They are Community property! I didn't even have to tell you about them!"

"None of our business?" Ryder snapped. "Of course it's our business! They are our brother and sister! We just want to know if they are alright! They wouldn't start a fight for no reason!"

The woman stood and glared hard at Ryder. "Get out of this building now before I call the Harmony Group!"

Evie's heart began to pound hard and she quickly stepped between Ryder and the front desk. "Ryder, let's go! Please, we can see them later!"

He gave a final hard glare at the woman before storming out of the Children's Unit with Evie quickly following behind. She was huffing behind him, trying to keep up.

"They wouldn't cause a fight for no reason! I bet you anything the other kids started it and they are being punished for it."

Evie was finally able to catch up enough to grab his arm, forcing him to stop. "Ryder, calm down! Please! As soon as we see them again, we will talk to them and figure out what happened."

With a huff, he continued walking down the road. Evie quickly took her place next to him and the two of them walked back towards the Laborer's Unit. "Maybe Huntley had something to do with this," Ryder said under his breath.

"It's possible, but we can't just assume that."

He sighed with defeat. "It's just fucked-up. I fucking hate the Community!"

"I do too. But let's at least take advantage of this time. Let's go back to that spot we went to last time. I have so much to tell you!"

Ryder led her back behind the housing unit and they sat on the ground. "Well, do you have any good news? Please tell me something positive so I can have something good happen today," Ryder said, his face in his hands.

Evie sighed and looked down at her hands. "There's no such thing as anything good happening in the Community, but I was able to look through Huntley's desk. I know how he found out about me and Aaron. How he knows everything about our family." Ryder looked up, and Evie continued to stare at her hands.

"Huntley leads the Harvesters. He ordered them to follow me. He has so many pictures of me and all of you. He's had the Harvesters stalking me for God knows how long." Evie fought hard not to cry. She finally looked up to see a look of horror on Ryder's face.

"That means he also ordered the raid on the Underground. All those people died because of him."

Evie nodded. Ryder shook his head in disbelief.

"So, there's no hope. No fucking hope of him leaving us alone. Of leaving you alone!" he exclaimed, almost yelling out the final words.

She turned to her brother and quickly grabbed his hands. "But that's not all! Ryder, you were right. There's hope to get out of here."

He looked up at her with a raised brow. "What are you talking about?"

"Eden! It's real! I saw a file in Huntley's desk. People in debt have been going missing for years, and it's not because they went to Medical Waste. Ryder, if you can find someone from Eden, you can get everyone out!"

He looked shocked. It took several minutes for a smile to finally reach his lips. "Are you serious? Evie, please tell me this isn't a joke. Eden exists?"

She nodded, returning the smile. "Yes! I'm not joking!"

Ryder was silent for several moments before the smile slowly faded from his face. "Evie, there's no way in hell I can even try to find someone from Eden with the Harvesters on our asses."

Evie bit her bottom lip and tried to prepare herself for her next words. "You won't. Which is why there's only one thing I can think of to make sure you can try to find someone."

Ryder sat back, his hands leaving hers. "What are you talking about? What are you thinking?"

She sighed and tried to stay strong. "I've been thinking a lot about this. Ever since I found out about Eden, I felt real hope for the first time. Hope for you all getting out and away from this place."

"Why are you acting like that doesn't include you too?"

She took a breath. "Because it doesn't. You won't like hearing this, but there is no hope for me getting out. At least, not right away. I can keep the Harvesters away from all of you, but not me. Not while Huntley has them following me."

"So what the hell are you planning?"

Evie felt her hands begin to shake. She wasn't sure if it was the chill in the air or because she was nervous to speak to her brother about her plan. "Ryder…the Community only keeps tabs on people in debt. Well, I'm assuming they do. Once you are free, our bracelets come off and we aren't numbers anymore."

"What does that have to do with getting us out of here?"

"I…I can make a deal with Huntley. I'll make a deal and get all of you out of debt. Hell, maybe I can even negotiate to get Aaron out. Once you are free, you can leave and the Community will stop keeping track of you. Then you will have more of a chance to find someone from Eden."

His eyes narrowed, his expression growing harsh. "What kind of deal?"

She sighed and looked to the ground in defeat. "I'll accept his proposal to marry him if he frees all of you."

Her brother inhaled, his face growing furious. Finally, he snapped, "No way in hell! Not happening! Not now or ever!"

Evie quickly wrapped her arms around him and rested her head on his shoulder. "Ryder, I know you don't like hearing this. I don't like saying it. But it's the only thing I can think of! There's no other way I can make sure they don't track you! Please, let me do this."

He grinded his teeth, not returning her hug. "No way am I accepting this! I'll look for Eden! I'll be careful, I promise!"

She pulled back and looked into his eyes, trying to keep her voice level. "There's no way you have a chance of finding Eden with the Harvesters watching me. You will be free, and I will keep my distance while you look. Once you find someone, you beg for them to help get everyone out. You, BB, CC, and Aaron."

"How can you ask me to leave you behind? I'm not leaving here without you!"

"But you know there is no hope for me! At least, not right now. Focus on getting BB, CC, and Aaron out. Maybe sometime in the future, I'll escape this hell too. But for now, we need to take this chance. BB and CC don't deserve to grow up here."

Ryder opened and closed his mouth several times. It was obvious he was trying to find another option for them.

"Evie…what happens if I can't find someone? What if you do all of this for nothing?"

She gave her brother a small smile. "Then at least you will all be free."

The cold crept into their bones, but neither of them seemed bothered by it. Their minds were too preoccupied with this situation and all that was at stake.
After a while, Ryder sighed. "You're going to do this even if I tell you not to, right?"

"Yes, I am. I'm sorry, but I don't know any other way."

Ryder leaned forward and placed his forehead against hers. "You just can't stop being so selfless, can you?"

Evie chuckled and wrapped her arms around her brother. "We can get out of here, Ryder. For the first time in my life, I actually have some hope."

Both of them stood and made their way back around the building.

"Let's head back. I want to get this over with," Evie said.

She began to step in the direction of the large gate when Ryder grabbed her arm.

"Evie… if I can't find Eden…then this could mean I'll never see you again."

Evie forced a smile. "I don't believe that. I'll see all of you again. I have faith! Find Eden and get everyone out. Then, maybe someday, I'll get out too."

His face once again fell, and they slowly made their way in the direction of Huntley's house. It was a silent walk, as neither of them had any words to say. When they finally stood in front of the large house, Ryder gave his sister a tight hug.

"I swear I'll find them, Evie. I promise you," he whispered into her ear.

Evie returned the hug, tears in her eyes. "I'll see you again, Ryder. I'll see all of you again. Tell them all I love them. Please, get everyone out of here!"

They finally broke apart and Evie walked into the house, wiping the tears away from her eyes. She made her way into the kitchen to see Mary putting away the dinner dishes. Upon seeing her, Mary looked at the clock and raised a brow. "You're back a little earlier than usual."

Evie nodded. "Is Huntley in his study?"

Mary slowly looked back to Evie. "Last I knew, he was."

Evie nodded and walked out of the kitchen, ignoring Mary's attempts to call her back. Her feet felt heavy as she made her way up the stairs. She tried to stand tall and be strong. She had made her choice. She wasn't going to cry or show any fear in front of the man who haunted her like a menacing shadow. Who led the Harvesters and created the Medical Waste Facility. She was done being afraid.

She stood in front of his door for several minutes before getting the courage to knock.

"Come in."

Evie shuddered and made her way inside. Huntley was sitting over his desk, scribbling on several different pieces of paper, as usual. She stood a few feet away from his desk and took a breath.

"Mr. Huntley, I have a deal for you."

Immediately, his writing stopped. He dropped his pencil and slowly sat up in his chair. This was the first time Evie had ever seen him look surprised.

"You have a deal for me?"

Evie steeled herself, refusing to look away from his face. "My brothers and sister are freed from debt. BB and CC are enrolled in a regular school in the Community so they can have a good life once they graduate. Ryder is given a good paying job and gets a home of his own." Huntley opened his mouth to speak, but Evie continued.

"And Aaron as well. You pay for Aaron's medical bills and his debt is erased."

Huntley's eyes narrowed.

"That's asking for too much, Evie."

She didn't back down and continued to stand tall against him.

"You owe it to him. You almost had him beaten to death for nothing. He deserves his freedom for the suffering you caused him. All because you thought I lied to you."

The sea of uncertainty and challenge surrounded them, tossing their resolves this way and that in a silent battle. But she wasn't going to give up.

"And if I refuse?"

Evie shrugged. "Then you refuse. I won't be accepting any other deal but this one. And we both know money isn't an issue for any of this."

He smirked. "No, it isn't. But you are demanding an awful lot."

"It's the only offer I have for you. I won't be accepting yours."

Huntley leaned back in his chair, the smirk still plastered on his face. "I can easily refuse yours, as well. Either way, I would win Evie. You are staying with me in this house for the rest of your life."

"You're right. I will be. But I'd always be Community property, not yours."

His face suddenly hardened, and she saw a flash of anger. Evie knew she had said the right thing. There was another tense silence between the two of them before Huntley finally sat straight in his chair, his eyes never leaving hers.

"Done."

Evie released a breath and felt her body slowly relax. "Say it. I want to hear you say it," Evie said, knowing she was pushing the issue. But she needed to hear him say the words.

Rather than be angry, he merely smiled.

"They all go free. Your twin brother and sister will be sent to the best school in the Community. Your older brother will be given his own smaller Labor Unit to supervise. It will include housing and a very nice salary. Your other *friend* will have his medical fees and debt erased. Once he is healed, I'll leave it up to your brother to either hire him into his group or if he will be left to find another job for himself."

Huntley said the word 'friend' as if it were disgusting.

Evie sighed and nodded. She felt that this was the only victory she would ever have over him. "Thank you, sir."

She turned, ready to leave the room when his voice stopped her.

"Evie."

She turned to look at Huntley. A huge grin had spread across his face. Evie suppressed the urge to shudder when he raised his hand and crooked a finger at her. "Come here." He was holding something small in his hand, but she couldn't see what it was. She held her breath and walked forward, stopping in front of his desk. He chuckled. "No. Here."

He was pointing to the spot next to him, behind his desk. A feeling of dread was taking over her as she made her way around the desk and approached him. When she moved closer to him, Huntley rose from his seat. He towered over her, and she felt his hot breath on her face.

She finally saw the small device he was holding in his hand. It was the remote for her bracelets. Her heart jolted at the sight of his finger going for a small button on the bottom. Before she could open her mouth to protest, she heard the small sound from the remote and her bracelets sprang open. Evie looked down at her wrists, completely surprised. Huntley dropped the remote onto his desk and carefully removed her bracelets completely.

"You don't need these anymore," he said gently.

Evie rubbed her wrists, feeling somewhat overwhelmed. The last time she had been without her bracelets was when she was waiting to be assigned to Huntley's house at the Distribution Center. It was a very odd but welcome feeling.

She couldn't bring herself to meet his eyes, and her gaze stayed down to the floor.

"Thank you, sir."

She tried to turn away but was stopped. He had raised his hand under her chin and forced her to look up at him. Her heart was pounding loudly in her chest as his finger tucked a loose strand of hair behind her ear. Huntley slowly lowered his head and he captured her in a kiss. Evie began shaking as his arms gently wrapped around her, forcing her to press up against him.

Before Evie could get her thoughts together, Huntley spun her around and her back was suddenly pressed against the edge of his desk. His lips never left hers as his hands began to roam her body. With no warning, he grabbed her legs, and she was lifted onto his desk with him between her thighs. His mouth finally left hers, and his kisses began to travel down her neck.

Evie forced herself to breathe and endure his touch.

Her mind was racing as he slowly began unbuttoning her blouse. With every kiss and touch, she told herself over and over again that it would all be worth it in the end. Her loved ones would be free. Ryder would have a better chance of finding someone from Eden and getting them out of the Community. And if not, then they could finally have lives outside of servitude and could seek their own happiness.

Huntley's lips returned to hers, and she forced herself to respond. He moaned while Evie held onto the edge of his desk to keep balance. One of his hands slid up between her breasts and gently wrapped around her throat. He applied no pressure, but Evie felt as if he could strangle her at any moment. His other hand lifted her leg further up to wrap around his waist. He raised his head and looked into her eyes.

"Tell me you're mine." Huntley began trailing kisses all over her face, and Evie felt his hand slightly tighten on her neck. "Say it!" he hissed into her ear. There was now desperation in his voice.

She didn't want to give him another victory over her. Not yet. Before his lips could reach hers again, she pulled away from him.

"No! Not yet!"

Huntley froze, his eyes darkening in anger and aggravation. His hand tightened around her neck more, not in an attempt to hurt her but to assert dominance. But she wasn't going to be intimidated by him.

"I won't say it. Not until you keep your word."

Huntley's eyes narrowed, but he kept his hold on her. He leaned forward, and Evie felt his breath on her face again.

"All it takes is a couple of phone calls, Evie, and it is done."
She placed a hand on his chest and attempted to push him back away from her.

"And until you make those calls, I won't say it. I'm Community property until you keep your word."

Huntley stared down at her for several moments before he slowly released her throat and stepped away from her. Evie quickly slid off his desk and hurried to the door while closing her blouse.

"I'll have everything taken care of tomorrow, Evie. Remember that."

Evie placed her hand on the doorknob, then turned her head to look at him, keeping her face stoic and unreadable. "And I won't say anything you want me to say until after it is done. Remember that."

Out of the corner of her eye, she could see the small smile on his face when she walked out of his study. She quickly made her way into her room and ran into the bathroom. In a flash, Evie was in front of the bathroom sink, rinsing her mouth out over and over again. Next, she grabbed her toothbrush and squeezed out a ridiculous amount of toothpaste on the brush. By the time she was done, she had a metallic taste in her mouth from brushing so hard. Evie could see a small amount of blood when she spit into the sink.

Once her mouth felt clean, she immediately stripped off her clothes and jumped into the shower. No matter how hard Evie scrubbed, she couldn't stop feeling his hands and mouth on her body. Especially around her neck. After her skin was red and she had no energy left, she dropped to the bottom of the shower and silently cried.

Evie knew she had to get used to his touch. She had two small victories over him today. But starting tomorrow morning, he would be the one to always win. Evie couldn't help but be thankful he didn't completely force himself on her. Huntley could have easily taken more from her. He didn't have to stop. Why he didn't force himself on her, Evie had no idea, but she was thankful. Although that could change after tomorrow morning.

After the water ran cold, Evie forced herself out of the bathroom and changed into her pajamas. She turned off the light and crawled into bed. She didn't care how early it was. She desperately wanted to sleep and try to drift away for a while. The only positive thought that helped her was knowing that tomorrow morning, all of her loved ones would be free.

Before Evie could even try to close her eyes, she heard heavy footsteps outside the bedroom and in the hall. Her heart began to pound in her chest as the footsteps stopped outside of the bedroom door. In the darkness of the room, Evie could see the light coming in from under the bedroom door, with the shadows from a pair of feet blocking it. Evie held her breath for several minutes until the feet finally walked away.

She didn't release it until she heard Huntley's bedroom door open and close.

Chapter 16

In the end, Evie couldn't sleep and got out of bed early in the morning. Since she couldn't sleep, she decided to surprise Mary with coffee and breakfast. The house was eerily silent as she crept downstairs. Not even her footsteps made a sound.

In less than half an hour, Evie had a fresh pot of coffee ready and began cooking eggs and bacon for breakfast. Just as Mary was walking into the kitchen, Evie had finished plating everything up.

"What are you doing up so early?" Mary said with her brows raised in shock.

Evie shrugged. "I couldn't sleep."

Mary and Evie sat down at the table and silently ate breakfast. It wasn't until they were almost done eating that Mary broke the silence.

"So, are you going to tell me what the hell happened last night?"

Evie stared at the table, not wanting to meet the older woman's eyes yet. "I'm going to marry Huntley…in exchange for him freeing my family and Aaron. After today, their debt will be paid."

"Will that make you happy?" Mary asked softly.

Evie had no answer. Her eyes never left the spot on the table. After several moments of awkward silence, Mary rose from the table with a long sigh. "Well, you do what you need to do, hun. We both know I can't stop you." Mary began gathering the breakfast dishes. "But don't think for one second that I'm going to call you Mrs. Huntley!"

She meant it as a joke and Evie knew it, but that didn't stop the poor girl from breaking down into tears. Evie's hands covered her face as she leaned over the table and cried. Mary didn't hesitate. She practically threw the dishes on the table, some of the pieces falling onto the floor and shattering. Mary wrapped her arms around Evie, desperately trying to comfort her.

"I'm sorry… I'm so sorry…" Mary said while stroking Evie's hair.

Evie wrapped her arms around Mary and sobbed harder. The women stayed like that for several moments until Evie finally took a few deep breaths and slowly released herself from Mary's hold. "It's okay. It will all be worth it. They will all be free and live their lives outside of the Community."

Mary looked confused and raised a brow. "What do you mean 'outside of the Community'?"

Evie stood and gave her a hopeful look. "Like I told you before, Eden is real!" she whispered to her. "It's real. When all of them are free, Ryder can try to find someone from Eden. They can all get out!"

Mary took a step back and gave Evie an exasperated look. "Evie, I know you want to believe such things are real, but it's just a rumor. Eden doesn't exist."

Evie glowered. "Then why does Huntley have a file of them in his desk?"

Before Evie could say another word, Mary's hand suddenly covered her mouth. "Hush! That never happened! You found nothing and you didn't see anything. Okay? Drop it! I never want to hear of this again."

Mary began grabbing the breakfast dishes, her eyebrow twitching in aggravation. Evie sighed and cleaned up the broken dishes while Mary cooked Huntley's breakfast. She had no idea why Mary would be in such denial that Eden existed.

Once Mary finished assembling Huntley's breakfast tray, Evie carefully took it and exited the room. As she made her way up the stairs, her heart began to pound and goosebumps ran up her arms. The thought of him touching her again made her sick.

She gently knocked on his door and waited for his response.

"Come in."

Evie opened the door and tried to be as polite as possible. "Good morning, Mr. Huntley."

He said nothing as she placed the breakfast tray on his desk. Before she could grab the dirty dinner dishes, he grabbed her hand and gently pulled her closer to him. She turned to face him as he stood. "I owe you an apology," Huntley admitted. Her brows creased in confusion while his eyes roamed her face. "Last night...I got carried away. I shouldn't have done that. I should have restrained myself."

She blushed and looked away. "Thank you, sir."

"Elias."

Evie turned back to face him, looking confused. "Sir?"

"My name is Elias. No more formalities between us. In a couple of hours, your debt will be paid. You will no longer belong to the Community."

She tried to keep a look of anger off of her face. "So, I will belong to you then."

He chuckled. "I suppose you will. After we are married."

Evie took a breath and fought the urge to step away from him. "And when will that be?"

"Soon. I have some things to take care of first. I'll be meeting with an old friend of mine later today to make arrangements for your brother and sister to attend school. I can also speak to her about getting a marriage license for us."

Evie nodded and tried to step away from him, wanting some distance between them as she felt it was hard to breathe properly in front of him. But he did not release her hand. Instead, he pulled her even closer and reached a hand inside his pocket.

"I remember every word you said to me in this room. You called me a monster." She felt her blood run cold as he leaned down over her. "I promise you, Evie, I am not a monster. There is another side of me. One I haven't shown anyone else. I would love to share it with you."

His hand come out of his pocket to reveal a small box. Releasing her hand, he pulled out a ring. Her eyes widened at the sight of the beautiful sapphire ring. It was a simple oval cut with small diamonds surrounding it on a silver band. Carefully, he lifted her hand and slipped the ring onto her finger.

"I keep my promises, Evie. I promise you that I will never hurt you. You will always be safe with me. You will have my protection. You will be the only one to see the real side of me."

Evie was taken aback. He actually sounded sincere. Huntley raised her hand and gave it a gentle kiss.

"The only thing I have ever wanted in this life was someone like me. Someone who sees things for what they truly are in the Community. I never thought I would find you, and I will never let you go."

Before Evie could respond, his lips pressed against hers while one hand held the back of her head and his arm wrapped around her waist. Her head was spinning and she felt dizzy. Not once had she thought this man could be capable of such softness.

After several moments, he slowly broke the kiss and looked into her eyes.

"I have a car arriving in an hour. By the end of the day, you and your family will be free." He finally released her, and she took several steps back. Evie could not speak. "Please inform Mary that I won't require lunch today. I'll be home in time for dinner."

Evie simply nodded and quickly grabbed the dinner dishes. She rushed out of the room with the sound of him chuckling behind her.

Once she was in the hallway, she fell to her knees. The tray laid flat on the floor as she forced herself to breathe. Slowly, she lifted her hand and looked at the ring on her finger. It was beautiful. She couldn't help but wonder how long he had the ring, waiting for her to accept his deal. Another thing that startled her was the sincerity is his voice.

"I never thought I would find you. And I will never let you go."

She shivered and wrapped her arms around herself as she remembered his words. Evie was now convinced that she would never escape from the Community. He would keep her too close to him. And she was sure that if he was away, the Harvesters would keep an eye on her for him.

"Ryder...please find Eden! Please find a way out of this place!"

With shaking hands, she grabbed the tray and returned to the kitchen. Mary was scrubbing the countertops when she entered.

"You okay?"

Evie simply nodded and began to fill the sink with water. Out of the corner of her eye, she saw Mary approach and stand next to her.

"Okay, stop lying. What's wrong?"

Evie couldn't find the words to say. Silently, she raised her hand and flashed the ring to Mary. The older woman's eyes went wide as she gently took her hand and lifted it up to get a closer look.

"Damn! That's a hell of a ring! Well, the man has good taste in jewelry."

Evie gently took her hand back and stopped the water. "I guess this makes it official now. He said by the end of the day, everyone's debt will be paid. And he's going to speak to someone today to get a marriage license."

Mary gently patted her shoulder. "It will be alright. Mr. Huntley sure as hell has his flaws and has done some terrible things, but he's honestly good to his wives. If you're lucky, you will just stay in your room and him in his. You will only have to see him on formal occasions. Well, that is if you host a party here."

Evie snorted. "Yeah, like I know anyone in the Community besides family that I would invite over."

Mary chuckled. "Yeah, that was a dumb statement. But no matter what, know that I'm here for you. I have your back no matter what happens."

Evie immediately turned and wrapped her arms around Mary. "I know. Thank you."

Mary returned the hug, rubbing her back in comfort. After several moments, they stepped away from each other and Evie turned back to the dishes.

"Take your ring off while you wash them, or while you work overall. You don't want something happening to it. Although, I'm not sure how much longer you will be working like this. Pretty soon, you won't be in his service anymore."

Evie laughed and slipped the ring off, placing it on the counter.

"I'm not leaving you to do all this by yourself. That will never happen."

Mary laughed as well, turning back to her task. "I had a feeling you would say that."

Once the kitchen was done, she slipped the ring back onto her finger and set to her task of vacuuming the hallway. After some time, she heard footsteps coming down the stairs. Huntley smiled as soon as his eyes landed on her.

"I'll be heading out."

Evie nodded. "Have a good day, sir."

His eyes flashed with an unknown emotion and he walked over to her. "What is my name, Evie?"

She swallowed and forced herself to continue staring into his eyes. "Elias."

He smiled. "There is no need to call me 'sir' ever again."

She nodded. "Sorry. Force of habit."

Huntley chuckled. "I'm sure you will be able to break it quickly." He leaned down and gave her a gentle kiss on her forehead before turning and exiting out of the front door. She tried to continue her task with no distractions, but her head was spinning.

"By the time Huntley comes back, I will be free. My debt will be paid. My family's debt will be paid. And Aaron's debt will be paid."

It was her dream for almost her entire life for her loved ones to be free from debt, but she had never dreamed of it happening like this. She couldn't help but smirk.

"I'm trading my freedom for my siblings' and Aaron's freedom. Four lives freed for one. At least I'm getting the better end of the deal."

She began lugging the vacuum up the stairs to begin on the second floor. Before she could plug the cord into the outlet, the sound of someone talking caught Evie's attention. Quietly, Evie crept around the corner and heard a light voice coming out of Mary's room. She could just barely make out the words Mary was saying.

"Just do it! Quickly!"

Before Evie could lift her hand to knock on the door, it was swung open and she was greeted with Mary's startled face. "Jesus, Evie! What is wrong with you? You nearly gave me a heart attack!"

"Sorry! I was just worried. I heard you talking in your room."

Mary raised a brow. "What are you talking about? I was just putting something away. I wasn't talking to anyone."

Evie looked puzzled as Mary stepped out of her room and closed the door.

"Sorry, but I swear I heard you—"

"I sometimes get carried away and talk to myself. You aren't always around to talk to." Before Evie could say another word, Mary walked down the hall and went downstairs.

Evie shook her head and went back to vacuuming.

Maybe she was hearing things.

Evening finally arrived and Mary had just finished dinner. Both women were eating their roasted pork chops and vegetables when they heard the front door open. Evie's heart began to pound, and Mary tensed up as the kitchen door opened. Huntley gracefully entered the room and smiled at the two women. Mary stood instantly.

"Welcome back, sir. I'll have your dinner tray done for you in less than ten minutes."

He gave Mary a nod then looked at Evie. "It's done. Finish your dinner, then we will talk."

Evie offered a nervous smile and he left the kitchen. She looked down to her half-eaten dinner and suddenly didn't feel hungry anymore. Her head felt light, and she felt a wave of overwhelming emotions.

"It's done. They are all free."

Evie took a long breath and stood from the table. "I'll finish this later, Mary. I'll take up his dinner and get this conversation over with."

Mary looked as if she wanted to object but said nothing. The old woman quickly assembled a dinner plate and placed it on the tray. Without a word, Evie grabbed it and made her way out of the kitchen. The closer she got to Huntley's study, the heavier her feet felt. She forced herself to continue moving forward. Goosebumps spread all over her arms when she gently knocked on the door.

"Come in."

She entered with the tray and walked to his desk. Out of the corner of her eye, she saw him raise his brow at the sight of her.

"Did you finish your dinner already?"

She released a small breath and forced herself to look at him. "I wasn't hungry. I promised Mary I would finish it later."

Huntley smirked. As soon as she placed the tray down, Evie took several steps back. She didn't want to be within arm's reach of him.

"You said you wanted us to talk. Would you like to wait until you've eaten?"

"There's no need. We can talk now." He sat back in his chair and clasped his hands over his crossed knees. "You are all free. As we speak, I have transport vans going to the Children's Unit. Your younger brother and sister will be taken to the boarding school across the Community. They have wonderful housing for the children. Your brother has been informed and, starting tomorrow, will be promoted to running his own labor force for the Community. Your friend has had his debt and medical bills paid as well. When he recovers, he can join your brother's labor force, if he wants to."

Evie felt as if a giant weight lifted off of her chest. All her years of hard work and pain finally paid off.

They were all free.

She gave him a small smile. "Thank you." There was silence as they stared at each other for several moments. She began to feel incredibly awkward. Evie tried to think of something else to say. "W-when will we be married?"

"My friend is obtaining a marriage license for us. It will be a couple of days. I'm assuming a small private wedding is acceptable to you?"

She nodded. "I don't exactly know anyone else I would want to invite that isn't family."

He chuckled. "No. I don't want a single one of the Community's leeches at our wedding. It will be small. I only need one friend of mine to attend. You may invite your family, if you wish."

Evie swallowed. "W-when will it actually take place?"

"This Saturday."

She began shaking and felt lightheaded. "So soon?" Evie whispered.

Huntley tilted his head slightly, a smile still on his face. "Is that a problem, Evie?"

She frantically shook her head. "No! Not at all. It—it's fine. I just wasn't sure what to expect."

He chuckled. "I would hope that wouldn't be a problem. Especially with all the effort I made today to free your family and friend." Huntley's eyes seemed to harden at the final word, and Evie understood the silent threat.

"No, there is no problem. This Saturday is fine."

"Good. Mary can accompany you to find a dress tomorrow, if you want her to. She can now easily take over the household tasks."

Evie's eyes narrowed. "No. I won't leave her to do it alone. We may be married soon, but that won't stop me from helping Mary."

To her surprise, he laughed. "I figured you would say that. Mary can go back to bringing me my meals. In the meantime, you should decide on some wedding details, such as your dress and any flowers you would like. It won't be a grand affair, but you can choose what you want for the wedding. Whatever will make you happy, Evie."

She clenched her fists and grinded her teeth together. "Yes. Thank you, sir—" Evie was cut off by a hard glare.

"What was that, Evie?"

She took a shaky breath. "Elias. Thank you, Elias."

He smirked. "You're welcome."

She had just turned to leave when his voice stopped her.

"Evie."

She looked at him to see a chilling grin on his face.

"Am I to receive no award for my efforts today?"

She shivered and forced herself to begin rounding his desk to his side, knowing what he wanted.

Huntley turned in his chair as she approached him. Every part of her wanted to smack the grin off his face. The man who was so sincere to her earlier seemed to be gone. He was now once again using underlying threats to get what he wanted from her.

Evie slowly leaned down over him and gave him a small kiss on his cheek. "Thank you," she whispered.

Before she could fully stand up, his hand was gently placed behind her head, keeping her in place. "Is that all?"

This time, she couldn't suppress her glare. He seemed amused as she leaned back down and gave him a tender kiss on his lips. Before she could pull away, he deepened the kiss. His other hand grabbed her arm and jerked her forward, forcing her to fall onto his lap. Just as she gasped in surprise, his lips fell on hers again. His arms wrapped around her waist, keeping her in place. She was shaking as he groaned at the contact.

After a few moments, he pulled away and sighed. His dark eyes stared intently into her blue ones. "Apologies if that was too forward."

Evie quickly scrambled out of his lap and glared at him while he laughed at her flushed face. "I seriously doubt you are sorry," she snapped.

"Is it wrong for a husband to kiss his wife in such a way?"

"You aren't my husband yet!"

"No, but I will be before the week is over."

She turned to leave, ready to be away from him. Just as her hand landed on the door handle, she heard movement from behind her. Before she could completely turn, a large hand landed on the wall next to her head. The other was against the door, stopping her from opening it. Evie could feel his breath on the back of her neck, and her legs began to tremble.

"I'm a patient man, Evie. I truly am. But right now, my patience is at its limit."

His hands lifted from the wall and the door. She suddenly felt one hand begin to stroke her hair. It took every ounce of control she had not to knock his hand away.

"I want you, Evie. That's no secret. You know I'm a man who keeps his promises. I will never hurt you. I will protect you until the day you die and never let you go." Evie whimpered as his hand slowly slid to the front of her neck and gripped her throat. She wasn't sure if breathing was hard because of his grip or because she was afraid. "But do not deny me what is mine. Not even the simple pleasures of a kiss. Or your touch. It will be mine before the week is over."

Evie felt a flash of rage and turned to face him, knocking his hand away.

"This morning, you told me you weren't a monster. You told me there was another side to you. One you wanted to share with me and only me." The fear of him faded as she saw a look of surprise on his face. "So tell me, *Elias*, which side is the real you? The side that was so sincere this morning when you made your promises, or the man that threatens my loved ones to get what you want? Or is it the side you show to the higher-ups in the Community? There are so many faces you have!"

He took a step away from her, completely astonished.

"You are getting exactly what you want! You win! You win it all, okay? So, stop with your demands and stop threatening me and my family!"

Evie couldn't stop herself. She quickly turned and fled the room, afraid of what he would say or do. She rushed through the hallway, barely missing Mary as she ran by. She could faintly hear Mary calling to her, but she did not respond. Rushing into her bedroom, she ran straight into the bathroom. She fell in front of the toilet ready to vomit, but nothing came up. Her stomach simply churned in pain and she curled up into a ball on the floor.

Perhaps she had no tears to shed anymore. All she could do was stay on the floor and shiver. It was impossible to tell if she was shivering from the cold floor or because of her fear. From outside of the bathroom, Evie heard the sound of frantic footsteps coming into the room.

"Evie?" She felt strong arms wrap around her and force her to sit up. She opened her eyes to see the face of a concerned Mary. "Evie, what's wrong? Talk to me!"

Without warning, Evie began to giggle. Mary sat back with a look of confusion. "Mary," Evie said between giggles. "Do you want to go dress shopping with me tomorrow?" Her giggling quickly dissolved into sobs as Mary wrapped her arms around her.

Chapter 17

It was another night of no sleep. Evie's head was pounding, and her eyes were sore. Mary had to drag her out of the bathroom to lie down in the bed. When they woke up, Mary took the task of delivering Huntley's meal to him. She was honestly surprised he was not demanding her presence in his study and contemplated going to him and apologizing. Her fear now was of him harming her loved ones because of her outburst.

Mary refused to allow her to do any chores and demanded that Evie try to relax. But that was impossible. Evie took her time in the garden, pulling every little weed she could find as well as slowly trimming the bush hedges. The entire time she worked, she ignored the chill in the air. It was obvious that it would start snowing in the Community at any time now. Evie swore she could feel Huntley's gaze on her while she was outside and knew she would have to face him at some point.

Occasionally, her eyes fell on the large sapphire ring on her finger. With a heavy heart, Evie decided to go to him in the evening. She would apologize and beg for him not to hurt her loved ones. She knew she was safe from his fury. It was her family and Aaron she was worried about.

After an unknown amount of time, Evie heard the backdoor open and saw a flushed Mary coming outside.

"Mary, are you okay?"

The older woman huffed. "I should be asking you that. You're the one going through hell right now. Not to mention you moping around here."

Evie wanted to argue back, but she bit her tongue. She didn't want to fight with Mary, even if she was being harsh. "Mary, I'm just trying to keep busy. I'm not moping around at all. I—"

"You need to take a walk."

Evie stopped and blinked at Mary. "Huh?"

Evie finally noticed the large black coat Mary was carrying. She held it out for Evie to take. "You should be wearing this anyway. Just take this now and go for a walk. Get out of here for a bit." Mary thrust the coat at Evie when she didn't immediately take it. "Put it on and get out of here for a while."

Evie sighed. "Mary, I can't. I need to go apologize to Huntley. If I don't, he will—"

"He is fine!" Mary snapped. "I mean it. His mood is just fine. If you want to apologize, then do it later tonight. But you need to get out of this house and get some air."

Evie knew she wouldn't budge on the matter and begrudgingly slipped on the coat. Mary followed her to the front door, and Evie buttoned up the large coat. "Please tell me this isn't one of his ex-wives' coats."

Mary snorted. "No, it's mine. I wouldn't do that to you."

As she opened the front door, she gave Mary a small smile. "Thank you. I'll be back soon. Maybe some air will help."

Without warning, Mary grabbed Evie and wrapped her into a strong embrace.

"Know this," Mary whispered into her ear. "Everything will be fine. For you, your family, and your young man."

They broke away from each other and Evie looked completely confused and overwhelmed. "Mary, what—"

"Now, get out of here. And take care of my coat!"

The front door closed before Evie could say another word.

"Maybe a walk around the park will help me breathe."

She turned and placed her hands in her pockets, ready to stroll along and try to forget the world for a while.

Elias hardly touched any of his paperwork. The memories of the previous night ran through his mind. Not once did he think her capable of expressing such anger to him. It was refreshing and exciting to him. He had no intention of making her afraid of him for the rest of her life. Perhaps he should learn more restraint.

After some time, he heard knocking on the door.

"Come in."

Mary entered with a tray of shortbread cookies and a cup of coffee. "Good afternoon, sir," she greeted politely with a smile.

He returned the smile and gave a polite nod as she placed the small tray on his desk. "Hello. Where is Evie?"

"She went out for a walk, sir. Said she needed some air."

Elias nodded. "When she returns, ask her to come and see me please."

Mary smiled. "I will, sir. Though, she did mention speaking to you this evening."

He raised a brow. "Did she mention why?"

"Well…she said something about owing you an apology. But I'm not sure why."

Elias chuckled. "I believe we owe each other an apology. Thank you, Mary. I'll speak with her when she gets home." He sat forward in his chair and grabbed the cup of coffee.

Mary nodded. "I'll let her know as soon as I see her."

She quickly exited the room and he casually sipped his coffee. No one else that had ever worked for him could quite make a cup of coffee as good as Mary could. He wondered if Evie could make it just as good.

The sound of his phone ringing brought him back out of his thoughts. He gracefully lifted the phone to his ear.

"Yes?"

"Elias, how are you?"

He smiled at the sound of Edith's voice. "Very well. How are you?"

"I am well, thank you. How is your bride-to-be doing?"

"As well as she can be, at the moment. But things will be better after the wedding."

"Ah yes, I'm looking forward to it. Your wedding certificate will be ready by Friday afternoon. It will be interesting to hear the gossip around town after you two are wed."

He chuckled. "I'm sure you will tell me all about it. None of them dare say it directly to me. But while I have you, I want to thank you again for helping me with my wedding present to her."

"About that. That's actually why I'm calling."

Elias raised a brow. "Is something wrong?"

"No. Well, I don't think so. I'm not sure. The twins that were released yesterday. Did you have them taken somewhere else last night?"

There was a strong silence before he answered. "No. Why?"

There was a deep breath on the other side of the phone.

"Well, I sent the van last night to pick up the children. I called the school this morning to confirm that they were settled and everything went well. The school confirms that they were taken to their housing, but their older brother apparently came and took them just an hour after they were dropped off."

He silently listened to her every word, trying to put together the puzzle that was just dropped in front of him. "The school allowed a man who claimed to be their brother to just take two children in the middle of the night?"

"The children themselves confirmed he was their brother. And, since he wasn't in debt, they didn't question it. None of the students there are Community property, so the school doesn't track visitor times and such. But they haven't returned yet. Didn't you tell me that you were freeing her older brother too?"

There was another hard silence, and Elias felt anger beginning to brew inside of him. "Edith, please let me make some calls. I will call you back as soon as possible."

"Understood. Thank you."

As soon as he hung up, his fingers quickly dialed the needed extension. It rang twice before someone answered.

"Laborer's Unit."

"This is Elias Huntley. I need some information on a man who was released and given a promotion. A man named Ryder Harmond. He was released from debt as of last night."

"Right away, sir!" He faintly heard the sound of clicking from a keyboard. "Yes, sir! Former number four-six-one-eight. Birth name was Ryder Harmond. Per orders from the council, he was released last night and told he would be leading his own smaller unit. But when he was given the offer, he rejected it and left."

"What do you mean he rejected it?" Elias snapped.

"I'm sorry, sir, but he rejected the offer. He said he would make his own way and left the unit. We have no idea where he went. And he isn't in debt, so there was no need to—" Elias had heard enough and ended the call, slamming the phone down on the receiver.

"The brother doesn't take the job, Fine. That's his stupidity. But why take the children? Where would they go? He can't provide for them without a job. Where did he take them?"

Another flash of anger made him lift the phone back up and punch in the next number.

"Community Central Hospital. How many I—"

"This is Elias Huntley. Connect me to the debt sector of the hospital."

"One moment please,"

His patience was wearing thin as the line rang. A feminine voice finally answered.

"Hello, this is—"

"This is Elias Huntley. I need information on a man who was released from debt and had his medical bills paid. The name is Aaron Carlen. He was in the Laborer's Unit."

"Just a moment please." More keyboard clicking could be heard from the other line. "Number five-eight-one-three, birth name was Aaron Carlen. Yes, his debt and medical bills were waived last night."

"Is he still a patient in your unit? Was he transferred to the other side of the hospital?"

There was an awkward pause. "N-no sir. He released himself last night."

"What do you mean he released himself? A man in his condition was allowed to release himself from the hospital?" Elias spat.

"Sir, I'm sorry, but he was no longer in debt! Unless you are in debt, we don't-"

"Where did he go?" he yelled through the phone.

Elias heard whimpering on the other side of the line. "Sir, we don't know! He was picked up by a man—"

He slammed the phone down in frustration and stood, pacing in front of his desk.

"This isn't a coincidence. This was planned. This all happens after their debts were paid. There is a puzzle here, and I can't see all the pieces!"

He paced as his thoughts surrounded him. None of this made sense to him, but he knew he shouldn't care. They were all free. If they wanted to waste the good fortune he had given them, then that was their stupidity. He kept his end of the bargain. He gave them freedom and opportunity while Evie—

Elias froze.

"She went out for a walk, sir. Said she needed some air."

Mary's words seemed to echo in his head and, for the first time since he was a boy, felt a rush of panic. In a flash, he grabbed the phone and punched in another number.

"Conner."

"Evie is in the Community walking around somewhere. Find her and bring her to me immediately!"

"Yes, sir."

Elias slammed the phone down, almost breaking it. His breathing was heavy, and his anger was out of control for the first time in years. If Evie wasn't safely returned to him soon, many people were going to find themselves heading straight to Medical Waste.

Evie had no idea how long she had been walking for. Mary was right. She needed the fresh air. Even the light snowfall was pleasant.

"It's time to accept how things are going to be. I need to apologize to Huntley. Apologize and just let things happen. My family and Aaron are free. Even if they don't get out of the Community, they will be free to have happy and normal lives."

With tears in her eyes, Evie looked up to the sky.

"Aaron, please find someone who will love you as much as I do. Please find happiness with someone."

She quickly wiped the tears from her eyes and began making her way out of the Community park. Just as Evie exited the property and stepped onto the sidewalk, she heard the sound of tires squealing and the roar of an engine. Her head spun to see a large van stop right next to her. It was a Harvesters van.

Evie's survival instincts took over and she turned to run, but it was too late. Two large men were quick to grab Evie's arms and she was being dragged into the van.

"I didn't do anything! Let me go!" she screamed.

Just as they dragged her into the van, the door closed, and the van took off. Evie fought with every bit of strength she had.

"Get off me!" she hollered at the men who held her arms.

A large hand covered her mouth, and one of the men's faces was suddenly inches away from her own. The second man was behind her, holding her arms.

"Stop screaming! We aren't with the Harvesters! If you want to see your family again, you need to shut up and calm down!"

Evie's eyes went wide and she stopped struggling. The hands on her slowly released their hold on her.

"W-who are you?" Evie tried to sound strong, but her question came out more as a whimper. The mention of her family scared her to death.

The man took a breath and seemed to calm down. "My name is Mark, and I'm here to help you."

The van was no longer driving erratically. Evie was able to steady herself and look around. She couldn't see the driver in front as a large black screen stretched across the vehicle. The man behind her finally came into view as he slid away from Evie. There was nowhere for them to sit in the back, so they were all forced to continue to rest on the floor of the van.

Evie looked at the other man. She couldn't help but think that he looked very familiar. He had almond skin, dark eyes, and short dark hair. The man named Mark had dirty blond hair and blue eyes. Both men had hard lines on their face which hinted at years of stress.

Her eyes darted from one man to the other. "If you aren't with the Harvesters, then who are you?"

Mark shrugged. "Just some people trying to help out others. If you let us, we can help you too."

Evie's eyes went wide again. "Are you with Eden?"

Mark exchanged a look with the other man. "Eden? What the hell is that?"

"There was a rumor going around about a group called Eden helping people in debt escape. Are you them?"

Both men looked at each other, then burst into laughter.

"Jesus, what kind of a name is that?" Mark chortled, throwing his head back.

"I wanted to be named the Liberation Squad!" the other man added, tearing up while he laughed along.

Everyone jumped when they heard someone pound on the dashboard in the front seat of the van. "Shut up back there! You never know who can hear you!" a feminine voice hissed.

The men rolled their eyes, and Evie finally looked at the man sitting next to her. "Were you in the Laborer's Unit? You look familiar."

The man looked at Evie in surprise. "No. I've never been in debt."

This confused Evie even more. "Then who—"

They were all startled when the van finally stopped moving. They heard the driver's side door open and close. Just a moment after, the side door to the van slid open.

"Let's go!" a strong voice commanded.

The men quickly climbed out of the van, and Evie slowly followed. It seemed as though they were in a dimly lit garage of some kind.

"Evie!"

Her head whipped around to see a familiar man running right for her.

"Ryder!"

Evie ran forward and wrapped her arms around him. She cried tears of joy while Ryder spun her around in excitement. Once he placed her back on her feet, her hands clutched the sides of his face. "What are you doing here?"

Ryder smiled as he gently peeled her hands off of his face. "You told me to get everyone out. I would never leave without you."

Before Evie could question him more, the sound of someone clearing their throat made them both turn their heads.

The woman was just a few inches taller than Evie. Her hair was thin, and dark bags hung from under her eyes. "If you're done with your little reunion, we need to move on," she snapped.

Evie took a step forward. "Who are you?"

The woman stood tall and proud. "We don't have a name, but everyone in the Community calls us Eden. We're here to help you."

Evie took a moment to finally get a good look at their surroundings. She noticed this was more of an abandoned warehouse rather than a garage. The windows were boarded up with planks. The only light source came from the electric lanterns spread through the room.

"We don't have much time," the woman said quickly. "You need to make a choice. You can either stay or let us help you escape."

Evie's heart began to pound in her chest. "I can't leave without my brother and sister! Or A—"

"They have already been secured," the woman said impatiently, cutting her off with a wave of her hand. "The choice you make now is for yourself. No one else."

Evie looked to Ryder. "Where are they?"

Ryder gave her a small smile. "They're safe. BB, CC, and Aaron. They're safe."

"Your brother, sister, and fiancée were extracted last night," the woman said, clearly annoyed. "They're waiting for us to meet with them. But you need to decide. Are you coming with us or staying here?"

Evie turned back to completely face the woman. "Who are you?"

The woman let out an exasperated noise. "My name is Anna. I was saved from the Community many years ago by the same group of people helping your family now. Our informant told us that it was imperative to save you as soon as possible. She gave us the opportunity to get you this morning."

Evie opened her mouth to ask, but the answer suddenly rushed into her head. "Mary?"

Anna nodded. "She's been helping us for years. Mary has helped save dozens of children during her time working for us."

Evie's heart pounded loudly in her chest. All this time they had worked together and not once did she ever think that Mary was a member of Eden. "Why? Why did she want you to help me?"

Anna tilted her head. "So, you want to go back and marry Huntley?"

Evie glared at the woman, her hands clenched into fists. "Of course not! But why would Mary risk herself like this?"

"You tell me!" a man snapped. Evie turned to the familiar looking man from the van. His eyes were filled with anger and sorrow. He went on, "You tell me why she thought you were worth it. I probably lost her because of you!"

Evie stared at his face for several moments. Upon looking over his face, she finally realized who he was.

"You're Mary's son, aren't you? You're Michael."

His gaze dropped to the ground, his expression growing dark. Mark stepped forward and placed a hand on his shoulder.

Anna turned to address him. "Mary knew the risks, Michael. You both knew."

It was the first time Evie heard Anna speak with compassion. Michael nodded and wiped the tears out of his eyes.

"Mary contacted us and said we must move quickly. She knew you would take Huntley's deal for your family. Mark contacted Ryder just before his debt was paid. Ryder was then informed to reject the job offer and go get your twin brother and sister.

As soon as we obtained them, he went to the hospital and helped Aaron discharge himself. They were out of the Community borders before the sun even rose for the day."

Evie sighed in relief, and Ryder stepped up behind her, his hands resting on her shoulders.

"We thought Mary had been under suspicion for a while, but we were wrong. Mary was able to help us for many years. But she couldn't let him win. She wasn't going to let you sell yourself when you and your family could be saved. Her last request to us was getting you and your loved ones out. You could say it was a final 'fuck you' to Huntley."

"He deserves a lot more than a simple 'fuck you,'" Evie hissed.

Anna surprised Evie with a small laugh. "You're right. He does. That man will pay for everything he has done one day. I am sorry you had to suffer. I still can't comprehend the monster he's become."

Evie raised a brow. "How do you know Huntley?"

Anna took a long while to respond.

"He's my brother."

Chapter 18

Mary sat at the small table in the kitchen, slowly sipping her coffee. Her eyes casually glanced at the clock every few minutes. Another cup of coffee sat hot and ready right across from her. After several moments of nothing but the sound of the clock ticking, Mary finally heard the kitchen door open from behind her. She continued to slowly drink her beverage as Elias's large frame entered her view.

"Mary," he greeted politely.

She gave him a polite nod in return. It was quite odd to see him in the kitchen, but Mary was expecting it. Elias gracefully took the seat right across from her and began slowly drinking the cup that was ready for him. The two stared at each other from across the table. Despite the circumstances, both still held a deep respect for one another.

Elias quickly grew tired of the silence. "How long, Mary?" he asked.

Mary didn't say anything for a while as she carefully considered her next words.

"I have no idea how long it's been now. Pretty much as soon as my Michael was saved. Took me a while to learn your routine before I could help them."

Elias tilted his head. "And by them, you mean Eden?"

Mary shrugged. "If that's what you want to call them."

Another couple sips of coffee were taken.

"I'm quite surprised," Elias admitted, eyes thoughtful. "I never noticed you going through my paperwork. I'm sure that's what helped you get out all of those children."

"Well, I've worked here for quite a while. It took me almost a year before I got the nerve to begin actually looking for anything useful."

He nodded and took another drink from his mug. "How have they been taking the children, Mary?"

She raised a brow and gave him a stern look. "We both know I won't answer that question, sir."

Elias smirked. "No. But if you're smart, you will answer my next question." He gently placed the coffee cup on the table and leaned forward. "Where is Evie?"

They stared at each other, both silently challenging the other. Finally, she sat back in her seat. "How do you know she still isn't taking a walk?" Mary said sarcastically.

The corner of his mouth twitched in aggravation. "I was alerted early this morning that her twin brother and sister did not stay at the school's housing unit after their older brother took them. And since their debt was erased, they were no longer being monitored. Same with her older brother. And her friend in the hospital checked himself out as soon as his bills and debt were paid last night. It doesn't take much to figure out what happened."

His eyes narrowed dangerously as he extracted the small flip phone from his pocket. "I found this hidden inside your mattress. You made the call and told them when they would all be free."

Elias placed the phone in the center of the table. Mary's eyes didn't bother to look down at it. She merely stared at him blankly.

"Now, tell me. Did Evie know to 'go for a walk' today?"

Mary scoffed. "Of course not. She never suspected a thing. I sent the poor girl out myself. Besides, we both know she never would have willingly gone if she knew her family was still in the Community. It would have been too dangerous for them. She never cared about her own safety."

He smiled. "Yes, you're right."

Mary took another small sip of her coffee, obviously wanting to savor every drop. "Why her? Why are you so infatuated with her?" she asked.

Elias raised a brow. "And how do you know it's just an infatuation?"

Mary tried to suppress a shudder, but failed. "Why her? Why do you want her so badly?"

He slowly released a breath and sat back in his seat. He knew there was no need to hide anything from Mary. His eyes began to scan the room. "I remember when I was a boy working in a home like this. I made sure my house is the largest in the Community but, at the time, the home I worked in was the largest. I worked for the worst bastard in this unit." Elias stood, his eyes looking over the appliances.

"One day, I was beaten for not having the lawn finished before noon. The sadistic fuck kicked me out of the house bloody and bruised, telling me not to return until the yard work was done. Every inch of my body felt like broken glass as I began to work." He suddenly stopped, his eyes staring at the light on the ceiling.

"Across the street, there was this house. It was just outside the Community Board Unit. It was such a cozy home. Perfect for a small family. It even had a white fence with flowers surrounding it."

He continued to look at the light while Mary leaned forward, listening intently.

"I saw a car pull up into the driveway. As soon as the man exited the car, his wife came out of the house and greeted him with a smile, holding their child in her arms. I could feel the love they had, even from across the street. It was real, genuine love. Something I never believed existed until that point."

Elias sighed and took his seat at the table, facing Mary again.

"After that moment, I knew that there was some form of love in this rotting place. All I ever wanted was someone who thought the same way I did. For someone who saw the rotting decay of the Community." His eyes darkened, and a smile spread across his face. "And I did. I found a woman who not only believes what I do, but who holds so much love inside her that she would give up everything she has for her family. It's everything I've ever wanted in my life."

There was silence in the kitchen for several movements while Mary tried to comprehend everything he had said. "So, the man who has destroyed so many lives wants the white-picket fence dream. A loving little family. No offence, sir, but I didn't take you as a family man."

He tilted his head. "You don't think I would make a good father, Mary? Evie will make a wonderful mother. I was hoping after the wedding, we could turn her room into a nursery."

Mary clearly looked disgusted and leaned away from him. "And you think after everything you've done, you deserve any of that?" she asked, incredulous.

Elias smirked. "No one deserves anything. If you want something, you need to take it as soon as you can. I learned that a very long time ago." He finally finished his coffee and leaned forward. "Tell me where she is, Mary. Tell me, and all is forgiven. Your debt will be paid and you will be free to go wherever you want. No one will know of your assistance in helping Eden and going against the Community."

Mary stared at him in disbelief. "And the ones that took her from you?"

"They will be dealt with. But the faster I find Evie, the more of a chance you have of seeing your son again."

Mary sighed and sat back in her seat, averting her eyes. "I accepted a long time ago that I would never see my son again. I know he's safe." Her face finally lifted, and she met Elias's gaze with a look of resolution. "You are right about some things. She really did used to be like you. And I do mean 'used to.' Evie found out about the existence of Eden thanks to you. She found the information in your study." She smiled at the flash of anger on his face. "So, I'm sorry if this disappoints you, but Evie suddenly had something you have never had before. Hope. Real hope. Maybe in some ways, she is still a bit like you, but not nearly as much as you once thought. And yes, Evie is a woman full of so much love that she would be willing to sacrifice everything she has for her loved ones. But it's not a love you deserve to have."

She leaned forward and sneered at him. "There is no chance in hell that I would ever tell you where to find her."

He said nothing for a long while. Elias still regarded her with respect, though he wasn't going to hide his disappointment and anger. He stood and slowly walked over to the kitchen door. Mary sighed as she heard the shuffling of two men entering the room. Elias made his way back to the other seat across from her. He didn't sit, but he stared down at her, frowning.

She knew exactly where she was going.

"Thank you for your years of service, Mary," Elias said with full sincerity.

Mary finished the last of her coffee and stood. "And thank you for helping me save those children."

Elias's eyes flashed with anger as the two men gently took Mary's arms and led her out of the kitchen. She walked out of the house standing tall and looking proud.

As soon as Mary was escorted out of the kitchen, another man stepped in. "Sir, we have news."

Elias's eyes darted to Conner, who had been patiently waiting outside the room. "What is it?"

"We caught surveillance footage of your fiancée in the park. Just as she was exiting the area, a Harmony Group van pulled up and dragged her into the vehicle. Somehow, they stole one of our vans, which we are currently investigating. Surveillance also confirms it was the same van used to pick up the former labor worker from the hospital. We haven't been able to find the location he and the children were taken to."

Elias couldn't stop himself from smiling. Eden was much smarter than he thought. They had taken advantage of the deal Evie made with him. He knew Evie had nothing to do with this plan, but it was brilliant of Eden and Mary to use Evie's deal to easily come in and take her family.

He finally looked at Conner, snapping out of his thoughts. "Do we have any leads on where they are?"

Conner nodded. "We found an old warehouse in the Laborer's Unit. There's evidence that it has been used by several people. Pictures were left behind. Pictures of the children that disappeared over the last several months."

"And the van they used?"

"We were able to track it. It's currently parked at another warehouse in the Lumber Unit."

Huntley grinned to himself. It was all coming together.

"Good. We need to move fast. They will try to escape anytime now. We need one of the rebels alive for interrogation. Evie is to be given back to me immediately."

"And the others, sir?"

"There is plenty of room for them at Medical Waste."

"And the children?"

Elias gave Conner a dark look. It was more than enough to answer his question. The man nodded to his boss and began to leave the room.

Elias called out, "The other young man with them…Aaron…"

Conner turned to listen and was met with a furious face.

"I want him torn for parts."

The answer was an easy decision for Evie. Her younger brother and sister were safely away, along with Aaron. All they needed to do was get themselves out. The sapphire ring that was once on her finger had been tossed on the floor of the abandoned warehouse.

Anna sat in the back of the large van with everyone else. Michael had decided to take a turn driving.

"Where are we going now?" Evie asked.

"The Farming Unit. We'll escape through the trees. From there, we have a small boat that will take us out of the Community lines. There's a ship waiting outside of the boarders. That's where the rest of your family are. No matter what happens to us, they're safe."

"They won't follow us out of the Community borders? I didn't think they cared about territory lines."

"We don't have a choice. But once we're on the ship, we have more people to help us. They're prepared with weapons and are ready to fight back. We also have another advantage. We disabled all the other boats in the area. It would take some time before they could even try to follow us. Then, we'll make our way to the Settlement. It was founded by people who escaped from the Community in the past."

Evie nodded. She was trying to stop herself from shaking but was failing miserably. Despite the heat running in the van, she felt cold.

"Are you really Huntley's sister?" Evie asked quietly. There had been no time for her to ask these questions earlier. They needed to move immediately. But now, Evie couldn't stop herself from asking. She could vaguely see some resemblances Anna shared with Huntley.

Anna's expression turned sour.

"Unfortunately, yes. We're twins. We were both turned in at the same time. Kind of ironic how each of us turned out," she said bitterly.

Evie looked to the floor of the van, unsure of what to say.

"Why did Huntley want to marry you?" Anna questioned next.

Evie shrugged. "He told me that we were alike in many ways. I guess in some ways, we really are. He said he was waiting for someone like me. I don't know or understand why he wanted me."

No one said anything after that. Everyone else around them had been listening intently, but now, there was nothing much else to say.

Everyone jumped when Michael pounded on the screen separating him and the rest of the crew. "Incoming! They found us!"

Evie's heart pounded in her chest as Ryder suddenly grabbed her and held her close.

Anna rushed towards the front of the van to speak to Michael. "How many are following?"

"We've got two Harvester vans and three motorbikes on our trail!"

Evie felt herself begin to hyperventilate. She wasn't sure how, but she knew Huntley was in one of those cars.

"How far are we from the unit?"

"We're almost there!"

Anna immediately turned to address everyone in the van, her eyes wild and desperate. "We will have to move quickly! The van won't make it to the docks but the motorbikes can! Once we reach the tree line, we have several of our own bikes waiting for us! Run to the bikes as fast—"

She was cut off by the van suddenly spinning out of control.

"They're ramming into us!" Michael hollered.

Evie held onto Ryder for dear life while he gripped a small bar on the side of the van so hard his knuckles turned white.

"We're about to crash! Everyone, get ready to run!"

They all braced themselves. It felt as if time had slowed down. Within moments, everyone was suddenly slammed into the side of the van as it crashed into the trees. Despite being dazed, Evie was astonished that Anna was still able to move as fast as she had. She crawled forward and forced the door of the van open.

"Everyone, move! Now!"

They all quickly climbed out of the van. Evie was then able to see that the opposite side of the van had collided with a large tree. Michael helped everyone get out of the vehicle with firm hands. All of them could see the large black cars and motorbikes closing in on them.

"The bikes are ahead! They can't follow us in the trees! Move it!"

Everyone wasted no time. They ran as fast as they could deeper into the trees. Sure enough, several feet in front of them was a small clearing where three motorbikes sat waiting for them. Ryder immediately jumped onto one and Evie quickly climbed on behind him. Anna slipped on the same bike as Michael while Mark got onto his own. Just before they began driving into the trees, Evie glanced behind them. The cars had suddenly changed direction, no doubt planning to try and cut them off. She considered them lucky that the trees were too thick for their larger motorbikes to follow through the tree line.

The small dirt path they took was very narrow and was hardly big enough for the smaller bikes. Evie held onto Ryder as tightly as she could while branches slapped into her arms. Thankfully, Mary's coat protected her from bruises and cuts. Ryder wasn't so lucky. His bare arms were scratched and bleeding but he didn't slow down.

It seemed like it had taken hours, but finally, they could see the end of the road. Just ahead was the water. As soon as they broke out of the trees, everyone dropped their bikes. No one even bothered to turn them off. Evie slipped and fell hard onto the dirt. Searing pain ran down her arms and could already feel bruises forming. That didn't stop Ryder from grabbing her and dragging her forward.

"We're almost there! Keep moving!" he yelled.

Evie gritted her teeth and forced herself to keep running. Her lungs burned, and her legs almost felt numb. Ahead of them was the boat on the docks. The other Community boats were floating around in the water, their motors removed. Michael and Mark hurried to untie the boat, ready to push off. Evie and Ryder had just jumped onto the docks when the vans and motorbikes seemed to burst out of the trees.

Evie was shoved inside the boat by Anna, who then rushed forward to push the boat away from the dock. Evie laid on the bottom of the boat, trying to catch her breath as everyone took their seats.

"Why haven't we moved yet?" Anna demanded, her voice coming out in a shriek.

"The motor won't start!" Mark yelled, desperately trying to pull the chain on the motor.

Evie began to panic as she heard the slamming of car doors opening and closing. The roars of the motorbike engines were cut off. After what felt like an eternity, the roar of the motor turned on and the boat jolted out into the water. They all heard the yelling of the men on the shoreline. Once they were a few feet away, the motor on the boat died and they stopped.

"Fuck!" Mark cursed, desperately trying to get it working again.

Evie stayed on the floor of the boat, shivering and trying to calm herself. She couldn't stop herself from screaming in fear as the sound of gunshots filled the air. Everyone quickly ducked, trying to avoid the bullets.

"Hold your fire!" a loud voice commanded.

The sound of gunshots finally stopped. Mark didn't hesitate and quickly began to work on the motor again.

"Evie!"

Evie felt as if her heart had stopped. Her blood ran cold, and she felt herself begin to hyperventilate.

It was Huntley.

"Evie, this isn't over! I will find you! No matter where you run, I will find you!"

Ryder quickly wrapped his arms around his sister and tried to cover her ears. "Don't listen! Don't listen to him!" he whispered to her. But Huntley's voice was too loud. Mark was still trying to start the motor.

"You're mine, Evie! I will never let you go!"

Evie began to cry, clutching onto her brother. Huntley's voice was finally drowned out by the sound of the motor starting. But the damage was done. His voice would haunt her for the rest of her life.

The boat roared to life, and Mark immediately led them away from the Community border. No one relaxed until the men on the docks were nothing but specks in the background.

Chapter 19

Everyone was still trying to catch their breath as the boat drove through the open water. The smell of salt water filled the air as they were speeding away from the Community. Evie hadn't moved once. Ryder stayed on the floor with her, holding her tightly against him. She was shivering uncontrollably due to fear and anxiety.

After about ten minutes, Evie finally sat up in the boat. Ryder followed, still keeping his arms wrapped around her. Anna was sitting in the seat just behind her. Evie was surprised when Anna rested a hand on her shoulder.

"It's over," Anna said in a comforting voice.

Evie wiped the tears out of her eyes and looked back at Anna. "It isn't over. This is far from over." She didn't say it to be rude; it was nothing but the truth. Anna gave her a weak smile, but her expression was full of deep respect.

"We got away too easily," Michael said. "They could have easily killed us all. Why the hell would Huntley tell them to stop firing?"

There was silence for a moment before Anna spoke.

"Because he couldn't risk killing Evie."

All heads turned to her. Anna was looking down at Evie with a soft expression.

"He didn't want to risk hurting you. Maybe you don't realize it, but I think you saved all of our lives."

She said nothing and leaned into her brother's embrace.

They were all quiet as the boat continued to wade through the water. After some time, Evie finally saw the large ship that was waiting for them. The large black structure looked to be well fortified with several armed guards on the deck.

As soon as they stopped the small boat, Mark and Michael helped Evie and Ryder climb up the small ladder to ascend onto the large vessel. As soon as their feet touched the deck of the ship, they heard their names being called.

"Evie! Ryder!"

She turned and was tackled by her twin brother and sister. Her arms wrapped around them and she began covering their faces in kisses with tears of happiness streaming down her face as she dropped to her knees. As soon as Ryder got on the boat, he knelt down and his arms wrapped around the three of them. None of them wanted to let go of each other. It wasn't until Michael spoke that Evie slowly began to release them.

"Your other friend is down below. He's still in pretty bad shape. First door on the left in the hallway."

Evie slowly stood and smiled at BB and CC. "I'm going to go say hi to Aaron."

The twins then turned their full attention to Ryder. As Evie made her way down the stairs of the ship, her heart began to pound. This would be the first time she had seen him since his attack. Upon reaching the door, she gave a light knock.

"Aaron?"

After several moments of no response, she carefully began opening the door. Once she stepped inside, Evie's hands covered her mouth, and she held back a sob.

Aaron was covered in several bandages. His right arm was in a cast, and his left eye was black and almost swollen shut. Evie stumbled forward and collapsed into the chair next to his small bed. She gently placed a hand on his chest and silently cried. When his hand covered hers, she jumped.

His eyes slowly opened, and he gave her a small smile. "Hey, Evie."
She tried to smile for him, but she couldn't help the hot tears rolling down her cheeks. "Aaron...I'm sorry...I'm so sorry..." she sobbed.

Aaron's hand tightened around hers. "It isn't your fault. It never was. I knew you would get out. I knew I'd see you again."

Evie finally smiled at him, and his face turned serious.

"What happened, Evie? What did he do to you?"

She forced herself to keep a straight face, shaking her head. "It doesn't matter. None of that matters now."

He narrowed his eyes. "Did he hurt you? Did he try anything? Please, tell me the truth."

Evie lowered her gaze to their entwined hands. "He hurt you because of me. I rejected his offer because I didn't want Ryder to be the only one to pay off BB and CC's debt. But he thought I rejected him because of you." Evie took a breath before forcing herself to continue. "Then, I found out everything about him. He started the Medical Waste Facility. He's also the one who leaks contraband into the Underground. And he's in charge of the Harvesters. So many evil things in the Community was created by him."

Evie could see his face beginning to turn red and his teeth grind together. "Did he force himself on you?"

Evie couldn't bring herself to look at him. Her thoughts went back to those moments in Huntley's study. He didn't need to hear anything like that right now.

"No. But the only way I was going to free all of you was if I married him." Aaron turned his head and glared at the ceiling. "I'm going to kill him, Evie. One day, I'm going to watch the light leave his eyes!"

Evie began to shake her head frantically. "Don't think like that! We never have to step foot in the Community again. We never have to see him again!"

It was a lie she was telling herself as well as him. A terrible feeling in her chest told her that none of this was over and that she would be seeing Huntley again. She just wasn't sure when.

Aaron sighed and looked back at Evie. "Well...I hope you're still okay with marrying me." With a shaking hand, he slowly slid his hand under the blanket and into his pocket. It took a moment, but he soon held up a small metal ring. "Not exactly a diamond. But maybe I can get you something better when we get to the Settlement."

Evie began to smile and cried happy tears at the sight. "How? How did you—"

"Had some help. The boys at the unit found some scrap metal. Took about five hours while everyone was asleep to make it. I had it with me the entire time. Even in the hospital."

Evie took the ring and slipped it onto her finger. "It's perfect, Aaron!"

She slowly lowered her head and gave him a gentle kiss. Very carefully, she broke the kiss and slid next to him on the bed. His arm wrapped around her, and Evie smiled at the warmth of his embrace.

The next couple of days seemed to drag on endlessly. BB and CC quickly adjusted to being able to sleep in rather than wake up early to begin lessons. Anna assured Evie and Ryder that they could attend a normal school in the Settlement. They still woke up early out of a habit well embedded in them from a young age. Aaron continued to stay in bed, as he still needed to heal from his injuries.

Evie sat on the deck of the ship well before the sun was due to rise. She heard the heavy footsteps of her brother approach her. He gently took a seat next to her, staring in the same direction.

"You doing okay?" he asked.

Evie thought for several movements. "I...I don't think I'm going to be okay for a while. I will be someday."

He smiled at her. "Yeah, I get it. I think there's hope for BB and CC, though. With some time, I hope they can forget the past. At least most of it, anyway."

She nodded and began twirling Aaron's ring on her finger. "It's not over," she said, still staring into the distance. "None of this is over yet."

He continued to stare in the same direction as Evie. "You're right. It's not. But for now, we need to take a break and try to move forward. It's all we can do."

Evie smiled as the sun began to rise for the day. They squinted their eyes from the blinding light. In the distance, the duo could see small buildings. They had reached the Settlement. Ryder's arm wrapped around her, and he pulled her close.

"I don't know what will happen from here, but we're all together now. We're all going to be okay in the long run," he said confidently.

They both looked up into the sky as the clouds drifted past. The sun shone brightly as it rose over the Settlement.

Evie's smile grew.

"Maybe there is a God after all."

Acknowledgments

Thank you for taking the time to read my story! I have been working on The Community for years and it's a dream come true to see it shared with the world.

When I was a kid, my dream growing up was to become an actor. I loved the idea of getting out of myself and emerging into another character and into another place and time. Well, that didn't work out well for me. I wasn't exactly getting leading parts in the high school plays. Those roles went to the popular kids. Or maybe I just sucked at acting. Either way, It didn't happen. So, I pursued my second love which was cooking. I earned my Associates Degree and have been in the culinary industry ever since.

Besides cooking, I had another passion. I'm sure you can figure out that it was writing. It's not a passion I have shared with many people. If I couldn't escape reality with acting, then I was going to write to escape by creating my own worlds and characters. The Community was the first story I could see clear as crystal. It's been a long journey and for the first time in a long time, I'm truly proud of myself for something. However, The Community wouldn't have gotten to where it is today without help. I would like to take the time to acknowledge those amazing people now.

First, some professional acknowledgments are in order.

Thank you to my editors Cara Flannery, Tracey McKinney and Ashley Olivier. They are amazing editors and I cannot thank them enough for their amazing skills and helping me professionally shape The Community. Thank you to all those who proofread and beta read my story. Your insight and critiques greatly helped me get the story to where it is today. I also wish to thank Aubrey Joy Rosales of Jai Design for the amazing cover design for the book. You can check out her other works on her Instagram page: designjai.

Now to my personal appreciations.

I want to thank my amazing parents, Russell and Melissa Meeker, for their love and support through this whole journey. Credit for naming the Harmony Group/Harvesters goes to my dad. To my friends that put up with me on a regular basis, I don't know how you do it and I thank you for suffering through my crazy antics. To my amazing husband, Erik, for your love and support. Even though you have no idea what my book is about, or even what the name of it is. I love you and I thank God I have you in my life.

And finally, to my beautiful little girl Saya. You have been my strength, my comfort, and my inspiration to keep moving forward. As cheesy as it sounds, I hope this proves that if you keep fighting and working hard, you can accomplish your dreams. Never give up on your goals and keep fighting to make them happen. I love you.

Thank you all again for giving this story a chance. I hope you all enjoyed and I hope you enjoy the next part of Evie's story.

ABOUT THE AUTHOR

Kristin Holm was born in Columbus, Ohio and raised in Whitehall, Ohio. After graduating from Whitehall Yearling High School, she attended the Columbus Culinary Arts Institute at Bradford School and earned her Associates Degree of Applied Science in Culinary Arts. She has been in the culinary industry for over ten years. Besides having a passion for cooking, Kristin has always had a love of writing and has strived to become a published author.

When not cooking or writing, she enjoys reading, creating chainmaille, playing Dungeons & Dragons, and spending time with her family and friends. She currently resides with her family in North Pole, Alaska and is working on the next installment of Evie's story.

Email: kristinholmauthor@gmail.com

Facebook: Kristin Holm - Author

Instagram: kristin_holm_author

CPSIA information can be obtained
at www.ICGtesting.com
Printed in the USA
BVHW031106271221
624881BV00001B/13